SOMEONE LIKE YOU

"Bretton, with her insightful observations, gets to the core of her characters in this novel about the many roles women play—wife, daughter, sister, mother, lover—whether by choice or by the force of circumstance. Commitment, avoidance, love, and guilt—Bretton, a master storyteller, superbly dramatizes a great range of emotions in this compelling tale." —*Booklist*

"Readers who appreciate a powerful character study that digs deep into cause and effect will want to read Barbara Bretton's fine, convincing tale." —*The Best Reviews*

CHANCES ARE

"A fine follow-up to *Shore Lights* . . . salt-of-the-earth characters . . . Alternately poignant and humorous, this contemporary romance gracefully illuminates life's highs and lows." —*Publishers Weekly*

"Barbara Bretton's myriad of fans will appreciate this solid contemporary sequel to *Shore Lights* . . . two delightful protagonists. Ms. Bretton provides a fine return to the Jersey shore with this warm family drama."
—*Midwest Book Review*

continued . . .

GIRLS OF SUMMER

"A moving romance . . . Barbara Bretton provides a deep tale of individuals struggling with caring connections of the heart." —*Midwest Book Review*

"A book readers will want to savor." —*Publishers Weekly*

"Insightful . . . Bretton excels at women's fiction that engages the emotions without manipulating them . . . I highly recommend that discriminating readers pay a visit to these *Girls of Summer*." —*The Romance Reader*

"Barbara Bretton is a master at touching readers' hearts. Grab this one when it hits the shelves! A Perfect 10!" —*Romance Reviews Today*

SHORE LIGHTS

"An engrossing tale of hope, promise, heartache, and misplaced dreams . . . Its uplifting message and smooth storytelling make it a pleasant read any time of year." —*Publishers Weekly*

"Bretton's warm, wonderful book presents complex familial and romantic relationships, sympathetic characters, and an underlying poignancy, and will please fans of Kathryn Shay and Deborah Smith." —*Booklist*

"Entertaining . . . Barbara Bretton bestows a beautiful modern-day romance on her audience." —*Midwest Book Review*

"Her women's fiction is well written and insightful with just the right blend of realism and romance . . . [*Shore Lights*] may be her best novel yet . . . A rich novel full of wry humor and sweet poignancy . . . The novel's magic comes from the author's ability to portray the nuances of human relationships at both their worst and best . . . powerful." —*The Romance Reader*

Just Like Heaven

BARBARA BRETTON

JOVE BOOKS, NEW YORK

THE BERKLEY PUBLISHING GROUP
Published by the Penguin Group
Penguin Group (USA) Inc.
375 Hudson Street, New York, New York 10014, USA
Penguin Group (Canada), 90 Eglinton Avenue East, Suite 700, Toronto, Ontario M4P 2Y3, Canada
(a division of Pearson Penguin Canada Inc.)
Penguin Books Ltd., 80 Strand, London WC2R 0RL, England
Penguin Group Ireland, 25 St. Stephen's Green, Dublin 2, Ireland (a division of Penguin Books Ltd.)
Penguin Group (Australia), 250 Camberwell Road, Camberwell, Victoria 3124, Australia
(a division of Pearson Australia Group Pty. Ltd.)
Penguin Books India Pvt. Ltd., 11 Community Centre, Panchsheel Park, New Delhi—110 017, India
Penguin Group (NZ), 67 Apollo Drive, Mairangi Bay, Auckland 1311, New Zealand
(a division of Pearson New Zealand Ltd.)
Penguin Books (South Africa) (Pty.) Ltd., 24 Sturdee Avenue, Rosebank, Johannesburg 2196,
South Africa

Penguin Books Ltd., Registered Offices: 80 Strand, London WC2R 0RL, England

This is a work of fiction. Names, characters, places, and incidents either are the product of the author's
imagination or are used fictitiously, and any resemblance to actual persons, living or dead, business
establishments, events, or locales is entirely coincidental. The publisher does not have any control over
and does not assume any responsibility for author or third-party websites or their content.

JUST LIKE HEAVEN

A Jove Book / published by arrangement with the author

PRINTING HISTORY
Jove mass-market edition / March 2007

Copyright © 2007 by Barbara Bretton.
Excerpt from *It's In His Kiss* copyright © 2007 by Barbara Bretton.
Cover photograph by Jupiter Images Royalty Free.
Cover design by George Long.

ISBN: 978-0-515-14262-4

JOVE®
Jove Books are published by The Berkley Publishing Group,
a division of Penguin Group (USA) Inc.,
375 Hudson Street, New York, New York 10014.
JOVE is a registered trademark of Penguin Group (USA) Inc.
The "J" design is a trademark belonging to Penguin Group (USA) Inc.

PRINTED IN THE UNITED STATES OF AMERICA

10 9 8 7 6 5 4 3 2 1

Just Like Heaven

One

Kate French shifted the phone from her left shoulder to her right and plunged her hand deeper into her lingerie drawer.

"Mom!" Her daughter Gwynn was no longer a teenager, but you would never know it from her tone of voice. "Are you listening to me?"

"I heard every syllable." Kate pulled out an orphaned hand-knit sock and a silky pink camisole carbon-dated from the disco era and tossed them onto the bed behind her.

"So what should I do?"

Unfortunately Kate had shifted into maternal autopilot five minutes into the conversation and had lost track. Was Gwynn still debating her roommate Laura's excessive devotion to the New York Giants or had she segued into an old favorite of all the French women: a dissection of Kate's nonexistent love life?

She bent down and peered deeper into the perfumed recesses. One pair of plain cotton panties. Was that too much to ask for? "Run it by me again, honey."

"I know what you're doing," Gwynn said. "You're answering e-mails while I'm pouring out my heart to you. I really wish you wouldn't do that."

"Gwynnie, I'm not on the computer."

"I can hear the keys clicking."

"What you hear is the sound of your mother searching her lingerie drawer for a pair of—"

"Hold on! I have another call."

The distance between the thirteen-year-old girl her daughter used to be and the twenty-three-year-old woman she was hadn't turned out to be quite as wide as Kate had hoped. She glanced over at the clock on her nightstand. *Come on, Gwynnie. I have things to do.*

"That was Andrew." Gwynn the daughter had been replaced by Gwynn the girlfriend. She sounded almost giddy with delight. The sound hit Kate's ears like fingernails on a chalkboard. "He called from the boat! Isn't that the—"

"I'm going to hang up now," Kate said. "I have an appointment down in Princeton and I'm running late. We can pick this up another time, can't we, honey?"

"But, Mom, I still haven't—"

"I know, I know, but this can't be helped. I want to hear everything you have to say, honey, but not right this minute."

"You're going to Princeton?"

"Yes, but not if I don't get out of here in the next ten minutes."

"If I leave now I could meet you for lunch at the Mexican place and I can tell you my news in person."

"I thought you were working lunch shift at O'Malley's during the week."

"Mondays are slow. They won't miss me."

"You can't just not show up, Gwynn. That's how you

lost your last job." *And when you do show up, you're always late. That's not how you get ahead.*

"You always do that to me."

"Do what?" She glanced at her watch. Was she the only one in the family who believed in punctuality?

"Keep score. Why can't you just accept that my career path isn't like yours and let me live my life my own way?"

"Gwynnie, do we need to have this conversation right now?" She was still on London time and not up for a discussion of individual rights and freedoms with an independent young woman who still expected Mommy to foot the bill for her car insurance.

"You sound pissed."

"What I sound is jet-lagged." She waited for the appropriate response from her only child, but none was forthcoming. "Did you forget I've been in England for almost ten days? I'm still on London time." *Does any of this ring a bell, Gwynn?* She liked to believe most daughters would notice when their mothers were out of the country.

"You've been gone forever. That's why I have so much to talk to you about."

"Honey, this can't be helped. I really have to go."

"Are you okay?" Gwynn asked. "You're not acting like yourself."

"We'll talk later, honey," she said and then disconnected.

Normally Kate would have felt guilty for cutting her daughter short, but today she only felt relieved. She loved Gwynn more than life itself, but her daughter's melodramatic outbursts had a way of sucking the oxygen right out of her lungs.

"Okay," she said as she tossed the cell onto the bed. "Let's get down to business."

There had to be something wearable in the house.

A ten-day trip to the U.K. shouldn't deplete a woman's reserves. She pulled out the second drawer of her lingerie chest and dumped the contents in a pile. T-shirts from various island paradises. A garter belt with tiny roses embroidered across the handmade lace, remains of a long-ago Valentine's Day celebration. More bras than any one 34B woman needed in three lifetimes. A puka shell necklace. The black lace mantilla she had found in a shop in Seville during her last married vacation. Ticket stubs, a McCarter playbill, a deflated balloon dachshund, and what was easily the worst birthday present her mother had ever given her: the infamous red lace thong.

Maeve had come of age at the start of the turbulent sixties, and she believed in shaking up the status quo whenever she had the chance. How better to ignite some passion in her forty-year-old daughter's life than to present her with outrageously sexy underwear in front of friends, colleagues, relatives, and a half-dozen prospective boyfriends? Unfortunately the passion Maeve ignited in her daughter had nothing to do with romance and everything to do with embarrassment. Kate had tried to be a good sport about it, but it had taken every ounce of self-control at her command to keep from throttling her own mother.

She held up the thong. It wouldn't cover a Barbie doll, much less a full-size woman. What on earth had Maeve been thinking?

She considered making a quick run to Target for a three-pack of Jockey for Women, but the clock was ticking and Professor Armitage wasn't known for his patience. And there was the fact that she was way beyond exhausted. Jet lag rarely bothered her, but today she was having trouble keeping her eyes open long enough to finish getting dressed.

She cringed her way into the scrap of lace and elastic

and then peered at herself in the mirror opposite the bed. That was better than a jolt of caffeine. The thong should have come with a warning sticker. This much reality so early in the morning was hard to take.

She looked closer. That couldn't possibly be right. The human body wasn't supposed to have quite so many indentations. Maybe they should add an instruction label too for the lingerie-impaired. She slipped off the thong, spun it around, then tried again.

A forty-one-year-old woman with a red lace wedgie was a sight to behold.

Thank God it was a sight nobody else on the planet would likely ever see.

Rocky Hill, New Jersey—9:45 a.m.

"Congratulations," the real estate agent said as Mark Kerry handed her four signed copies of the contract. "It's now official: your house is sold."

It was also officially the point of no return. "Now what?" he asked, wishing he felt more enthusiastic about the sale.

Bev scanned the signature pages and then slipped them into a large folder. "We have a tentative closing six weeks from today. I'll arrange for the appraisal, the home inspection, radon testing, smoke alarms, yadda yadda yadda. All you have to do is pack for your move," she said with a cheery smile.

"And dig up the township permits for the new roof."

"See?" Bev rolled her eyes. "I'd forget my head if it wasn't attached. We'll need the roof permits, the signed lead paint disclosure, and your attorney's name. You can fax copies to me and I'll pick up the originals."

"So far it's been almost painless."

"Five days from listing to contract," Bev said, clearly

pleased, "and we managed to get top dollar. It doesn't get much better than that."

She gave him a contact sheet with pertinent phone numbers and a metaphorical pat on the back.

"You look shell-shocked," she said as he walked her down the gravel driveway to her car. "I promise you the hard part is over."

Easy for her to say. When Memorial Day weekend rolled around, he would be on his way back up to New Hampshire to find out if you really could go home again.

Where was home anyway? This small stone cottage in New Jersey didn't have much going for it, but somehow over the last two years it had become home. Or as close to it as he was likely to get.

Two postage-stamp bedrooms. Small kitchen. No dining room. No family room. A basement with its own share of troubles. When he walked through the front door he knew he was where he was meant to be.

But nothing lasted forever.

The other contract he needed to sign was propped up against the toaster, along with a note from his old friend Maggy Boyd, who was shepherding him through the process.

The funny thing was, he thought he would have more time. Bev had warned him to be patient. The New Jersey real estate market wasn't as hot as it used to be and the whole thing might take a while.

It didn't.

Kris and Al Wygren showed up on Sunday for the first open house and fell head over heels in love with the place. They loved the wonky windows, the big stone fireplace, the squeaky floorboards, every single thing. He had pointed out all the flaws and they only loved it more.

The Wygrens were all of twenty-five or twenty-six.

Newly married. Newly pregnant. Ready to build a nest of their own.

He and Suzanne had been just like them. Young and in love with their entire future spread out before them like a field of wildflowers. Not that he would have ever thought of the wildflowers simile. That was pure Suzanne. She had seen life through a prism of joy that even in memory still amazed him.

Her mother used to say that God had been feeling generous the day he made Suzanne. He had granted her beauty and wit, intelligence and a kind heart, a sense of humor that could still make Mark smile across the years.

But the one thing God hadn't seen fit to grant her was the one thing that would have made all the difference: a long life.

When she looked at him, she saw a hero. The kind of man his father had been, the kind of man he wanted to be. But time hadn't been on their side. She had been taken from him while he was still very much a work in progress.

At least Suzanne never saw him stumble and fall. She never saw him flat on his face on their front porch, stinking of cheap whiskey and pain. She hadn't been there to see him try to outrun the memories of their past. The lost days, those dark nights, belonged to him alone, and for that he was glad.

She never found out her hero was only a man.

Coburn, New Jersey—around 10:30 a.m.

Kate was stopped in traffic near the Bedminster exit on Route 287 when a wave of something uncomfortably close to nausea swept over her. Jet lag on an empty stomach was bad enough, but for sheer misery she would put her money on the thong.

Traffic eased up as she neared Bridgewater Commons Mall, but the cell phone calls kept coming. Her assistant, Sonia, called twice. Clive phoned from England to tell her she had left a pair of sunglasses behind. Armitage's secretary wanted to make sure she was on schedule. Jackie the furniture refinisher had another one of her minor emergencies designed to boost her going rate another ten percent.

They all called for different reasons, but every call ended the same way. *You sound exhausted . . . You need a vacation, not a buying trip . . . I'm worried about you . . .*

Bless call waiting, the greatest exit strategy ever invented. What was wrong with everyone? Sure, she had noticed the dark circles under her eyes, but that was genetic. Maeve had them and Maeve's mother before her. And unless she missed her guess, Gwynn had something to look forward to. Kate wasn't twenty any longer. Not even Estée Lauder could turn back the clock.

She shifted around in the driver's seat, tugging at the elastic band pinching her hip bone. Her mother had promised her that the thong would release her inner goddess and turn her into a siren capable of luring men away from ESPN and repeats of *Baywatch*, but so far her inner goddess was missing in action.

Her cell burst into the *William Tell Overture* as she neared the Route 1 exit. Her mother's theme song.

"What did you say to Gwynn? She called me, sobbing."

"Hello to you too, Mom. I thought you were in New Mexico."

"I am and our girl woke me up with her tale of woe. What is going on back there?" Maeve was on the other side of the country, touring for her latest self-help tome, but family drama transcended geography.

"It was Gwynn being Gwynn," Kate said. "She wanted to talk, I needed to finish dressing and get on the road."

"You hurt her feelings. She had some news she wanted to share with you."

"I cut her short once in twenty-three years and it's a major incident?" She took a series of deep breaths and tried to calm herself. "I haven't slept in almost thirty-six hours, Maeve, and my body thinks it's the middle of the afternoon."

"You don't sound like yourself," Maeve observed. "What's going on, sweetie? We're worried about you."

"Is Mercury in retrograde again or something? There's nothing wrong with me that a good night's sleep won't take care of. Why is everyone suddenly asking if I'm okay?" Jet lag was hardly a new concept.

"Maybe because it's clear you're not yourself. You've seemed a little depressed, forgetful—"

"Ma!" Kate practically shouted into the tiny cell phone. "I think your imagination is running away with you."

"You might be entering perimenopause," Maeve volunteered.

The morning was actually deteriorating. She wouldn't have believed it possible.

"So how did things go in London with Liam? Any sparks?" Her mother was nothing if not resilient.

"We had tea together my first day. That was it."

"Sharon said he would be perfect for you. She'll be so disappointed."

"Next time why doesn't Sharon fix you up with the Liams and Nigels of this world. I keep telling you I'm not looking for a man and I mean it."

"You might not be looking but you wouldn't turn down a good one if he popped up."

"I'm not sure there are any good ones," she said, "at least none that I'd be interested in."

"That's not normal, honey. You sound like you've given up."

"Mom, this is old news. I'm perfectly happy being on my own, even if that seems to bug the living daylights out of everyone else in the world except me. Can't we just leave it at that?"

"Sara Whittaker's son is back in town. He's been working in Tokyo the last few years, a graphic artist. I think you two might hit it off."

"Mom, I have another call. We'll have to pick this up later."

"You don't have to use the call-waiting excuse with me, sweetie. I know when you've had enough."

Kate had to laugh. "It's a real call this time," she said as her irritability lifted. "I'll call you tonight. I promise."

Paul Grantham, old friend and confidant, was next in the queue.

"Took you long enough, French."

"Thank God it's you," she said, adjusting the headset. "This thing hasn't stopped ringing since I got off the plane."

"So how was the big buying trip? Is there anything left on the other side of the pond?"

"Not much," she admitted. "I may have struck gold." She told him about the stack of Revolutionary War–era letters she'd found in a tiny shop near Lincolnshire written to a colonel's wife in New Jersey.

"When will you know if you found the mother lode?"

A truck, horn blaring, appeared out of nowhere in her blind spot. "Oh, damn! Sorry!" She veered back into her lane, heart pounding wildly. "What were you saying?"

"Are you okay?" he asked. "You sound a little out of breath."

"I'm not out of breath. It must be the connection." That and her surging adrenaline.

She held on while Paul answered an assistant's question.

"Sorry," he said. "Crazy morning. We're still on for the Hospital Gala this week, aren't we?"

"I take it Lisa's no longer on the scene."

"Lisa is looking for somebody who's willing to go the distance," he said, "and we both know I'm saving myself for you."

It was an old joke between them, but lately she had the feeling there was more behind her old friend's words than either one of them cared to acknowledge.

Paul was a partner in a prestigious Manhattan law firm, another one of the Coburn High School Class of 1982 who made good. He had been in her life for as long as she could remember, part of their crowd from kindergarten through high school. He had hung out with them at Rutgers, where Kate had struggled unsuccessfully to combine marriage, motherhood, and college, and he had stayed a good friend even after their respective marriages fell to the divorce statistics. They had tried dating once early on but the absurdity of dressing up and staring at each other over candlelight and a bottle of Tattinger had pushed them both into helpless laughter, which was pretty much where they had stayed.

Or so she had thought until recently.

"Oh my God," she said through clenched teeth. "I almost rear-ended a cop."

"You sure you're okay?" he asked. "Maybe you should take the day off and catch up on your sleep."

"That's something you say to your aging aunt," she snapped. "I'm not ready for the nursing home yet, Paul."

"Tell you what," he said. "How about if we're not both hooked up by the time we hit retirement, we pool our Social Security checks and move in together."

"Sweet talker." She rolled to a stop. "No wonder Lisa's not going to the gala with you this weekend."

"She's twenty-eight. I don't have time to wait for her check."

She tried to think of something suitably witty to say in response, but her mind was filled with nothing but air.

"Kate?" Paul's voice poked through the fog. "Are you still there?"

"Sorry," she said yet again. "I don't know what my problem is today."

"Did you eat anything? You're probably hungry."

"I grabbed a brownie and a Frappuccino at the airport while I was waiting for my bags to get through customs."

"And now you're crashing. Pull into a McDonald's and get an Egg McMuffin."

He sounded uncharacteristically solicitous, which made her wonder how bad she sounded.

"I don't have time. Armitage expects me there in twenty."

"Screw Armitage. Get something to eat. You're running on fumes."

Another wave of nausea gripped her. Maybe he was right. "I'm coming up on Princeton Promenade," she said, easing over into the right lane. "They have a great food court." She could grab some protein and a bottle of water and be on her way again with time to spare.

"Good thinking."

"Oh, wait! I don't have to stop. I have some nuts in the glove box." She leaned across the passenger seat and popped open the glove box in search of smoked almonds, survivors of her last trip down the shore for the semiannual Atlantique City extravaganza. The Atlantique City trade show was a must for New Jersey antique shop owners, and Kate was no exception. French Kiss maintained a prominent spot twice a year. She sifted through her insurance card, registration, and owner's manual and pushed aside a small flashlight and an open packet of tissues. Where were the almonds?

She veered toward the fender of a white Escalade and quickly steered back into her own lane to a chorus of angry horns.

"What the hell is going on?" Paul asked. "It sounds like you're at the roller derby."

She caught sight of herself in the rearview mirror, and the odd feeling in the pit of her stomach intensified. A single bead of sweat was making its way down her forehead toward her right eye. It was barely seventy degrees outside. Nobody broke into a sweat in seventy-degree weather, least of all her.

"You're right," she said. Everybody was right. "I'm a menace. I should get off the road."

"Want me to drive down there and get you?"

She turned on her blinker and made the right into the parking lot of Princeton Promenade. "Don't be silly. You're in Manhattan. I'll be fine after I get something to eat."

"I'll send a car for you. We use services all over the tristate area."

She zeroed in on a spot two lanes over and headed for it. "I'll stop. I'll eat. I'll be fine."

"I'm gonna hold you to it."

She whipped around the head of the third lane from the entrance and zipped into the spot as a dented blue Honda angled itself behind her. "Uh-oh," she said.

"What's going on?"

"Some guy in an old blue car is glaring at me. He seems to think I stole his spot."

"Did you?"

"He didn't have a turn signal on." She hesitated, replaying the scene in her head. "I might have."

"Where is he?"

"Stopped right behind me."

"Blocking you in?"

She slunk down low in her seat. "I never do things like this. I'm the most polite driver on the planet."

"Is he still there?"

"Yes."

"Want me to call mall security? I can use another line."

She hesitated. "Maybe you—oh, thank God! He's driving away." She watched through the rearview mirror. Good-looking men in her own age demographic had no business wearing Grateful Dead T-shirts.

Paul wanted to talk her into the mall and out again but her cell battery was running down. The only way he would let her go was if she promised to phone him after she saw Professor Armitage.

Normally she would have told him to back off, but so far nothing about the morning had been even remotely normal. It wasn't like him to be so solicitous. The last time he had sounded that worried was when one of his daughters said she wanted to become a model.

A vague sense of dread wrapped itself around her chest and it wouldn't let go.

"Okay," she said out loud. "Don't go getting crazy."

The problem was so obvious that it was almost laughable: she needed food and water and she needed them right now. The food court was located near the multiplex at the south end of the Promenade. A huge round clock mounted to the left of the Sushi Palace sign offered up a reality check she didn't need. Armitage expected her at his front door in exactly thirteen and one-half minutes. Even if she ditched the search for protein she would never make it on time.

Why hadn't she just cancelled out earlier this morning when she was trapped at the airport waiting for her boxes and bags? Why had she been so hell-bent on squeezing as much from the day as was inhumanly possible?

She swallowed hard against a sudden, acrid burst of nausea at the back of her throat. The air was soft and sweet with spring promise and she swept huge gulps of it into her lungs in an attempt to clear away the discomfort, but that didn't help either.

She flipped open her phone and said, "Call Armitage," then waited while it attempted the connection.

"Call Armitage," she said again.

No luck this time either.

She would have to find a pay phone in the food court and—

And what?

Professor Armitage. That was it. *Concentrate!* The thought of facing the professor's wrath wasn't half as unnerving as this weird, disconnected feeling that seemed to be growing more intense. Unless Armitage wanted to assess the documents in the emergency room of the nearest hospital, he would simply have to understand.

Understand what? She went blank for a second as scattered images flooded her brain. Professor Armitage's woolly gray beard. His fierce little eyes. The cold, slick feel of the metal box in her hands. The way that stupid thong pinched exactly where no sane person wanted to be pinched. The whooshing sound inside her head . . .

Don't faint! she warned herself. She would die of embarrassment if the EMTs saw what she was wearing under her peach cotton twinset and pearls.

A shiver ran up her spine and she pushed the thought as far from her mind as she could. Clearly her imagination was as jet-lagged and out of whack as the rest of her, hopping without warning from one bizarre thought to the next.

She didn't know the first thing about being sick. Her last hospital stay had been twenty-three years ago when she gave birth to Gwynn. She was the one who visited patients and brought them flowers and candy and trashy magazines to while away the hours. She was always the one who got to go home when visiting hours were over.

The thong pinched when she took a step, then pinched harder when she stopped. What she wanted to do was duck between the parked cars and make a swift adjustment, but wouldn't you know it: the man she'd beat out for the parking spot was two aisles over and looking right at her.

Bad enough she was wearing underwear ten years too young and two sizes too small for her. Imagine being caught fiddling with it in public by an angry man in a Grateful Dead T-shirt. They locked eyes for a second and she looked away. His look was disconcertingly direct but it wasn't angry, and that unnerved her. She had expected anger or irritation, but she saw neither. His look wasn't flirtatious, but there was something there, something she couldn't put her finger on. She couldn't remember the last time a man's gaze had unsettled her this way. The stupid thong was even affecting her judgment.

She shot him another quick glance. Tall, lean. Thick dark hair that caught the sunlight and held it. A deeply intelligent face alive with open curiosity aimed in her direction and a smile that—

Okay. Enough of that. The smile was for whoever was on the other end of his cell phone connection. Besides, the guy was wearing a Grateful Dead T-shirt. What more was there to say?

A woman with three small children in tow raced past her in a cloud of baby powder and soap. Her stomach lurched at the sweet smell and for a second she thought she was about to faint. She tried to steady herself with another deep breath of spring-fresh air but suddenly her chest felt tight, as if some unseen force were wrapping a band around her rib cage and pulling tighter and tighter, and she knew she was going down.

Or was she down already? She wasn't sure. The world had gone all soft-focus on her except for the sickening smells of pickled ginger, old Juicy Fruit, and motor oil.

I'm asleep, she thought. What other explanation could there be? This had nothing to do with real life. *Open your eyes, Kate. You really don't want to be having this dream.*

The room smelled like a Dumpster. The mattress was hard as a rock and the covers were all tangled up around her legs and she felt as if she were being—

She opened her eyes and screamed. Actually she *tried* to scream, but she couldn't draw down enough oxygen to manage more than a loud whisper.

The guy in the Grateful Dead T-shirt, the same guy she had beat out for the parking spot, was bent over her, tugging at the hem of her skirt.

"Glad you're back with us," he said, as if they were chatting over cocktails at T.G.I. Friday's. "I was starting to worry."

He tugged again and she tried to strike out at him, but her arms seemed weighted with lead.

"Whoa!" He pretended to duck. "Take it easy. I'm on your side."

She thought of a half-dozen remarks she could make, but none of them found their way to her lips. What was wrong with her? Usually she could deal out a smart remark at the speed of light. "Get your hands off me," she managed. *That's the best you can do? Pathetic.*

"You don't want all of Princeton to see that red lace, do you?"

Oh God . . . the thong . . . just leave me here so I can die of embarrassment . . .

"So what happened? Did you trip? One second you

were walking toward the Promenade and the next—" He made a falling gesture with his hand.

Couldn't he see she wanted to roll under a car and disappear? Why was he trying to make conversation?

It wasn't a hard question, but she couldn't seem to figure out the answer.

"Does this sort of thing happen a lot?"

"Never." She cleared her throat. "Absolutely never."

"I'm going to take your pulse again."

Again?

"It was over a hundred when I checked your carotid artery. That's not great."

Not every Deadhead could use "carotid artery" in a sentence with such ease. Was it possible he actually knew what he was doing?

"No thanks." But she wouldn't mind an extra-strength Advil. Her shoulder. Her back. Her hand. Even her teeth hurt from the fall. Her left jaw was actually throbbing.

"I'm a licensed EMT." He pulled some cards from his pocket and she pretended to examine them, but the truth was she couldn't focus on the text. "Fifteen years' experience. New Hampshire and New Jersey."

"This really isn't necessary," she said. Or at least that was what she tried to say. She was having trouble following the conversation and even more trouble synching her thoughts with her words.

"Do me a favor and lie down. You look like you're going to pass out again."

She wanted to protest, but suddenly the thought of lying flat on her back in the middle of the Princeton Promenade parking lot sounded like the best idea she'd ever had. He opened a newspaper wide and spread it down on the ground beneath her head, but the combined smells of pickled ginger, motor oil, and chewed-up bubble gum seeped through and made her retch.

He placed two fingers on the pulse point in her inner wrist and monitored the second hand on his watch. "One twenty. Any nausea?"

She nodded. *You felt queasy in the car. Maybe you should tell him that.*

"Any underlying medical conditions that might have some bearing on this?"

She was perfectly healthy. Why couldn't he see that for himself?

"Are you on any medication?"

"Vitamins."

"Are you in pain?" The man was relentless.

"Not—not exactly pain."

"Discomfort?"

Oh God. Even through the fog swirling around her, she could see where this was going. "Yes." *Admit it, French: you're in big trouble.*

"Where?"

"My back."

"Sharp pain?"

"Not sharp . . . pressure." Three words and she was totally wiped out. What was happening to her?

"Okay. I'm not trying to worry you but we need to call nine-one-one." He pulled a cell phone from his back pocket and punched in the numbers.

The band around her chest tightened and she broke into a sweat.

". . . Yes, I'll stay here with her . . . thanks." He jammed the phone back into his pocket. "You're probably right. I'll bet it's nothing too but I know you'll feel a lot better if you hear that from a doctor and not some guy in a Dead shirt."

She wanted to laugh at his joke, but all she could manage was a quick smile. She was sweating. How could that be? She wanted to say, "This isn't really me," but that required more energy than she could muster up. He wiped her forehead with the back of his hand, and she almost wept from the gentleness of the action. "Heart attack?" she whispered.

"Yes," he said. "There's a good chance that's what it is."

"Lie to me," she managed. "I don't mind." She tried to force another laugh, but the iron band around her rib cage wouldn't let her.

He didn't pull his punches, but the deep compassion in his eyes made her feel safe.

"It could be indigestion, a panic attack, a sprained muscle. But if it *is* your heart, we need to get help sooner rather than later."

"Are you sure you're not a—"

She was going to say "doctor," but the pain exploded and it blew everything else away. Deep crushing pain from the center of her body that stripped her of her identity, her memories, her future, stripped her of everything but bone-deep terror.

"Oh God . . . oh God . . ." Was she saying it or just thinking it? She didn't know. She felt as if she were floating above the parking lot like a helium balloon on a very fragile string.

He leaned closer. She could feel his warm breath against her cheek. "What is it? Do you want to say a prayer? Is that what you're saying?"

No . . . no . . . make it stop . . .

"Stay with me." His voice flew at her on the loud rush of wind inside her head. "I'm not going to let you go."

Don't let go . . . don't let me go . . . I'm scared . . . this is really happening . . . oh God . . . Gwynnie . . . I've got to see Gwynnie . . . I have to tell her I love her . . . I don't even know your name and you're the one who'll have to tell my daughter . . .

"The ambulance is on its way . . . you're going to be fine . . . just hold on a little longer . . . I'll stay with you . . ."

I can't hold on . . . I want to but I can't . . . don't let me go . . . don't let me go . . .

"Talk to me . . . come on . . . look at me . . . open your eyes and look at me . . . grab my hand and hang on . . . I'm not going to let you go . . ."

Somewhere in some other universe he took her hand and held tight, but it was too late. His words were the last ones she heard.

Two

He knew the moment it happened. The spark that made her all that she was went out. The ambulance was still a good six or seven minutes away. She didn't have six minutes. The window of opportunity was shrinking with every second.

"Come on!" he urged her. "Don't leave us now!"

She wasn't breathing. That rapid pulse was still.

"What's going on?" A woman with two kids paused to look.

"She passed out," he said as he stretched her flat and tilted her chin up. This wasn't the time for full disclosure.

"What's up?" A man leaned out of his open car window to look.

"He says she passed out," the woman said.

"Does he know what he's doing?"

The woman with the kids moved closer. "Do you know what you're doing?" she asked.

"CPR," he said as he cleared the airway. "I'm trained."

"Is she sick?" another voice from behind. "Want me to call somebody?"

He cleared the redhead's airway and tried to block out everything but the task at hand.

"What's he doing?" a man asked. "Did anyone call the cops?"

"She's having a heart attack. The ambulance is coming."

"Who are you?" the first voice demanded again. "Do you know what you're doing?"

They were all talking at once and the voices got tangled in the wind and the birdsong and the low roar of cars moving along Route 1 while the red-haired woman drifted farther out of reach.

Focus, he told himself.

In the far distance he heard a siren.

Block everything else out and focus.

He checked her carotid artery for a pulse. There was no sign of respiration.

A surge of anger filled his chest. This wasn't her time. He knew it in his bones. Nothing happened without a reason. God had put them in this place at this moment and it was up to him to take it from there.

He filled his lungs, tilted her head back, pinched her nose, and then slowly blew air into her open mouth and watched her chest slowly rise.

He waited a second, refilled his lungs, and then did it again.

Still nothing.

The sound of the siren grew closer.

He placed the flats of his hands on her chest and pushed down hard and fast.

Onetwothreefourfivesixseveneightnineten . . .

"You're hurting her!" A shrill voice pierced his concentration.

"He knows what he's doing." A different voice, also nearby.

Nothing. Still no pulse. No respiration.

He tilted her head back, pinched her nose shut, and then tried to breathe life into her still body, once, then twice.

Again he placed his hands on her chest. Her bones felt delicate and breakable. She would have bruises when this was over. He positioned his hands and pushed down quickly again and again and again. "Come on . . . come on . . . I'm not going to let you go . . . work with me . . . breathe . . . you can do it . . . breathe!"

The commentary around him didn't let up.

"That's not how you do it."

"Yes, it is."

"He doesn't know what he's doing."

"She moved! I saw her arm move!"

. . . eleventwelvethirteenfourteen . . . fifteensixteen-seventeen . . .

The sound was harsh, rasping, the most beautiful sound he had ever heard. She was breathing on her own. Her pulse was shallow but it was there, and he sent up a prayer of gratitude. Her lips were moving, but he couldn't make out what she was saying. It didn't matter. She was still with him.

"You're going to be okay," he said as the ambulance screeched to a halt a few feet away from them. "Help is here."

Their eyes locked. He started to say more, but realized his words didn't matter. She was looking straight through to his heart. He took her hand and she clung to him, and for a moment nothing else in the world mattered.

"So what have we got here?" a tall female responder asked. The name *Emily* was embroidered across her breast pocket.

"Possible heart attack," Mark said. "She stopped breathing and I did CPR."

"Good thinking. How long was she gone?"

"Ten seconds. No more than that."

Emily bent down over the red-haired woman. "I'm Emily and that's Bill over there. We're here to make you comfortable. Are you in pain?"

Her hazel eyes fluttered closed then open again.

"I'll take that as a yes. Can you tell me your name?"

She tried but couldn't. Her grip on Mark's hand tightened. Her breathing was rapid and shallow, and he could sense that she was slipping away again. Her hands were long and slender. Her nails were painted a pale pinkish ivory color. Her only jewelry was a man's round-faced watch with a black leather strap. Emily reached for the small shoulder purse slung across the red-haired woman's body, opened it, and looked inside.

"Good. She has a wallet. Admissions can check for ID."

Emily pushed back the crowd of onlookers. Bill pulled a stretcher from the ambulance and wheeled it over. The two technicians quickly lifted the red-haired woman onto it and rushed her back to the ambulance.

"You can't go with us," Emily said to him. She was a physically intimidating woman. He had no doubt she'd use force if she had to.

"I'm not leaving." Not with the red-haired woman's hand gripping his. Not with her hazel eyes fixed on him as if he were all that stood between her and the great unknowable.

"I promised I'd stay with her," he said.

"Are you related?"

He shook his head.

"Sorry. You can follow if you want."

"I'm staying with her," he said, then pulled out his own ID and flashed it. This was a promise he didn't intend to break.

Emily looked at it and shrugged.

"I guess we can make an exception," Bill said, looking over Emily's shoulder.

It was a tight fit inside the ambulance. Bill climbed back behind the wheel and Mark tried to stay out of Emily's way as she affixed the leads to the red-haired woman's chest and legs. They were going to attach a twelve-lead EKG that would transmit information straight to the ER via cell phone so they could take her to the best facility.

"Shit." Emily checked her monitors.

Fear turned his blood to ice. "What's wrong?"

"I can't get a good connection. We'll have to take her straight to St. Francis and let them sort it out." She shook her head in disgust and reached for the receiver attached to the side wall. "The connection's down . . . We're bringing her in . . . female . . . thirty-five . . . breathing on her own . . . pulse one twenty-two . . . respiration seventy-eight . . . BP ninety-eight over fifty-two . . . complained of chest and back pain, nausea before she passed out . . . passerby administered CPR after she stopped breathing . . . We're four minutes out . . . okay . . . will do."

A light film of sweat covered the red-haired woman's face. Her beautiful hazel eyes were wide with fear and pain.

Emily opened a packet and popped out a pill. "Chew this." She forced the white tablet between the woman's lips. "It's aspirin. It won't hinder further treatment."

The red-haired woman looked up at him and he nodded. He felt ridiculously happy when she started to chew. He wondered if she understood what was going on or if she was running on autopilot. It had been a long time since he had been this important to anyone. Not even to himself.

"We're almost there," he said to her, his mouth pressed

close to her ear. "They'll run an EKG, check your blood gases . . . you don't have to worry . . . it's all going to be okay."

This wasn't the place for the truth. He didn't know if she would be okay. This was the real world, a place where unspeakable things happened to people who deserved so much better. You had to hold on to something bigger than yourself, a belief in something that could make sense out of chaos.

If he could give her that much, he would be happy.

She was trying to say something, clearly frustrated by her inability to make herself understood. He leaned closer still, but he couldn't make out her words. The oxygen mask hissed softly. A lock of auburn hair lay across her cheek, silky and cool to the touch, and he gently tucked the strands behind her ear. She smelled of spring. He didn't want to know that.

She pressed on his hand and looked past him. He turned around and saw the metal box resting on a jump seat. "That's yours, right?" Again the closed/open movement of her eyelids. "I'll make sure it stays with you."

The ambulance wheeled into the driveway at St. Francis and braked to a stop at the entrance to the ER. The back doors swung open and the woman was swept away from him on a wave of urgency. She cried out, whether from surprise or pain he didn't know. He grabbed the metal box and ran after her but was turned away at the door.

"Patients only," the burly security guard said. "Use the entrance around the corner."

"Look, can't you make an exception? I promised I'd stay with her. She'll—"

"She's not going anywhere. Use the other entrance."

He ran full out to the corner and then realized it was the wrong corner. He doubled back, maneuvered around a pair of ambulances, turned the other corner, and waited for the automatic doors to open into an empty hallway posted with signs for the cafeteria, radiology, physical therapy, and emergency. He wound his way through a labyrinth of corridors with offshoots leading deeper into the interior of the hospital. He flagged down an intern, who assured him he was running in the right direction.

He passed the turnoff for radiology and had just cleared the door to physical therapy when he heard his name.

"Mark? Mark! Hey, man, I thought that was you."

He looked over his shoulder. Jacob Margolies, one of his neighbors, was grinning up at him from his wheelchair, fresh from physical therapy.

"Jake, I'm in a rush. Can we catch up later?"

"Is everything all right? You don't look—"

He loved Jake like a brother, but he didn't have time. He barreled around the corner, down the straightaway, and burst into the waiting area to the emergency suite.

"How can I help you?" A pleasant-looking woman in a security guard uniform sat at a plain beige desk. She slid a sign-in sheet toward Mark.

"I'm looking for someone . . . a woman, cardiac . . . They just brought her in by ambulance."

"Name?"

"Mark Kerry."

A small smile. "Her name, sir."

"I don't know." He quickly explained the situation.

The guard checked her computer screen. "I'm not showing any female cardiac patients admitted this morning."

"They took her in the back way. It was just a couple minutes ago."

"It would still be on the screen, sir."

"Can I go back there and look?"

"Let me see what I can find out." She lifted a pale-green receiver and pressed a series of buttons. "I'm looking for a female cardiac . . . just admitted . . . thanks." She looked up at Mark. "She's gone."

His head emptied of everything but despair.

"Oh God, I'm sorry." The guard touched his hand. "I don't mean gone that way. They moved her to another hospital."

Relief almost brought him to his knees. "Where?"

"Oops." She picked up the phone and dialed again. "The cardiac transfer, where did they take her . . . Well, where is Jen . . . She would know . . . So you didn't log her in . . . Okay . . . Thanks anyway."

He didn't need a translator. "You don't understand. I've got to find her." *I made a promise. I said I wouldn't let her go.* "I'm holding something of hers. It should be checked in with her belongings."

"Well, I don't know what to tell you, sir. She's not here, so I guess you'll have to hang on to it. I'm sure you'll find her."

But he knew life didn't work that way. Sometimes people slipped through your fingers and you couldn't bring them back no matter how hard you tried.

Kate's hospital room—four days later

They all said it was a miracle, that God had been watching over her, and Kate supposed there was some truth to that. A complete stranger had stepped out of his own life long enough to save hers. Even she had to admit there was an element of the miraculous at work.

She remembered accidentally swiping a parking spot from a guy in a pale-blue car and then the next thing she knew she was in the CCU wondering what all the fuss was about. Something life-changing had happened between those two events and she wished she could remember what it was.

"The details will come back to you," Dr. Lombardi had said to her. "You've been through a traumatic experience. Just give it time."

But the thing was she wanted to know now. The story of a Good Samaritan in a Grateful Dead T-shirt who had performed CPR in the parking lot of the Princeton Promenade was attaining the status of suburban legend. A rescue squad worker told a receptionist who told another rescue squad worker who told the admitting clerk who told the emergency room nurse who told Dr. Lombardi who told her.

She was one of the lucky ones. Her heart attack had been a minor one and the swift administration of a lowly aspirin coupled with a powerful clot buster and a diagnostic angiogram had stopped the attack in its tracks before there was permanent damage.

The whole thing was nothing more than an interruption, a small detour along an otherwise smooth highway. She had been absolutely fine before the cardiac incident and she was absolutely fine now. In fact, if not for the fact that she was currently a guest at Central Jersey Medical Center, it would be as if nothing at all had happened.

That was the good news.

The bad news? Her mother, her daughter, her colleagues, her friends, and the entire South Jersey contingent of aunts and cousins did know what all the fuss was about and they had converged on her hospital room to explain it to her.

"God saved you for a reason," her aunt Pat said as she wolfed down a handful of truffles from one of the many open boxes of candy scattered throughout the room. "Now you need to look into your soul and figure out what that reason is."

"Actually God didn't save me," she said. "Apparently it was a guy in a Grateful Dead T-shirt who did the honors."

"Don't say that!" This from her cousin Dorothy. "Of course it was God who saved you! He was just God's emissary."

The sign of the cross broke out on the far side of the room and spread fast.

"God has a plan," Mary Fran the ex-nun offered. "We just have to open our hearts to the possibilities."

"I said a rosary for you," Aunt Sheila announced from the sofa near the door. "I asked the Blessed Mother to strengthen your heart so you can withstand the trials ahead."

"Thanks, Aunt Sheila. I appreciate it." *I don't need it but I'm trying very hard to appreciate it.* "I don't think there are any trials ahead, but it's nice to know I'm covered."

"I asked Father Loughlin to add you to the prayer chain at Blessed Sac." Cousin Dorothy wasn't going to be outdone by anyone. Kate was surprised she didn't claim a private line to the Vatican.

"Really?" Sheila's expression was decidedly unsaint-like. "Father Barrett promised to mention Kate at the early mass tomorrow."

Kate was starting to feel like a volleyball during a holy playoff game. "I appreciate the concern, but you don't have to do this. I'm as good as new. I don't need to have masses said for me."

You would think she'd stripped down to her red lace birthday thong in the vestibule of St. Patrick's, the way they looked at her.

"Your cousin Linda cried when I told her I was having a mass said for her, that's how happy she was." Sheila eyed the two-pound box of chocolate truffles at her right elbow as if it were a consolation prize for Kate's ingratitude. "She says it cut her recovery time in half. If you ask me, I think it was definitely a—"

Please don't go there. If they started talking miracles

again, she would be forced to jump out the window. From miracles it was only a Hail Mary to Mother Teresa, and before you could say "Holy Trinity" they would be trying to drag her into their scheme to canonize Pope John Paul II and name him the patron saint of South Jersey widows.

"Anyone for politics or sex?" she mumbled under her breath. Either topic would be a relief. Had her family always been this church-crazy, or had she lost the ability to block them out?

Pat made a show of looking around the room. "Your mother and Gwynn aren't here with you?"

Not unless they're hiding under the bed. "They drove over to the mall to pick up my car. It's been sitting there since Monday."

"Your car's been at the mall since *Monday*?" Dorothy sounded downright gobsmacked, but at least it took her mind off religion. "You actually think it'll still be there?"

"Princeton has a very low crime rate," Kate said. "I'm sure it's fine."

Dorothy started to argue, but Sheila gave her a poke. "Kate's heart," she stage-whispered. "Don't get her upset. We don't want anything to happen."

"My heart is good as new," she said, wishing she didn't sound like a ten-year-old kid begging to stay up to watch Letterman. "I'm not going to go into cardiac arrest on you."

"Whatever you say, dear." That was Sheila again. "You know best."

Clearly she didn't, because if she had known best she would have gone to pick up her car herself and left Maeve and Gwynn here to cope with the rest of the family.

"So what's the chaplain here like?" Maeve's younger sister Gloria asked, steering the conversation right back into troubled waters. "Jeannie Lapinski told me he looks like a young Merv Griffin."

Don't laugh. She means it as a compliment.

"The one at St. Francis is a living doll," Gloria's daughter Rebecca chimed in. "He came to see me when I had Brandon and he really put the birth into perspective for me. He was so compassionate."

They turned toward Kate, who was beginning to understand why deer in the headlights looked the way they did.

"I don't know what the chaplain here is like," she said. "I haven't seen him."

"You haven't seen him?" Gloria looked outraged. "What kind of chaplain is he? He should make it his business to visit all of the Catholics in this hospital. I have a good mind to speak to one of the—"

"He did his job just fine," Kate interrupted. "He wanted to stop by but I told the head nurse it wasn't necessary."

Gloria and Dorothy exchanged horrified glances.

"Not necessary?" Dorothy's voice held exactly the right tone of amazement. "Of course it's necessary. I'm just surprised they didn't give you the Last Rites when your heart stopped beating."

Her heart was definitely beating now. "I didn't need Last Rites," she said through gritted teeth. "I needed CPR."

"And thank God you got it," Sheila said.

"No," Kate said, "thank the man in the Grateful Dead T-shirt that I got it. He's the one who saved my life."

If only she could find him and thank him herself.

Three

Who knew there were so many hospitals in central New Jersey?

He was on his seventh go-round with the good people at St. Francis and getting nowhere fast.

"I'm sorry. I know how frustrating this is but I couldn't give you that information even if I had it." The woman on the other end of the line was kind but not forthcoming.

"Sarah, listen—" He was on a first-name basis with the administrators by this time. "I'm the one who called nine-one-one for her. I'm the one who administered CPR when she crashed. She asked me to ride with her to the hospital. You can check my story. You've seen my credentials. I'll give you my cell number and the time of the call. The EMT unit will vouch for me."

"I wish I could help but there's absolutely nothing I can do. We would have to contact the patient in question and ask permission before we release information and she just isn't here."

"I know that, but somebody has to know where they sent her to."

"Not necessarily. If she wasn't admitted, she won't be in our database. You could try calling the rescue squad."

"I would if I knew which one it was."

"You didn't catch the team's number?"

"I didn't even catch her name," he said. "Listen, I don't have an ulterior motive. All I want is to return property to its rightful owner."

"Fax me some ID, your cell number, and the time of the call, and I'll see what I can do."

"I faxed Jessie my ID yesterday."

"Jessie has issues. Fax it directly to me."

"You don't know how much I appreciate this."

"Don't thank me yet. I'm not making any promises."

At this point he was convinced it would be easier to get Oprah's home phone number.

He hung up, thought about nuking some leftover pizza, thought better of it, leaned over the kitchen sink, and looked out the window. He was going to miss those woods. At first he had liked them because they reminded him of New Hampshire, but then, with time, he liked them because they were pure New Jersey.

FedEx had dropped off the contract earlier in the day. Maggy Boyd had explained everything in a long, chatty e-mail: where to sign, where to send it, what issues were still outstanding. It would take him all of five minutes to sign on the dotted line and slip it into the return envelope, but right now that other life seemed very far away.

Images from the other day were still fresh in his mind. The woman's pale peach sweater . . . her beautiful hazel eyes . . . the scarlet thong a better man wouldn't have noticed . . .

Women were definitely full of surprises.

Maybe she didn't make it.

The world was filled with uncertainty. He knew that firsthand. Maybe that was the reason for the bureaucratic runaround he had been getting. Death was the flip side of the coin of life. It was always an option in the real world. But would God help him save a life only to snatch that same life away a few hours later? His training told him that wasn't the way it was supposed to be, while his experience reminded him that sometimes that was the way it was and nothing in his bag of tricks could change it.

The thing to do was let it go, but that was the part of the job that always screwed him up. He got involved in people's problems; he let them into his heart, tried to keep communication going long after the other side was ready to move on.

Whoever she was, she wasn't his responsibility. The only thing he knew about her was that she drove a Miata, looked smoking hot in a thong, and liked the color red.

A lot.

What in hell was he supposed to do with that? The metal box of papers hadn't yielded any clues at all to her identity. It was clear at first glance that they were potentially valuable. They appeared to be authentic Revolutionary War–era letters written in a surprisingly clear hand. No business card. No receipt of any kind. No letters, notes, or memos written after 1778.

Wait a minute.

He straightened up. He was leading a meeting tonight and afterward he would share an early supper with some friends, one of whom was a retired cop who knew his way around the Department of Motor Vehicles.

License tags could yield a lot of information. He knew

it was a long shot, but maybe her car was still parked at the Promenade.

And, if not, he would think of something else.

Back at the hospital

"What on earth did you say to Dorothy and Sheila?" Maeve asked when she and Gwynn returned from their rescue mission. "We bumped into them in the parking lot and they were apopleptic."

"I didn't say anything." Kate, who had been engrossed in *As the World Turns*, reluctantly left Oakdale for New Brunswick. "Okay, so maybe I did tell them I hadn't been to mass since nineteen nincty-three, but that wasn't exactly a secret." She aimed the remote at the television and clicked OFF. "So do I still have a car?"

"Of course," Maeve said with an impatient wave of her hand. "Mission accomplished. I followed Gwynnie back to your house. We left it in the driveway."

Gwynn, who had been inspecting the latest additions to the massive floral displays multiplying on every level surface in the room, looked over at her mother.

"I'm fine, Gwynnie," she said with a laugh. "You don't have to look at me that way."

"What way?"

"Like I'm about to disappear."

Gwynn fiddled with a stem of stephanotis. "I don't think I've ever seen you sick in bed before."

"I'm not sick."

"But you are in bed," her daughter persisted, "and it's a little—" She lowered her head and started to cry.

Kate leaped out of bed and gathered her grown-up child in her arms. "Hey, none of that. This was just a little scare, that's all. There's nothing to cry over, Gwynnie."

"Your heart stopped!" Gwynn sobbed against her shoulder. "What if that guy hadn't been there to help? What if—" She sobbed harder, and for a second Kate was a young mother again trying to soothe her frightened little girl.

Kate stroked her daughter's hair and hugged her close. "But that didn't happen, honey. I'm right here with you and I'm not going anywhere." She glanced over Gwynne's shoulder toward Maeve and was shocked to see her mother weeping into her hands. "You're both making way too much of this, both of you. Nothing's changed. Everything is exactly the same as it was. I promise you."

To her amazement, her daughter sobbed louder.

"It's so unfair," Gwynn managed. "I told Gran—"

"Oh, that's water under the bridge," Maeve said through her tears. "We don't need to go there, Gwynn."

"But you said—"

"Said what?" Kate looked from her daughter to her mother.

"We were just talking before," Maeve said. "It's nothing for you to worry about."

Which, of course, made Kate worry. "What did you tell your grandmother that she doesn't want you to tell me?"

Gwynn sniffled twice. Kate grabbed a tiny box of tissues from her nightstand and handed it to the young woman.

"Gwynn?" she prompted.

"You could have died all alone," Gwynn said, bursting into a new round of tears. "Without anybody to love you."

She might as well have kicked her in the stomach. "People love me," she said. "You love me, don't you?" Gwynn nodded. "Maeve loves me." She grinned. "Most of the time, at least. I have good friends and colleagues. I don't understand how you could—"

"Gwynn means you don't have a man," Maeve broke in. "A lover, to be specific."

Kate met Gwynn's eyes. "Is that what you meant?"

"Yes." Gwynn looked defiant. "I hate to see you so alone."

"I can't believe you said that."

"Well, it's true," Gwynn said. "All I know is that I don't want to end up your age with nobody to hold me at night or care if I live or die."

"Gwynn! That's a terrible thing to say." She loved her life. She enjoyed living alone. Why would her daughter and her mother think otherwise? "I'm completely happy with things the way they are."

"That's the worst part of all," Gwynn said as Maeve watched from the sidelines. "You don't even know what you're missing."

"And you do?" Kate's voice rose despite herself. "I don't think you could possibly have any idea how—"

"Andy and I are getting married."

For a moment Kate thought she would need CPR for the second time that week. "Not funny."

"She's not trying to be funny," Maeve said. "Surely you saw this coming."

Saw it coming? Gwynn fell in and out of love on a regular basis. For the sake of her sanity, Kate had long ago stopped trying to keep track of the ever-changing cast of characters.

She wheeled around to face her mother. "You knew about this?"

Maeve nodded. "She told me—"

"I told Gran about it in the car today," Gwynn said, taking charge. "I wanted to tell you the other day—remember I said we should have lunch in Princeton?—but that's when you had your . . ." Her words trailed off.

"Had my heart attack," Kate said, aware that her heart hurt more right this second than it had during the worst of the MI. She cast around for the right thing to say, but she wasn't sure those words existed in her vocabulary. "I thought you were planning to start grad school in September."

Was she imagining it or was Gwynn actually blushing? "My plans have changed."

"Your plans have changed? When? In the last ten minutes? You've been accepted. You were going to share an apartment with Tanya and Britt. You were going to intern in your dad's office next summer. Have you told him? Have you told Tan and Britt? Have you told the school yet?" She paused for breath. "Andy's a fisherman, honey. He lives on the docks."

"What does that have to do with anything? I love him," Gwynn shouted, "and I don't want to wake up one day and wish I hadn't taken the easy way out."

"The easy way? Going back to school isn't the easy way, it's the smart way. If it's real, Andy will still be there when you graduate."

"And he'll still be living on the docks, right? Go ahead! Say it. You think I can do better."

"Of course I think you—"

Maeve shot her a warning look, and for the first time in years Kate heeded her.

"I'm sorry," she said. "I didn't mean to take it that far."

Gwynn was poised somewhere between tears and anger, and the look in her eyes made Kate feel ashamed of herself. She had meant every word, but she wished she had found a kinder way to express it.

Thank God for Maeve.

"Gwynnie, I thought you were going to duck out for some veggie wraps. That deli across the courtyard looks promising."

Gwynn hesitated. Maeve pushed. Kate was too upset to do anything at all except stand there as her daughter's future crumbled around her feet.

Maeve turned to Kate. "You can have a veggie wrap, can't you? Low cholesterol, no trans fats, it should be okay."

Kate nodded. She would have nodded yes to a bacon-wrapped cheeseburger at that point if it meant she would gain some breathing room.

Gwynn grabbed her purse and disappeared without a word to Kate.

"I'm glad you reined it in," Maeve said as Gwynn went in search of sustenance. "Gwynn is a free spirit. She's also a grown woman. You have to let her find her own way."

Kate sank down onto the bed. "If you keep saying things like that, I might have a relapse."

"Gwynnie and I are very much alike," Maeve went on. "Another Moonchild. That's why I understand her."

And that was exactly what scared her. She could see her daughter thirty years from now with a string of marriages under her belt. "She's flighty, immature, and irresponsible."

"She's also highly creative, high-spirited, and searching for the right path." Maeve poured herself a glass of water and plucked a shiny red apple from the basket near the radio. "The truth is, she's nothing like you, honey, and that isn't a crime."

"And what exactly does that mean?"

"Look at you," Maeve said, her Balinese dancer earrings jiggling with the movement of her head. "You had a heart attack four days ago—and an angioplasty, no less—and you act like nothing happened."

"It was a minor heart attack," Kate reminded her. "Angioplasties are outpatient procedures. No big deal."

"It's a very big deal," Maeve persisted. "You needed CPR. Most people in your shoes would be wrestling with some major life issues right now."

"I thought you raised me not to be like most people."

"Quite frankly, honey, this isn't normal. You're in denial."

"Now you're telling me I shouldn't bounce back so easily?"

"Well, it does strike me as a tad odd." Maeve bit into the apple and chewed with great gusto. "This should be a time for reflection and renewal."

"You reflect on it," Kate said, wishing she had an unlisted hospital room. "Personally I can't wait until I get home and everything gets back to normal."

She had the feeling she was the only woman in the world with more than a passing affection for normal.

Maeve considered her for what seemed like forever. "I went wrong somewhere with you, but I can't figure out what my mistake was."

"Six husbands might be a good place to start."

"That never bothered you. I married good men. You liked them all."

"They were terrific guys, but that doesn't mean it didn't bother me. I would have liked it better if you'd let one of them stick around long enough to unpack."

"You never said anything."

"I got pregnant and married at seventeen. That should've been a clue."

"There were options available to you," Maeve reminded her. "You could have chosen a different path."

"I was a practicing Catholic then. There were no different paths."

"We always have choices," Maeve said in her best New Age Guru voice, the one she used on book tours and speaking engagements. "What we don't always have is the guts to own those choices."

Emotional confrontations were her mother's lifeblood.

They invigorated Maeve and brought her closer to the other person and the universe.

Emotional confrontations made Kate feel as if she'd been run over by a UPS truck, and as a rule she did her best to avoid them.

She leaned back against her pillows and met Maeve's eyes. "So she told you this afternoon?"

"I'd had my suspicions," Maeve said. "Didn't you?"

"Nope," said Kate. "Not a single one. I thought he was just one of the crowd where she works."

"She's been seeing him for a few months."

"Yes, but she secs lots of people. I had no idea he was special."

"Then you haven't been listening, Kate."

Score one for the alpha female in the family.

"So tell me about my car," she said, putting aside Gwynn's earthshaking decision for the moment. "Any dents, scratches, or parking tickets I should know about?"

"Your car is fine but an odd thing happened while we were there." Maeve put down the half-eaten apple. "Some guy was checking it out."

"Tell me you're joking."

"He was parked right behind your car. He stayed there for ten seconds, then drove away."

Who needed a nuclear stress test when you had family to do the job? "I stole a spot from a guy in an old blue car."

"The plot thickens," Maeve said. "This guy was in a beat-up blue Honda."

"Now that's scary. What sane person would nurse a grudge over a parking space?" A flicker of memory tickled the back of her mind, then receded. "Did you ask him what he was doing?"

"By the time we wound our way around to where you were parked, he was gone."

"Did you see what he looked like?"

Maeve closed her eyes. For a second Kate was afraid her mother was trying to channel the guy, but then she said, "Dark hair. Maybe late thirties. Sad eyes. I could see that all the way across the parking lot."

The hairs on the back of her neck lifted just enough to catch her attention.

. . . hold on to me . . . I won't leave you . . .

"I think that was him."

"Our Good Samaritan?"

"He was the only man around at the time. I was walking across the parking lot and I saw him leaning against his car, talking on his cell phone. He looked over at me and I saw he was wearing a Grateful Dead T-shirt and I was afraid he was going to start up over the parking spot—"

"And—?" her mother prompted.

"And nothing. That's all I can remember." She aimed a look in Maeve's direction. "I wish you'd managed to talk to him."

"We don't know this is the same man, Kate. Gwynn thought he might be a car thief sizing up your Miata."

"And it might have been the man who saved my life."

"And what if it isn't? You can find out just about anything on the Internet. We don't want some nut showing up on your doorstep."

"I don't think it's some nut," Kate said. *I want him to find me, Mom. Can you believe it? I actually want a stranger to track me down.*

"It's all part of the grand plan," Maeve said. "If you're meant to see him again, you will, and if you're not, there's nothing you can do to change your fate. It's all been pre-ordained."

Was Maeve going Buddhist again? At least during Maeve's Wicca period, there had been spells and charms designed to goose fate along a different path.

They both looked toward the door at the sound of a familiar laugh. It was Gwynn, aglow with excitement. "You won't believe who I found wandering the halls!" She poked her head back out into the hall. "It's okay. She's awake."

Ed Bannister stood in the doorway, barely visible behind an armful of more larkspur and wisteria than Kate had ever seen any place short of a botanic garden in paradise.

On a surprise scale of one to ten, the appearance of her ex-husband with her favorite blooms was off the chart.

"Ed!" Maeve leaped to her feet. She had always had a soft spot for her former son-in-law. "It's been too long."

Ed handed Gwynn the flowers, then enveloped Maeve in a bear hug. "I read your latest on the plane, Mae." He mimed wiping sweat from his brow. "Nobody warned me you were X-rated these days."

Maeve laughed as she hugged him back. "A healthy sex life promotes a healthy life," she said, "and that isn't limited to people under sixty-five."

Maeve's current book promoted the sexual, social, and psychological benefits of Tantric sex for the senior citizen. Kate was proud of Maeve's success, but there were times she wished her mother wrote under a pseudonym.

"How cool is this?" Gwynn said, clearly delighted with the impromptu family reunion. "The elevator doors opened and there he was, wandering the halls looking for Mom."

Gwynn was an unapologetic daddy's girl. Kate braced herself for the pangs of jealousy that usually followed one of these father/daughter get-togethers, but this time she felt only regret that they hadn't been able to make it all turn out the way their daughter obviously still wanted it to.

"We're going to need two vases for all of these," Gwynn said, then dashed off with the flowers to the utility room down the hall.

"I thought you were in the outback," Kate said to her ex-husband. She could still see the teenage boy she had married in the grown man who stood before her, and probably always would. Once, a very long time ago, she had believed she would grow old with him.

"Marie tracked me down through the bush pilot who flew me in." He had met and married Marie a few months after their divorce became final.

Poor Gwynn. Romantic impetuosity ran in both sides of the family.

"You didn't have to do this."

"Of course he did," Maeve piped up. "We're family."

"We *were* family," Kate reminded her mother. Thirteen years was a long time to be divorced.

"You share a child together. That makes you family, no matter what the courts say."

For a woman who had danced through a half-dozen marriages and more engagements than anyone cared to count, Maeve retained an old-fashioned reverence for the institution that was as charming as it was illogical.

"Sit." Kate gestured toward a chair near the window. "You look exhausted."

"Good idea." Ed stifled a yawn. "I came straight from the airport."

"I'm going to strangle our daughter. What did she say to Marie anyway that pulled you out of the outback?" Gwynn could turn a root canal into major neurosurgery. Kate could just imagine what she could do with a heart attack.

He looked at her as if she had lost her mind. "She said you had a heart attack. I didn't need more than that."

"I'm fine, Ed. Stop looking at me like I'm going to disappear."

He didn't crack a smile. "Gwynn said you flatlined and a stranger gave you CPR in the parking lot."

"That's the story, but I don't remember the details."
*They said he held on to me when I thought I was going to
slip away and he didn't let go . . .*

"You should call and take him out to dinner when you're
back on your feet," Ed said. "There aren't many Good
Samaritans out there. They deserve a little recognition."

"I wish I could, but I don't know his name."

Maeve looked up from her knitting. "Kate thinks he
was wearing a Grateful Dead T-shirt."

"A Deadhead?" Ed threw back his head and laughed.
"I'd pay good money to see Kate with a Deadhead."

"You make me sound a little judgmental." Kate's feelings were seriously wounded. "I wouldn't judge a man by
his T-shirt."

Her ex-hippie mother couldn't resist. "Honey, you came
out of the womb with a scorecard in your hand and God
help anyone who doesn't measure up."

She considered the source. This was Maeve French
talking, the woman who made her living with her imagination, a copy of the *Kama Sutra*, and a deck of tarot cards.

"Oh, don't look at me like that," Maeve said, waving a
bejeweled hand in the air. "You are a formidable woman,
but somebody has to tell you the truth."

Ed had been around the French women long enough to
know better than to allow himself to be drawn into one of
these impossible-to-win discussions, and feigned a catnap.

"Your heart was trying to tell you something," Maeve
said. "You need to let some whimsy into your heart."

"I'll tell Dr. Lombardi," Kate said. "He's leaning toward Lipitor."

Maeve, who was very good at ignoring cheap shots,
plunged ahead. "This is a sign from above that it's time
for a change."

"A sign from above? I thought your goddesses were all
earthbound."

"A woman's belief system isn't meant to be parsed like a subordinate clause." Maeve looked toward Ed for support. "Besides, a little spirituality wouldn't hurt you, Katherine Margaret."

"I agree." So much for Ed's fake catnap. "Marie and I decided a few years ago to start going back to church. Best decision we've ever made."

Kate didn't even try to mask her surprise. "I suppose you went back for the kids' sake?" Ed and Marie had three children, all under the age of twelve.

"That's how it started," Ed said, "but I think we've gotten more out of it than they have."

"So you're a practicing Catholic again." She couldn't have been more surprised if he had told her he'd decided to take up ballet.

"Hard to believe, isn't it?"

"Yes," she said with a laugh. "I thought twelve years at St. Aloysius had pretty much beaten it out of you too."

"I found I missed the ritual."

"You always did like the smell of incense." She meant it as a joke, but nobody laughed. What on earth was going on today? A sense of humor was definitely an endangered species.

"I'm not talking about the theatrics of religion," Ed said as Maeve nodded in agreement. "I'm talking about the sense of continuity." Apparently for Ed it was about family, about his own history, about taking strength from something bigger than he was, bigger than any problem life could throw his way.

It was a side of him Kate had never seen before, and she was intrigued. Funny how you could know a man your entire life, share a ten-year marriage and a beautiful child, and still not begin to understand what made him tick.

"You never miss it?" he asked her.

She thought about it for a moment. "Last Christmas

I thought about going to midnight mass but I stretched out on the sofa with some eggnog and the feeling passed."

"My daughter the comedienne," Maeve said with a shake of her head. "The closer you get to her authentic self, the more she makes with the jokes."

"I don't do that."

"Yes, you do."

"Organized religion isn't for everyone," she said, wishing she didn't sound quite so defensive. "I think I'm managing to lead a decent and productive life without it."

"But are you as happy as you could be?" her mother prodded.

"Is anybody?"

"Some people are."

"I don't see what religion has to do with my happiness."

Ed raised his hands in surrender. "I didn't mean to start a holy war, ladies."

"Don't worry. You didn't start anything, Ed. This is an ongoing skirmish," Maeve said. "My daughter doesn't think much of my spiritual quests."

"Maybe I'd think more of your spiritual quests if they didn't always end up with a new wardrobe and a six-figure book deal."

They were all grateful when Gwynn floated back into the room carrying two plastic vases overflowing with Ed's very expensive flowers. Gwynn herself overflowed with funny stories and observations, all tailored to amuse her father and remind him that his firstborn still needed his attention too.

Kate couldn't help but wonder when Gwynn planned to drop the Andrew bomb on poor, unsuspecting Ed.

Then again maybe Ed wasn't half as clueless as she had been and was prepared. His emotional radar had always been more well developed than hers. He had known she wanted to leave him before she was willing to admit that the marriage had run its course. She doubted he would be as blindsided as she had been by Gwynn's news.

Kate pretended to doze as conversation washed over her. All of this emotional Sturm und Drang was exhausting. Her heart attack had made everyone else just the slightest bit crazy and they were wearing her out.

She finally convinced Ed that she wasn't going to have a relapse and that he should go home to his family and catch up on his sleep.

"You should eat something first," Gwynn said. "Why don't we go get something in the courtyard before you go?"

Ed hesitated, but something in his daughter's eyes and tone of voice persuaded him to go with her. No surprise there. Kate had chosen the father of her only child very well. Ed was a terrific father, and her only regret was that they hadn't been able to grant their daughter's greatest wish: that her parents would stay married.

"He's good with her," Maeve said after Ed and Gwynn left. "She'll listen to what he has to say."

"Ouch," Kate said. "That hurts."

"She's a daddy's girl, sweetie. Always was, always will be. There's nothing you can do about that."

"Do you think he can persuade her to go home and get back to work?"

"I hope so," Maeve said. "She's on the phone with Andrew from the moment we get to your place until we leave the next morning."

"A slight exaggeration, Mom?"

"She sleeps with her cell phone on the pillow so they can breathe for each other."

"Oh God. I thought we left that behind when she turned eighteen."

"She's a romantic. Some of us never leave it behind."

"And how about you?" Kate asked. "You should get back to your book tour."

Maeve looked surprised. "And leave you to fend for yourself?"

"I don't need anyone to take care of me. I'll be going back to work next week."

"I thought Dr. Lombardi told you to take three weeks off."

"I don't know where you got that from. He hasn't mentioned anything like that."

Maeve tapped her earrings with her index finger and set them dancing, the way she did whenever she was about to make a big announcement. "I cancelled my tour, honey. I'm going to stay right here and take care of you until you're back on your feet, no matter how long it takes." She leaned over and kissed the top of Kate's head. "It will be like a mini-vacation for both of us."

Was forty-one too old to run away from home?

Four

Friday meetings could go either way. Sometimes it was standing room only, everyone looking to stockpile support against the uncertainties of the weekend ahead, while other times it was the leader and a handful of longtime members who found strength in routine, not numbers.

Mark had been leading the group for almost a year and he'd grown used to the ebb and flow. Ultimately it had nothing to do with him and everything to do with everybody else.

They were an eclectic group of cops, lawyers, doctors, writers, teachers, housewives, ex-cons, and a priest on sabbatical, with one thing in common: they were all recovering alcoholics who wanted to stay sober and were willing to do whatever it took to make that happen.

He'd been to groups that were nothing more than an aggregation of individuals linked by an acronym. But this one was different. He'd found some real friends and he wasn't looking forward to telling them that the New Hampshire job had come through and he'd be leaving Memorial Day weekend.

He switched off the lights and locked the door. Scott, Matty, and Ann were waiting for him in the parking lot for the weekly run to Zaslow's for pastrami and fellowship.

"I've got news," he said after they'd settled into a booth and placed their orders.

"You won the Megabucks lottery," Ann said.

"You're trading in that Honda for a Pinto," Matty chimed in.

"You sold the house," Scott said, "didn't you?"

"I signed the papers Wednesday morning," he said. "We close the Thursday before Memorial Day."

"Shit." Matty didn't even try to hide his disappointment. "That was fast."

Ann elbowed Matty in his well-padded ribs. "You knew this was going to happen sooner or later."

Scott gave Mark one of those ex-cop looks that had scared hell out of a generation of perps. "You got the job?"

"I got the job."

It was a bittersweet moment for all of them. They had all known he would go back sooner or later, but it surprised them just the same. He told them about the timeline his real estate agent had laid out and about the equally stringent timeline Maggy had set for his return to New Hampshire.

"I don't see what they've got that we haven't got," Matty said. "Maple syrup? You can get that at Costco."

Ann shot him a look. "We all have fences to mend. Mark's happen to be in New Hampshire."

The waitress brought their orders and they tucked into pastrami sandwiches while they caught up on the last week. Matty had had a root canal. Ann's traffic dispute was headed to court. Scott's insurance work might take him to Dallas next week, but he wouldn't know until Sunday night.

"We already know what your week was like," Ann said, reaching for a kosher dill. "You're pulling up stakes and leaving us behind."

He looked up from the remains of his sandwich. "Actually there's more." And he told them about the red-haired woman in the Miata.

Even he had to admit it was a damn good story. It had drama, a hint of sex, a touch of *ER* and *Grey's Anatomy.* What it didn't have was any kind of resolution.

"You went all the way to the hospital with her and you never got her name? What a moron!" Ann was the tactful one of the group.

"I had other things on my mind." Her life had seemed more important than her identity at the time.

"So why are you looking for her?" Scott probed. "Idle curiosity or is it something else?"

He didn't answer right away, which was an answer in itself. "She was carrying some Revolutionary War documents in a metal box. I brought them with us on the ambulance but—" They knew the rest.

"You've got a problem, pal," Scott said as the others exchanged meaningful looks. "No name. No ID. You don't even know where they took her."

"You could take out an ad in the paper," Ann suggested. "If those papers are valuable, somebody's bound to know about them and see it."

"What you need is a plate number," Scott the ex-cop said. "If you had that I could run a trace for you."

Mark reached into his pocket and withdrew a folded piece of paper and slid it across the table toward Scott. "I was hoping you'd say that."

*　*　*

To Kate's surprise she was able to convince both her mother and her daughter that she could manage without them for one night and persuaded them to go home a little after five p.m.

Gwynn got all teary when they were saying good-bye. "Be happy for me," she whispered in Kate's ear as they hugged. "I know what I'm doing is right."

Kate hugged her back, but the words Gwynn wanted to hear wouldn't come. "Don't forget to call Aidan O'Malley," she said instead. "He's not going to hold your job forever."

She regretted her comment as soon as it passed her lips. Gwynn's slender body stiffened in her arms and Kate felt a wall rise between them.

Maeve shook her head in obvious disbelief. Kate didn't blame her. Of all the things she could have said to her daughter, all the words of wisdom or love or comfort she could have offered, she had opted for the practical with a side order of implied criticism. *Better hold on to your waitress job, honey, because Fisherman Andy will never earn enough money to support you both.*

They had had their differences over the years. What mother and daughter hadn't? But she had never felt the sense of isolation that she felt right now.

For the first time since her heart attack, Kate was alone, and she settled back down against the pillows.

Sleeping in the middle of the day was still an alien concept. She envied people who could shut out the world and nap while the sun was shining. She flipped through the stack of books and magazines on her nightstand, but nothing caught her interest. Judge Judy was dispensing rough justice on one of the local television stations, but she wasn't in the mood for battling families and their operatic confrontations. She had had enough of that already today.

She looked at the clock. The evening crush of visitors was still an hour away. Paul had been there every night, driving all the way down from Manhattan through rush-hour traffic. Her assistant, Sonia; her accountant, Liz; Max the refinisher; Haoyin from across the street; Lydia, the clockmaker; Cookie Moore, the fiber artist from Clinton; even Marilyn Perrone, who had tried to put her out of business last year and wasn't the least bit apologetic about it: they all made it their business to turn room 405 into Party Central.

She wasn't a big fan of early evening. Everyone rushing around, heading home, heading out, hooking up with friends and lovers, planning the night ahead. It was the only time of day when she ever felt lonely, when the choices she had made didn't fit quite as well as they did the other twenty-three hours of the day.

It had been different when Gwynn was little and there had been all of the chaos and drama of after-school activities, making supper, supervising homework and bath time, signing permission slips, making costumes, sitting by the window trying to pretend she wasn't waiting up for her daughter to come home from a date. She had been secretly glad when Gwynn decided against going away to school and opted for Rutgers instead. Not that she dreaded an empty nest, but there was something to be said for delaying the inevitable as long as you could.

French Kiss was her top priority now, and the hard work and long hours were paying greater dividends than she had ever imagined. She couldn't wait to get back to the shop and start unpacking all of those boxes and crates she'd brought back from England. It would be like Christmas all over again.

There it was again, one of those flickering buzzes of memory just out of reach. An appointment? A meeting? Something important but she couldn't pull it up from the darkness no matter how hard she tried. Lombardi had told her not to worry about the gaps in her memory, that most of the missing bits and pieces would fill themselves in, and even if they didn't, she had suffered no permanent damage.

Still, she had been down in the Princeton area for some reason, but for the life of her she couldn't remember what that reason was.

She was grateful for the interruption when Janine, her favorite nurse, breezed into the room with an armful of red roses.

"Good," Janine said. "You're awake."

"It's only five-thirty," Kate said with a rueful laugh. "Of course I'm awake."

"Should I give you the standard lecture on resting up while you're here or would you rather talk about these gorgeous flowers?"

"Definitely the flowers."

"That's what I thought." Janine buried her nose in the abundant blooms and breathed deeply. "We took a vote and decided this batch says a whole lot more than 'Get well soon.'"

Three dozen bloodred roses in a cut crystal vase did make a statement.

"Are you sure they're for me?" There wasn't anybody on her romantic horizon and hadn't been for a long while.

"Honey, who else could they be for? You've cornered the flower trade around these parts." Janine plucked a card from the center of the profusion of roses and handed it to Kate.

Kate read the card and laughed out loud.

Let's give 'em something to talk about. —PG

"So who is he?" Janine asked as she made room for the roses on the windowsill. "That's one very major statement the guy is making here."

"Nothing romantic," Kate said, laughing at the look of disappointment on the other woman's face. "Just my friend Paul trying to stir up trouble."

"Which one is Paul?"

"The one who sent pizzas up to the nurses' lounge yesterday. I've known him since I was five years old." She slipped the card into the top drawer of the nightstand. "Trust me, there's nothing romantic going on." *Thirty-six red roses? What were you thinking, Grantham?*

"A major hottie sends you a boatload of roses and you're telling me there's nothing romantic?"

It did sound ridiculous, but this was Paul they were talking about. He was like her brother.

"We found out a very long time ago that we work better as friends."

"And he's not gay?"

"Definitely not gay."

"Then I'd rethink this if I were you. A man doesn't send three dozen red roses to a pal. Looks to me like you're wasting an opportunity."

Close friendship between a straight man and a straight woman would always be suspect. The hopeless romantics of the world, and there were an awful lot of them, usually hoped for more and were invariably disappointed by people like Kate.

Romantic love wasn't high on her list of priorities. She had never experienced that rush of excitement at the sound of a man's voice or the touch of his hand that sent Maeve's and Gwynn's blood racing on a regular basis. The romantic gene that defined the other French women had clearly skipped a generation and left her immune.

Janine was halfway out the door when she stopped and turned back. "What's wrong with me? There's someone here to see you but he wanted me to make sure you weren't napping first."

Her family believed in an open-door policy even when the door in question was locked and bolted. Her friends and co-workers didn't stand on ceremony either. Only a stranger would worry about whether she was sleeping. Wouldn't it be terrific if it was the Good Samaritan in the Grateful Dead T-shirt?

Instead, a perfectly pleasant-looking man in a black turtleneck and black slacks smiled at her from the doorway. Doctor? Lawyer? Renegade therapist?

"I'm Father Boyle. I apologize for just dropping by, but Sheila Fennessey said you might want to speak with someone."

For the second time that day Kate considered making a run for it, but twelve years of Catholic school education were hard to ignore so she stayed put, even though "Catholic" was more of a historical reference point than a current description of her religious beliefs.

"I'm afraid my aunt Sheila sent you out here on a wild-goose chase." She shook his hand and motioned for him to take a seat. "She probably forgot to tell you that I haven't been inside a church for anything other than a wedding in at least twenty years."

"God doesn't keep a calendar on us."

"That isn't what Sister Michael Maureen said back at St. Aloysius." She meant it as a joke, but the joke carried a slight sting.

She had to hand it to him. He didn't flinch. "I'm sure Sister Michael Maureen has updated her perspective since you last talked to her."

Clearly he had never met Sister Michael Maureen, but she restrained herself from saying so. She might not believe the way she had as a child, but respect for his religious vocation curbed her tongue. In many ways, once a good Catholic schoolgirl, always a good Catholic schoolgirl. Old habits died hard.

He inquired about her health and she ran through the story for what felt like the fiftieth time that day.

"Looks like God has other plans for you," Father Boyle said when she finished. "You've been given a second chance."

Why did the notion of second chances get under her skin the way it did? "Maybe it just wasn't my time."

"Isn't that the same thing?"

"I don't know, Father, and to be honest I'm not sure it matters." Where was it guaranteed that you wouldn't make even worse mistakes the second time around?

"Most people find themselves with a renewed sense of faith after an experience like yours."

"To be honest, all I've found myself with is a renewed sense of boredom. I can't wait to get home and back to work."

"You've been through a life-changing experience. Don't minimize its effect on your spiritual and emotional life. It takes some people longer than others to process all of the changes. Fortunately God has infinite patience with us."

"You sound like my mother." She didn't mention that Maeve dabbled in Wicca or that her daughter was exploring the Kabbalah. The man had his ecclesiastical hands full enough with her.

"Faith can be a comfort in troubled times."

"I know," she said, taken aback by the catch in her voice. Since when did she get all emotional about religion? "I wish—" She shook her head.

"Go on," he said. "I'm here to listen." Father Boyle settled back in the chair as if there were no other place in heaven or on earth that he'd rather be.

"I wish my daughter weren't dating a fisherman. I wish I could remember what I was doing in Princeton on Monday. And I wish I had something interesting to say, Father, but I don't. The heart thing was a minor problem, they took care of it, and I can't wait to get back to normal."

"No, I want to know what was it you stopped yourself from saying."

"You're good," she said with a small laugh. "I thought I covered pretty well."

"You did," the priest said. "We often hold back from saying the thing that's most important to us."

"Okay," she said, taking a metaphorical deep breath, "I wish I could thank the man who saved my life, but they rushed me out of St. Francis so fast that we lost each other. That's what I was going to say." And she wished she hadn't. Saying it out loud that way hammered home the enormity of what had happened to her and she preferred to keep it an arm's length away.

"Chaplains have a pretty good network. I might be able to find out something for you."

"I appreciate that, Father, but I think it's a lost cause at this point."

Father Boyle was a smart guy and he knew the brush-off when he heard it.

"Would you mind if I said a prayer for your continued recovery?"

To her surprise, she didn't mind at all.

He stood up next to her bed and bowed his head. The words were simple and direct. She didn't know where those words went or who, if anyone, actually heard them, but to her surprise the gesture touched her mending heart.

"Call me if you'd like to talk," Father Boyle said. He propped a business card against the telephone on her nightstand, then said good-bye.

Her days at St. Aloysius seemed a very long time ago, and for a moment she almost missed them.

It had been nice to believe that someone was out there watching over her.

Five

Dr. Lombardi scrolled his way down the screen of information, then turned toward Kate. "Looks perfect," he said, breaking into a smile. "You're a free woman."

"You mean, right now?" she asked. "This minute?"

"As soon as I can fill out the paperwork and you can find yourself a ride home."

"And I can go back to work on Monday?"

"I didn't say that."

"You said everything looks perfect. I feel wonderful. My shop is less than a mile away. It's almost silly not to go back."

"Sit down, Kate. You're going home but you're not in the clear just yet."

He explained her situation, the slim odds of a recurrence, the steps he wanted her to take to avoid one, the regimen of meds and physical exercise that would be part of her daily schedule, some behavioral modifications he hoped she would adopt.

"I'll do my best, Doctor, but I have to tell you I've tried meditation and it didn't work."

"Try again."

"It stressed me out more than the problems I was dealing with."

"I highly recommend you keep trying. It will help you deal with the emotional aftereffects that accompany MIs."

"Everyone keeps mentioning these emotional aftereffects, but I have to tell you that I just plain don't know what on earth you're talking about. I feel the same as I did before this happened."

"No euphoria?" he asked. "No renewed appreciation for life?"

"I wish I could say yes, but life seems pretty much the same as it did before this happened." Which wasn't a bad thing. She liked her life just fine.

"Well, there are exceptions to everything, but as a rule my patients have a period of intense euphoria and renewed joy in life."

"Is the euphoria permanent?"

"No," he said. "Sometimes it lasts a few days, sometimes a few weeks, and it disappears without warning. I warn my patients not to make any big decisions for a few weeks because their judgment may not be as keen as usual. Most stick close to home and family, but I've had a few patients who married, divorced, quit their jobs, and ran off to Tahiti in those first few postcardiac weeks. You need to take care."

"You just described my family," she said. "I had the heart attack, they're suffering the aftereffects."

"Just take it slow," he warned again. "This isn't the time to make life-changing decisions."

"Doctor," she said, unable to hold back the laughter, "believe me, I'm the last person you have to worry about."

Rocky Hill—later that same morning

There had to be a limit to how many times a man could check his e-mail without causing serious damage to the motherboard.

He'd clicked SEND/RECEIVE so often since breakfast that the touchpad was showing signs of wear.

Three new messages.

TO: mark.kerry@mklj.net
FROM: mboyd@nh2day.net
SUBJECT: revised contract attached

WHERE'S THE CONTRACT????? pls sign it asap and send it to Bishop Clennon so he can put the final stamp on it.
What are you waiting for?
Maggy

He wished he had an answer to that question.

TO: mark.kerry@mklj.net
FROM: annie-s@aol3.com
SUBJECT: meeting

The church basement will be closed next week—renovations. Temple Beth Israel said we can use their auditorium, but not Friday. Any ideas?
Ann

He'd get back to her.

TO: mark.kerry@mklj.net
FROM: scott5367@ppd-ret.gov
SUBJECT: info

Room 405 - Central Jersey Medical Center
Katherine Margaret Lee French
dob 01-06-65
622 Indigo Lane
Coburn, NJ

Good luck.
SCOTT

He couldn't stop smiling as he printed out the note.

Sometimes God didn't just show a man the way. Sometimes He handed him a road map.

* * *

"We're going to miss you," Janine said as she gestured Kate toward the obligatory wheelchair. "The last time we had this much fun was when Robin Williams came to visit a friend."

"And all that chocolate," one of the nurse's aides piped in. "We'll need to start a Weight Watchers group."

"You were all great to me," Kate said. "I can't thank you enough."

Janine rolled her onto the patient elevator and pressed G.

"So did Lombardi give you the big farewell speech?"

"He did. I think he's a little concerned."

"Concerned? We should all have charts like yours."

"I don't seem to be following the emotional profile of the post-MI patient. He seems to think I might suddenly turn into an emotional loose cannon."

"It's been known to happen but it's usually nothing more than excessive weeping and hugging everyone in sight."

"Highly unlikely in this case," Kate said. "I've never been one for a lot of emotional displays."

Janine rolled her across the lobby and out the front door into the late-afternoon sunshine.

"Last stop. Everybody out!"

Kate threw back her head and took a deep breath of sweet spring air. "Oh God, I'd forgotten how wonderful the air can smell." Five days of recycled hospital air had made her hungry for the real thing.

"You have your meds?" Janine asked.

Kate jiggled the paper bag on her lap. "Check."

"Instruction sheets?"

"Check."

"Follow-up appointment schedule?"

"Check."

"Then that's it. You're officially discharged."

Kate stood up and gave Janine a bear hug. "I'm really going to miss you."

Janine hugged her back. "Who's picking you up: your mother or your daughter?"

"Neither one." She gestured to a black Mercedes moving slowly toward them around the curved driveway. "Paul of the red roses."

Janine's eyes widened. "The plot thickens."

"I hate to disappoint you, Janine, but he was in the neighborhood."

It would make a funny story to tell Paul on the drive back up to Coburn.

* * *

The black Mercedes rolled away from the hospital entrance and a silver Toyota took its place. Mark angled around the small car, rounded the driveway, then found a parking space in the covered lot across from the emergency services area. A pair of elderly ladies in Easter-egg-pastel dresses were making their way slowly toward the elevator. They clutched each other's hands at the sound of his footsteps behind them, a flash of insight into old age and vulnerability.

He slowed his pace as he came even with them.

"Good afternoon, ladies. How are you today?" He kept his tone upbeat, his cadence even and unthreatening.

They turned to look at him and he was rewarded with twin looks of relief.

"We're just fine," the taller of the two said with a winning smile.

He fell into step with them as they exchanged pleasantries about the weather. He sneaked what he hoped was a discreet look at his watch but they caught him in the act.

"You don't have to worry about us," the taller one said, "but we've enjoyed your company."

"I'm sure you have important things to do," said the other with a flirtatious wink of one blue-shadowed eye. "Don't let us stop you."

He wished them well, reminded again of how much he enjoyed the company of old people, then took off for the lobby at a run.

A crowd waited at the elevator bank. He ducked into the stairwell and took the steps two at a time until he reached the fourth floor and room 405.

It was empty.

He grabbed the first nurse he saw. "I'm looking for Katherine French."

"Sorry," the young man said, "she was released about fifteen minutes ago."

"You mean she's gone?"

"That's what I mean." He flagged down a laughing nurse. "Hey, Patty, 405 checked out, right?"

"Right," the nurse named Patty said as she hurried past. "Janine wheeled her downstairs."

"She's okay?" Mark asked.

The male nurse shrugged. "Doubt Dr. Lombardi would let her go if she wasn't."

Relief shifted into determination.

"Do you know where Coburn is?"

Time for Plan B.

* * *

"What was that all about?" Paul asked as he exited the hospital grounds. "The nurse winked at me."

"You're famous," Kate said, delighted to be out of bed and in a moving vehicle. "Between the pizzas and the roses, you were the talk of the fourth floor."

"Did you like them?"

"You know I did, but three dozen? That was a bit showy even for you."

He didn't laugh. That should have told her something, but she was so intoxicated on freedom that it slipped right by her.

"So how did you end up pressed into delivery service?" Kate asked as he merged with traffic on Route 1.

"I volunteered," he said. "Gwynn is at ShopRite stocking up on low-fat, low-cholesterol goodies for you."

"And Maeve?"

"Burning sage on your windowsills."

It was the best laugh Kate had had in weeks. "You're kidding, right?"

"Actually she did say something about burning sage." He shot her a wicked grin. "Right after she reorganizes your underwear drawer."

"Oh God!" Kate sank down in the passenger seat as far as the shoulder restraint would allow. "She told you about the thong?"

It was his turn to laugh. "What was it our mothers used to say about clean underwear?"

She rolled her eyes. "Like wearing freshly laundered undergarments provided some kind of mystical protection against being hit by a truck."

"Guess you proved that wrong."

"The truck that hit me was only metaphorical," Kate said. "Besides, I'm not sure thongs qualify. They're more ornamental than functional."

"You don't hear me complaining, do you?"

She gave him a friendly whack on the forearm. "Try wearing one."

"You know you had us pretty worried."

"I think you've all gone just the slightest bit nuts."

"How're you handling it?"

"Me? I'm good as new." She swiveled around in her seat to face him. "Did you know Ed showed up straight from the outback?"

"Gwynnie told me."

"Did she tell you her news?"

"She's moving in with the fisherman."

"When did she tell you?"

"She didn't. I'm her godfather. I saw them together at Easter."

"They were together at Easter?"

"She brought him to Maeve's for dinner." He frowned in her general direction. "You don't remember?"

"Sort of," she lied. Gwynn's boyfriends were legion and, unfortunately, not terribly memorable. "And you saw there was something between them?"

"What am I, blind?"

"I didn't suspect a thing."

"No surprise there."

"What does that mean?"

"You know you're not exactly clued in when it comes to stuff like that."

"She's my daughter. If there'd been something to see, I would have seen it."

"There was and you didn't."

"That's beside the point." She fiddled with the fan adjustment. "Did you predict an engagement too?"

He whistled. "They're getting married?"

"That's what she says."

"What about school?"

She mimed flushing a john.

"Ouch," he said. "When did you find out?"

"She told Maeve and me yesterday and I assume she told Ed over an early dinner last night."

"Unless he told her his news first."

"Ed has news?"

"You really are out of the loop, French. Marie's expecting number four."

Kate felt her jaw drop into her lap. "Number four? Marie's older than I am."

"And obviously still fertile."

"I don't know what to say." There she was recovering from a minor heart attack while Ed's second wife dealt with morning sickness. It boggled the mind.

"Feeling any pangs?"

"No! God, no! Ed and I never had a fraction of what he and Marie have together."

"That's not what I meant. Haven't you ever thought about having another child?"

"Not since Ed and I divorced."

"You don't have to be married to have a child," Paul reminded her.

"Bringing up a child alone is hard work. I don't think I'd want to do it again." Even though Ed had remained an involved parent, she had still been the one who shouldered most of the day-to-day responsibilities.

"I miss the chaos," Paul was saying. "I would've liked another two or three."

She knew how tough it had been for him to adjust to seeing his kids only on alternate weekends.

"You're a man," she consoled him. "You could start another family when you're seventy-five."

"Gotta love biology," he said, and she rewarded him with another poke in the arm. "Maybe we should get together and give it a try while there's still time."

It was another old joke and one that usually didn't require a response.

"What do you think?" he pressed. "We're older and wiser. We don't expect fireworks. Maybe we should give it another shot."

"Very funny. I'm not sure postcardiac care includes practical jokes."

"I'm not joking."

She stared at him in utter disbelief. This couldn't possibly be happening. Paul was her old friend, her movie buddy, the pal she unloaded on when work or family or just plain life took a sharp turn toward crazy. She knew what had gone wrong with his marriage to Jill, why Edie broke off the engagement, what his four kids gave him on his last birthday that had brought him to tears.

"I love you, Katie."

Oh God. Why didn't he just drive them off a bridge and be done with it?

She reached over and patted his arm. "And you know how much I love you, Grantham."

Please let it go, Paul. If you stop now, we can just pretend this never happened.

"That's not what I mean."

"Where is this coming from?" she demanded. "When I left for England you were thinking of asking Lisa Dennison to go to Barbados for the weekend. Now you're saying you're in love with me. What happened?"

"Your heart attack happened," he said, changing lanes. "Suddenly everything was crystal clear."

"I'm the one who's supposed to be on an emotional roller coaster, not you."

"Back off, French," he said. "I'm having a moment here."

She had to laugh despite herself. "Do you have any idea how utterly ridiculous this will sound a few weeks from now?"

"Maybe it won't," he shot back. "Did you ever think of that?"

"I like being on my own, Paul. You know that."

"So do I," he said, "but life is short. Do you want to spend the rest of it alone?"

"I guess I always assumed that's exactly how I would spend it." She had Maeve. She had her daughter. She had good friends. Wasn't that enough? Being alone had never held any fear for her. She was strong, self-sufficient, content with who she was and what she had achieved.

Some women were given the whole package, romantic love and family and success, and some were given a portion of the whole. She understood that and was okay with it. Two out of three wasn't bad. If she were a baseball player, she would be in the Hall of Fame.

Besides, how could a woman miss what she didn't understand? Clearly she wouldn't recognize romantic love if it hit her in the head with three dozen American Beauty roses.

"Humor me, Kate. Keep an open mind. Have dinner with me tomorrow night and let's see what happens."

"We tried the romantic dinner thing ten years ago. We laughed so hard the candles guttered."

"Ten years is a long time. We've changed."

"Paul, have we met? Romantic gestures are lost on me and you know it." Love at first sight. Soul mates. Two hearts beating as one. She was clueless when it came to the Hallmark school of romantic love.

"Maybe you're a late bloomer."

"Maybe I'm happy the way I am."

He grinned over at her. "Maybe you're afraid I might be on to something."

She started to say something cutting, but a flash of insight cut her short. *He's lonely,* she realized. Beneath the smart remarks and veneer of sophistication, her old friend was lonely and that knowledge touched her deeply.

Intellectually she understood what he was feeling, but she had no firsthand knowledge of the emotion. This wasn't the kind of loneliness you erased by going to a movie with an old friend. This went far deeper into terra incognita. Maybe you had to have opened your heart wide to another person at least once in your life in order to feel that kind of loneliness.

Maeve had, many times. So had Gwynn. The only men with personal knowledge of Kate's heart were Dr. Lombardi and the man in the Grateful Dead T-shirt.

She tried to imagine what it would be like to feel that kind of deeply intimate connection with a man, Paul for example, but the best she could do was conjure up the same deep friendship and respect she felt for her ex. Hardly the stuff of everlasting love.

And definitely not the stuff of high romance.

Paul made a hard left onto Indigo Lane and her heart leaped at the sight of the carriage house nestled at the end of the block in a stand of oaks and maples. *Home,* she thought. Her small and wonderful home for one.

"Think about it," he was saying as they approached the driveway. "By tomorrow night you might be looking for a break from Mother Maeve."

"Okay, okay," she said, too preoccupied with excitement at being home again to argue. "We'll go out to dinner tomorrow night."

"I wouldn't mind more enthusiasm." He pulled in behind Maeve's crazy purple VW and turned off the engine.

"I don't have a romantic bone in my body. It's nothing personal." She unlocked her seatbelt and sighed as she looked across the yard. "I feel like I've been away for a century."

"Go on in," he said. "I'll bring your bags."

She leaned over and kissed his cheek. "You're a good friend."

He gave a short laugh. "That's a lousy thing to say."

She took her time walking across the front yard, letting the sunshine warm her shoulders, filling her lungs with the smell of newly cut grass. Her mother's laughter spilled through the open windows and beneath it she heard her daughter's chuckle. And there was a male voice too. An unfamiliar male voice. Startled, she stopped halfway up the path and looked back toward the street.

A pale blue Honda was parked midway up the block, behind Greg Kormac's flashy Navigator. She had stolen a parking spot from a car exactly like it on Monday. Maeve and Gwynn had seen its twin parked behind her Miata at the Promenade yesterday. And now here it was on Indigo Lane.

A burst of something close to pure joy spread through her chest. *He found me!* She hurried up the path and burst through the front door.

Maeve popped into the hallway. She looked like a teenager, aglow with excitement. "You'll never believe who—"

"Hello, Kate."

The world faded away. Everything, her mother, her child, her best friend, the floor beneath her feet, the very air in her lungs, it all vanished at the sound of his voice.

. . . I won't let you go . . . I'll never let you go . . .

She knew his voice, the smell of his skin, the way his hands felt against her skin, the taste of his mouth, everything that mattered. Everything she would ever need to know about him. Her heart surged, new and untried, with something painfully, scarily close to joy.

She ran to him, or maybe he ran to her. One moment she was standing alone in the middle of her hallway and the next she was in his arms, cheek pressed against his broad chest, breathing in his smell, listening to the quick and steady beat of his heart.

How long was it since she had been held in a man's arms? Months, years, maybe forever. She didn't know. She didn't care. Heaven existed. She could say that now as a natural fact.

His laughter rumbled beneath her ear. "Come on, Kate," he said in the same rich baritone she remembered, "let me see your face."

Laughing herself, she reluctantly leaned back in his arms and looked up at him.

"Oh my God!" she cried out. "You're a priest!"

Six

She jumped away from him as if she had been poked with a cattle prod. Who knew a Grateful Dead T-shirt inspired less horror than a clerical collar?

If anyone ever wanted to know if the fates had a sense of humor, she finally had the answer.

"This is Father Mark Kerry," Maeve said, hovering near them. "He showed up at the door about fifteen minutes ago."

"I'm so embarrassed," Kate said, trying frantically to forget the feel of his lean body pressed against hers. "It's just that I was—I mean, I was so excited to see you again." What was wrong with her? That was totally the wrong thing to say.

The tension between them was strong, almost irresistible. It took all of her willpower to keep from hurling herself into his arms again.

"The last time I saw you, you were on a stretcher attached to a twelve-lead EKG." He assessed her openly and his smile widened. "You look great."

"I feel great," she said, "but it's all because of you."

"I was in the right place at the right time," he said. "I'm glad I could help."

"So were a lot of other people, but they didn't save my life."

Their eyes met and she felt herself lifting right off the ground and sailing up to the ceiling with sheer happiness. His eyes were beautiful, sad and curious, the blue of sapphires.

He's a priest, Kate, remember he's a priest.

He took her hand and their fingers interlaced.

He's a priest . . . he's a priest . . . he's a priest.

"I've been trying to find you for days," he said. "I called every hospital in New Jersey looking for you."

"I tried to find you too."

You're holding hands with a priest, Kate. Stop it!

She heard her mother talking in the background, Gwynn's voice, the sharp tone of Paul's words, but nothing was getting past the staggering shock of recognition she was experiencing. She finally understood what all the fuss was about and wouldn't you know it? The guy was a priest.

"I finally went back to the Promenade and took your license plate number down. An ex-cop friend of mine ran it through DMV."

"Maeve and Gwynn went to pick up my car and they saw a car parked behind mine and I knew that was you."

Another minute or two, one missed traffic light or wrong turn, and they might never have found each other. The loss seemed so enormous, so overwhelming, it took her breath away.

"I'm glad," she said. "I—what I mean is . . . what I'm trying to say is that I'm so grateful that you—"

It took her a full second before she realized that the strangled, gasping sound she heard was the sound of her own sobs. Her entire body shook with the force of them as they ripped their way through her chest, tore at her throat, then broke free. She covered her face, helpless before a riptide of emotions that had caught her completely off-guard. Nothing in her life had prepared her for this. Not marriage. Not childbirth. Not even the heart attack when she was sure she was about to die.

The touch of his hand, the sound of his voice—that was all it took to send her free-falling into the world of romantic chaos, the one place she never thought she would be.

And the scariest thing of all was that she liked it.

* * *

She had been fine, emotional but fine, until she looked up and those wide hazel eyes of hers landed on the collar and the dam burst.

He was no stranger to people in emotional turmoil. Part of his job, an important part, was to be there in times of great pain and great joy. He was there to welcome new souls into the world and to help ease old ones into the next. He sat quietly next to hospital beds, prayed over problems that could shatter a man's soul, said the words that helped turn a man and a woman into a family with all that meant. He knew when to talk and when to listen. He could take a step back from the storm and wait for the sky to clear.

But he was helpless before Kate French's tears.

She was sobbing into her hands and nothing anybody did seemed able to stem the flow of tears. Her mother, clearly worried, tried to steer her toward a chair but Kate wouldn't budge. Her daughter, a time-capsule version of Kate twenty years ago, fluttered around with a bottle of Gatorade and talk of electrolytes. And the man, whoever he was, looked as if he would have knocked Mark flat on his ass if he hadn't been wearing a clerical collar.

Sometimes that collar was better than a Kevlar vest.

What he wanted to do was pull her back into his arms and hold her for a lifetime or two, feel her heart—her mended, powerfully beating heart—against his chest, bury his face in her hair, pile sensation upon sensation, memory upon memory, against a future without her.

Instead he did what he did best: tried to make sense from chaos.

"Maeve is right," he said. "You should sit down."

She looked up through her tears and nodded. "Okay."

Her mother and daughter exchanged looks, and then Maeve gestured him back toward the living room. He took Kate's hand to lead her toward the sofa and the shock of recognition, of completeness, hit him again and this time it almost brought him to his knees.

He had never felt the presence of God more powerfully than he did right now with her hand in his. He could scan back and re-create the chain of seemingly unrelated events that had brought them together five days ago in the parking lot of the Princeton Promenade. He had breathed life back into her body, felt her still heart start beating again. The inevitability of it all was as overwhelming as it was undeniable.

"Are you going to stand there all day?" asked the guy near the door.

Maybe they could stand there all day. He could think of worse fates. But the world didn't work that way and somehow they found themselves sitting next to each other on a squashy yellow sofa near a huge wall of windows that overlooked a garden. There were other people in the room. He heard them talking. He saw them as if from a great distance when they entered his line of vision, but they never really registered. Kate was his only reality.

She told him about her hospital stay, making him laugh at things nobody had ever made funny before. She was bright and witty and she cast so much light he almost had to look away.

It took him fifteen minutes and two cups of coffee before he remembered why he was there.

* * *

He was out to his car and back in again before Kate could get her bearings. He handed her a shiny metal box of papers, and the missing pieces began to fall into place.

"They looked valuable to me," he said, watching her closely as she sifted through the documents. "I wanted to deliver them in person."

"I don't know how to thank you."

"You don't have to. You're home and you're well," he said. "That's good enough."

And the funny thing was she knew he meant it. There was nothing of greed in his tone, no veiled glimmer of mercenary lust. Then again, he was a man of the cloth, and men of the cloth were supposed to be above such things, weren't they? Religious types operated on a higher plane.

Of course that didn't explain the intense pull she felt toward him, the bone-deep attraction. *Inappropriate* didn't begin to cover it. And you could add *unlikely*, *unexpected*, and *uncharacteristic* and that was just for starters.

They had warned her that this might happen, but she hadn't believed a word of it until now.

"Well, that's not good enough for me," she said. "The least I can do is invite you to lunch next week." She felt her cheeks redden with embarrassment. "I mean, this isn't a date or anything . . . I went to Catholic school . . . I know what's what . . ." She stopped, horrified by the run of nonsense spilling from her lips. "A priest *can* go out to lunch, can't he?"

If you judged by the explosion of laughter, she was ready for the big rooms down in Atlantic City. Who knew she was a budding stand-up comic?

"I don't get the joke," she said.

"Mark is an Episcopal priest," Maeve said. "He can have lunch *and* date if he wants to."

"Great," said Paul in his least friendly tone of voice. "Now that we've got that settled, where do you want your bags, Kate?"

Startled, she noticed her overnight bag dangling from his right hand and her matching tote dangling from his left. She had completely forgotten that her best friend was standing there. And to make matters worse, her mother and daughter were watching closely and taking notes.

"You can leave them in the foyer, Paul," she said, feeling instantly contrite and more than a little guilty. "Thanks for bringing them in."

"Upstairs is better," Maeve said. "Show him where, Gwynnie, would you?"

Gwynn cheerfully led an unhappy-looking Paul upstairs while Maeve mumbled something about checking the stove and disappeared, leaving Kate and Father Mark alone together.

"I'm not usually that big an idiot," she said. "I don't know why I got so flustered." She laughed nervously. "I mean, it's not like I've never spoken to a priest before."

"It's the collar," he said, laughing with her. "I should've worn the Dead shirt."

"Everything else about that day is still kind of murky but that shirt was unforgettable."

Their eyes locked again and a delicious shiver rippled through her.

"You saved my life," she said as tears welled up again. "I wouldn't be here today if you hadn't been there."

"I'm glad I was."

She grinned at him. "I'm gladder."

He grinned back. "No contest there."

The man was as close to perfect as they come. A tall, dark, handsome, kind, funny holy man.

Why couldn't he be a doctor or lawyer or your average run-of-the-mill bartender? Somebody she could curl up and fantasize about without feeling like she needed to go to confession.

"I'd like to make a donation to your church," she said, trying to elevate her thoughts to higher, more spiritual ground. "A small thank-you for returning these papers."

"I appreciate the thought," he said, "but I'm between assignments right now."

A priest who was between assignments? There must be a story in that. She wondered if she would ever have the chance to hear it. "If you have a favorite charity . . ."

"You mentioned lunch."

"You'd come for lunch?"

"If the invitation still holds, I would."

"Of course it holds! I'd love to have you come for lunch. When do you work—I mean, I know Sundays are probably pretty busy, but do priests have regular days off?" She was babbling again. Why did his religious vocation make her so profoundly uncomfortable? "I can make lunch any day you want. All you have to do is tell me. In fact, you don't even have to tell me right now. You can call me and let me know. Why don't you—"

"Tuesday."

"Tuesday," she repeated. "Okay. Tuesday."

"Tell me the time and I'll be here."

They settled on one o'clock, then exchanged cell numbers, e-mail addresses, and IM screen names just to be on the safe side.

Maeve glided into the room. "I made a nice Caesar salad with grilled chicken. We'd be delighted if you'd join us."

"Maeve always makes way too much," Gwynn called out from the kitchen. "We could feed an army."

Paul didn't offer any encouragement.

Mark hesitated and for a moment Kate thought he was going to say yes, but he didn't. Maeve gave him a huge bear hug and blinked back more than a few tears of gratitude. Gwynn planted a kiss on his cheek and got all choked up when she tried to share what was in her heart, which of course made Kate start crying all over again.

Paul grunted something that was either "Nice to meet you" or "Drop dead."

She walked him outside, feeling more like a giddy teenager than the serious middle-aged woman she used to be. They lingered at the foot of the front walk, not saying anything of consequence and definitely not saying good-bye.

"I should let you get back to work," she said finally.

He inclined his head toward the house. "I should let you get back to your family."

Maybe it was the smell of lilac or the buttery warm sunshine spilling over them. Maybe it was lack of depth perception or temporary insanity, but she leaned toward him just as he leaned toward her and a friendly kiss on the cheek became a quick brush of her lips against his.

They leaped back, startled and wide-eyed. She mumbled something and he mumbled something else in return. One of the things they mumbled must have been good-bye, because seconds later he was sprinting across the driveway to his car and she was beating a hasty retreat to the front door.

Her mother was waiting for her in the doorway, and from the look on her face it was clear Maeve had seen the whole embarrassing incident.

"Don't say a word," Kate warned her. "Not one single word."

Maeve didn't have to. Her smile said it all.

As far as Maeve was concerned, the red lace thong had worked its magic.

* * *

It was after eight when Mark finally got home. As a rule the first thing he did was start a pot of coffee, strip off his collar, and flip on the television, but today he headed straight for the computer.

Did high-speed Internet connections have their own patron saint? If not, they should. His e-mail was downloaded and ready seconds after he walked through the door.

TO: mark.kerry@mklj.net
FROM: mboyd@nh2day.net
SUBJECT: RE: revised contract attached

forwarded the contract to bishop clennon. hope house sale still going okay. I'd start packing if I were you. we need you back here asap
did you ever find the owner of that box of docs? inquiring minds etc
Maggy

Friendship between a man and a woman could be a tricky thing in the best of times. He had never lied to Maggy, even with half-truths, but he wasn't sure how much of this afternoon with Kate he was willing to reveal.

A few e-mail newsletters. The requisite spam. A half-dozen notes from clergy friends, congratulating him on rejoining the fold after his prolonged sabbatical.

But nothing from Kate French.

He had no business being disappointed. The woman

was only a few hours out of the hospital. She had other things to do besides write e-mails to an Episcopal priest between assignments. They had nothing in common. Just because God had brought them together at a critical moment didn't mean they were going to become pen pals. She didn't have to do it, but she had asked him to lunch. Wasn't that enough? What was he expecting, menu approval?

Still, he had really thought she would write to him. Something had happened between them this afternoon, something worth noting.

What's stopping you, chief? If you have something to say, there's the keyboard.

He'd start with the easy stuff.

TO: scott5367@ppd-ret.gov
FROM: mark.kerry@mklj.net
SUBJECT: RE: info

There's a place in heaven for you, friend, and a steak dinner w/all trimmings at The Old Grist Mill tomorrow night for you and Marcy.
Thanks.
MK

Build up to something a little more substantive.

TO: annie-s@aol3.com
FROM: mark.kerry@mklj.net
SUBJECT: RE: meeting

The Unitarians say we can use their meeting place at the corner of Locust and Grant from 5–7 p.m. Friday night. Would you post it to the list? See you then.
MK

Then get down to the real business at hand.

TO: kate@frenchkiss.biz
FROM: mark.kerry@mklj.net
SUBJECT: ~~Best wishes Hello~~ [no subject]

Sskdjeuncnfksloeooweoewpwqepwepwepwela';a'a
;'a;a'

He was hopeless. He couldn't even come up with a
workable subject header, much less a coherent message.
She had him tied up in knots, knocked completely off
center. The sweet fresh smell of her skin, the way she had
looked in the sunlight, the full-bodied sound of her laughter. Stronger men had been felled by weaker arsenals.

And that kiss . . . what was that all about? He hadn't
planned it, and from the look on her face neither had she,
but it had happened just the same. He had spent his career
trying to explain the coexistence of predestination and
free will, but he hadn't expected to experience it on a Saturday afternoon in Coburn, New Jersey. The choice was
his but he had the feeling the outcome was out of his
hands.

Seven

"Dinner tomorrow," Paul said as she walked him to the door. "I'll call The Old Grist Mill and make reservations for seven."

"Dinner?" His words caught her by surprise. "We're going to dinner tomorrow?"

"I asked you on the way home and you said yes. Remember?"

Clearly she didn't or she wouldn't be standing there wishing she could come up with a way to back out of it without hurting his feelings any more than she already had.

"It's been a long day. Everything's all jumbled up." She forced a laugh. "I'm not sure I remember my own name."

He nodded and tried to put a good face on it, but she could see the embarrassment in his eyes and she felt terrible. From the moment she walked through the front door and into Mark Kerry's arms, everything else had fallen away.

She didn't have the heart to tell Paul that after all these years he was five days too late.

"What's wrong with Uncle Paul?" Gwynn asked when Kate went back to the house. "He didn't seem very happy."

"He isn't," Maeve said. "He saw what happened here and he's jealous."

Gwynn's eyes widened. "Uncle Paul?" She looked over at Kate, who was wishing she had bypassed the kitchen and gone straight to her room and stayed there. "Since when are you two—?"

"Since never," Kate said, pouring herself a glass of orange juice from the fridge. "My hospital stay seems to have made more than a few people around here crazy." She glanced over at her mother. "Paul thinks he's in love with me."

Maeve was silent for a long moment. "I was afraid this would happen."

"So was I," Kate said. "I told him it's a by-product of my heart attack, but he thinks it's the real thing."

"Are you going to dinner with him tomorrow?" Maeve asked.

"How do you know about that?" Even Kate had managed to forget the invitation.

"He told me while you were out there saying good night to Mark."

"There was no polite way out of it," Kate said. "Besides, he's my best friend. He'll snap out of it."

"Tread softly," Maeve warned. "Our boy's heart is a lot softer than he wants anyone to think."

Was it? Paul's heart had seemed pretty resilient to Kate. He hadn't spent a Saturday night alone since his divorce.

"Did you really invite Father McDreamy to lunch?" Gwynn asked over her shoulder as she poked around the fridge for anything fattening and now forbidden. "I couldn't believe what I was hearing."

"You weren't even in the room."

"I was in the hallway." She flashed Kate the same grin she'd flashed as a seven-year-old learning to ride a two-wheeler. "Eavesdropping."

That smile, those twinkling eyes, that impish grin. Where did the time go? A rush of love swelled up inside Kate's chest, and for the tenth time in the last few hours she burst into tears which, of course, tipped her highly emotional daughter into tears and ultimately dragged her mother along for the ride.

"I hate this," Kate said, wiping her eyes with a paper towel. "If this is what I've been missing, I could do without it."

"This is good for you," Maeve said, ripping off two pieces of paper towel for herself and for Gwynn. "You've always been so bottled up, so self-contained. It's good to let your emotions flow through you. It's healthy for body and soul."

"It doesn't feel good," Kate said as a new torrent of tears rolled down her cheeks. "I feel like I'm totally out of control."

Maeve and Gwynn exchanged looks.

"I saw that," Kate said, reaching for another square of paper towel. "And I saw the last three looks too." She blew her nose and tossed the towel into the trash. "You're wrong."

Gwynn looked as innocent as a five-year-old. "I didn't say anything."

"We don't have to say anything," Maeve pointed out, "because she knows it's true."

Kate rinsed her juice glass and set it in the dish drainer to dry. "We're not having this discussion."

"Maybe you aren't," Maeve said, "but we've been having it since that gorgeous holy man showed up on the doorstep this afternoon. I have never seen chemistry like that between two people in my life."

"Gran is right," Gwynn said. "I thought the two of you looked smokin' hot out there."

Kate tried to think of something suitably funny and sarcastic to say in response, but unfortunately "Do you really think so?" was what came out.

She could hear their delighted laughter all the way upstairs in her second-floor bedroom, where she had fled in horror. If Maeve and Gwynn had seen the sparks flying between her and the priest, then there were sparks. Maeve made a living analyzing, encouraging, and celebrating sexual attraction. And Gwynn was a born romantic, hopelessly enamored of anything that even hinted at a possible love story. Kate was the one who was tone deaf when it came to the music of love and always had been.

But not this time. She had heard a symphony when their lips touched, complete with a choir of angels and Pavarotti in his prime. An entire opera of emotion was playing itself out inside her and all she could do was let it happen.

She probably shouldn't have invited him to lunch the way she did. She had put him on the spot in front of her family and Paul. What could he say but yes? Driving up to Coburn to have lunch with a woman he'd found facedown in a puddle of pickled ginger had to be the last thing he wanted to do on any given Tuesday. If she really wanted to thank him for saving her life, she would make a donation to the Episcopal Church and offer him an escape hatch.

The more she thought about it, the more convinced she was that this was the way to go. Nothing good could come of seeing him again. He was a man of the cloth and she hadn't been near a church in a few decades. For all she knew he was a married man with a devoted wife and five kids and a golden retriever, and those sparks they had generated were a big fat occasion of sin they would both do well to avoid.

Then again maybe Catholics were the only ones who

viewed the world in terms of sinning possibilities. Most of her information about Episcopalians came from reading the Mitford books, and her priest didn't look anything like Father Timothy. Since leaving St. Aloysius after high school she had kept religion, organized and otherwise, at a respectful distance.

This was the kind of research job the computer was made for, but where to begin? She could start with an overview of the religion, its basic tenets, its liturgical calendar, or she could do what every red-blooded American woman in her position would do: Google Father McDreamy and find out if he was married.

"Mark Kerry" was a popular name. There were thirty-two thousand six hundred twenty-one websites with mentions of Mark Kerry. She narrowed it down to Episcopalian Mark Kerrys with New Jersey ties and found three, two of whom were dead. The third was seventy-three.

Okay. So maybe this wasn't such a great idea. She had his telephone number. She could always call him and give him the opportunity to gracefully bow out of their Tuesday lunch.

He has your number too, idiot. If he wants to back out, he can call or e-mail or instant-message. You gave him everything but your Social Security number.

Then again, maybe he already had.

She clicked over to Outlook Express and waited for the screen to populate.

Downloading 273 messages . . .

She hadn't logged on since Monday morning, just before her life turned itself inside out.

Get well soon.
Get well soon.
What the hell happened?? Fill me in
I can't believe you had a heart attack

What about my Majolica vase
WTF?????
Did you find that Roseville urn we talked about
Hope you feel better reeeeeally soon

She skimmed the list of messages in her inbox but there was nothing from Mark Kerry. Not that she was expecting anything, but that didn't stop her from sobbing like she had just lost her dog, her best friend, and her 401(k).

"This is the twenty-first century," she said to the screen as she wiped her eyes with her sleeve. "You're a grown woman. If you have something to say to him, say it."

She reached for the piece of paper with his contact information taped to her mirror, then propped it up near her keyboard.

TO: mark.kerry@mklj.net
FROM: kate@frenchkiss.biz
SUBJECT: Lunch

~~I hope I didn't put you on the spot when~~

Too defensive. It made her sound like one of those wishy-washy types she hated.

~~Let's confirm Tuesday lunch Monday night.~~

Too businesslike.

I can't stop thinking about you. Something magical happened today, didn't it? I mean, I'm not crazy. I may not have a lot of experience with magic but I know—

Too honest.
The thing to do was shut down the computer before

she did something even more horrible than be caught wearing a red lace thong by a gorgeous Episcopal priest in a Grateful Dead T-shirt. Something she might actually regret a few weeks from now when she was feeling more like her normal, practical self.

Sunday evening—The Old Grist Mill

"Window seats," Paul said as they followed the hostess to their table. "With a view of the stream."

The trees had been strung with tiny white fairy lights that illuminated the soft spring night with romance.

This time last week she would have been oblivious to the twinkling lights and soft music, but tonight all she could think of was how wonderful this would be with the right man.

And, to her regret, her dear friend would never be that man.

The hostess went to pull out Kate's chair for her, but Paul leaped into position and did the honors. Normally they would have jockeyed playfully for the best seat but here in bizarro world he was acting like a *boy*friend instead of a *best* friend. Flowers. Compliments. She was afraid he might break into song at any moment.

It was going to be a long evening.

"I've always loved this place," she said after the hostess hurried away to seat another customer. "If it weren't in the back of beyond, I'd come here all the time."

"Best porterhouse steaks in the Northeast."

She winced. "I'm afraid it's broiled haddock for me."

"Damn," he said. "I should've taken you to Luigi's for seafood."

"They have fish on the menu here. I'll be fine."

She sneaked a glance at her watch. Two minutes and forty-three seconds had passed since the last time she looked. If she could keep the conversation firmly centered on her dietary restrictions and not on their future, alone or together, the night might not be a total disaster.

John, their server, offered a wine list. Paul zeroed in on his favorite merlot, which Kate declined.

"No wine?" He looked surprised.

"I forgot to run it by Dr. Lombardi," she said. "He has me on a few different meds and I'm not sure about interactions with alcohol."

Paul nodded. "Better safe than sorry."

"Isn't this the kind of conversation our grandmothers had over pots of tea?"

"We're getting older, French," he said. "Next stop is the AARP card."

So far, so good. This was the kind of thing they did best. No posing. No posturing. No trying to impress each other. Just two old friends, getting older by the day, out for dinner and friendship.

Provided, of course, you could ignore the twinkling lights outside, the candlelight inside, and the fact that he suddenly couldn't seem to take his eyes off her.

"I owe you an apology," he said after the busboy cleared away their salad plates and refilled Kate's iced tea.

"For eating those gorgeous shrimp in front of me?"

"Okay," he said with a smile, "so I owe you two apologies."

She shifted in her seat, wishing she could find a way to defuse this situation before he said something they would both regret. "You don't owe me anything, Grantham."

"I shouldn't have dropped everything on you yesterday." He dragged his hand through his wavy hair, a gesture she knew very well. "Believe it or not, I had a plan."

"A plan?"

"I was going to drop it on you tonight, somewhere between the salad course and dessert."

She glanced toward the exit some eighty feet away. "You're lucky I'm wearing heels. Otherwise I'd make a run for it."

"I'm spilling my heart out to you and you're making with the jokes."

"It's what we do," she reminded him. "It's what friends do."

"Think about it," he said. "No secrets. No drama. No bullshit. There would always be somebody at your back."

"Don't we have that already?"

"I want more."

"So do I."

She wasn't sure which of them was more surprised. Suddenly she realized that she wanted the secrets, the drama, the flowers, the fireworks, the whole nine yards.

Who knew?

On the other side of the restaurant

"I tried to get us a window seat," Mark said as he followed Scott and Marcy into The Old Grist Mill, "but they were completely booked." He had even played the clergy card, something he never did, but to no avail.

"Same great steaks no matter where we're sitting." Scott placed a beefy hand at the small of his wife's back as they waited for the hostess to seat them.

"We would have been happy with Sizzler, Father Mark," Marcy said. "This is way too fancy for us."

It was also Scott's favorite place, which made it a no-brainer.

He ordered a pitcher of iced tea for the table and settled back in his chair while Scott and Marcy debated sharing a Caesar salad or steamed clams and mussels. The restaurant bustled with conversation and laughter and music. A fire crackled in the stone hearth at the far end of the room, one of the last before the spring nights turned balmy and they opened the doors to the patio. He had been here twice as a guest and both times he had been shocked at the prices and impressed by the food and service. Not that he was an expert. Takeout Chinese, pizza, and frozen lasagna were more his speed.

He hadn't remembered The Old Grist Mill being a big date place, but tonight the restaurant overflowed with couples at various stages of courtship behavior. Young lovers whose dinners grew cold on the plate while they gazed into each other's eyes. New parents out for the first time since the baby's arrival, happy to be together but anxious to get home to their precious offspring. Empty nesters like Scott and Marcy in the rediscovery stage of marriage when, if you're lucky, the old becomes new all over again.

He had turned away from God after Suzanne's death, unable to reconcile an all-loving Creator with the shocking end of a young woman's life. He had lost his wife, his lover, his confidante, his future, and his faith the day she died.

"Hey," Scott said, after they placed their orders, "your redhead must be pretty special to rate this kind of thank-you."

Marcy gave her husband one of those wifely "shut up" looks that made Mark laugh out loud.

"I was glad to get those papers back to their rightful owner."

"I'm not buying it," Scott said, pressing hard.

"Ignore him," Marcy broke in. "There's nothing worse than a retired detective. He's always looking for the hidden story." She turned toward her husband. "I left my cell in the car. Would you get it for me, please?"

"It's not in your purse?"

"If it were in my purse, would I ask you to get it from the car?"

Scott, grumbling but in a good-natured kind of way, set off to retrieve his wife's cell phone. Marcy watched his progress to the exit with a look of love and bemusement on her face that brought a lump to Mark's throat.

"You like him," he said when Marcy caught him smiling at her.

"Him?" She laughed, but the affectionate look in her eyes was unmistakable. "I was just making sure he didn't trip on his shoelaces."

Mark laughed with her but he knew love when he saw it.

Eight

Kate and Paul were halfway through their entrées when something across the room caught his attention.

"You're not going to believe who's sitting at a corner table." He had that cat-that-ate-the-canary look she remembered from high school when he scored higher on the math SATs than she did.

"Maeve and Paul Newman."

"Not even close."

"Gwynn and an investment banker."

"You wish."

"I hate guessing games."

"Your Good Samaritan and his wife."

She spun around in her seat so fast she had to grab the edge of the table to keep from slipping off. "Oh my God!"

"Nope," said Paul, "but definitely one of the disciples."

The woman sitting opposite Mark was somewhere in her midforties, pleasant looking and conservatively dressed, exactly how Kate envisioned the perfect minister's wife.

She finally had something worth crying about and the tears were conspicuously absent. Go figure.

"You didn't know he was married?" Paul sounded gleeful.

"I still don't know he's married."

"The only thing missing is the booster seat for their youngest."

She had to admit the signs pointed toward wedded bliss. The comfortable familiarity between Mark and the woman was obvious. They weren't falling all over each other but there was an obvious connection between them. No sparks, not like yesterday, but—

"He should be excommunicated," she mumbled into her glass of iced tea. If Episcopalians didn't currently excommunicate, they could test the waters with Mark Kerry. If she was going to burn in hell, she would rather it be for missing Sunday mass than for coveting another woman's husband. That was just plain unforgivable.

* * *

Scott and Marcy went out to grab a smoke while Mark took care of the bill. The server had forgotten to add in Scott's medium-rare T-bone and had been pathetically grateful when Mark pointed it out to him.

"You don't know what it's like around here," the server said as he recalculated the bill. "They count every piece of dead cow back there and make us foot the difference."

"That image will stick with me a while." He added the tip and signed the credit receipt. "Thanks."

"You have a good night."

He might have had at least a decent night if he hadn't chosen that second to turn around for one last look at the old couple laughing over coffee near the stone hearth and seen Kate French and her friend approaching him.

"Looks like The Old Grist Mill is the place to be," Kate greeted him.

She didn't look surprised to see him. Her friend, the angry guy, shot him the kind of look usually confined to boxing rings and WWF conventions.

"Good to see you." He debated shaking her hand but decided against it.

Besides, she didn't offer.

The angry guy made a show of looking around. "Where'd your wife and friend go?"

He frowned. "My what?"

"Your wife," the angry guy persisted. "Nice-looking woman, light brown hair, probably answers to the name Mrs."

The thing about redheads was they couldn't hide anything. If their tempers didn't give them away, their skin did. Kate's throat and cheeks flamed crimson.

"You're talking about my friends Scott and Marcy Reilly. Come on," he said. "I'll introduce you."

He had pretty much put one-upmanship to bed by the time he was old enough to vote, but tonight he couldn't help himself. Watching the angry guy, aka Paul Grantham, deflate as he shook hands with Scott and Marcy was worth the price of a dozen steak dinners.

Kate, however, was clearly delighted to meet his friends. She embraced Marcy warmly and kissed Scott on the cheek. "I've never been so happy to have my privacy invaded in my life," she said and everybody laughed. "Those letters are very important to me."

"Wish I'd seen them," Scott said. "I'm a Revolutionary War buff myself."

"You can't grow up in this area and escape it," Marcy said. "George Washington slept around more than my cousin Amy."

The night air was cool and clear, a welcome change

after the warmth of the restaurant. The sky was a deep rich inky black studded with stars. It had been a very long time since he'd noticed a sky like that and even longer since he'd given a damn. But tonight those stars pierced him straight through to his heart. He wandered toward the far end of the lot without realizing it.

"They're getting along well." Kate popped up at his right elbow. "I think they've forgotten all about us."

"That's what happens when you put a lawyer together with a retired cop and his social worker wife. Hope you weren't in a rush to go home."

"It's such a beautiful night. I could stay here forever."

He gestured toward the debating threesome on the other side of the parking lot. "Good thing, because they don't sound like they're ready to call it a night."

They leaned against the side of his car and looked up at the sky. The sounds of music and laughter drifted out from the inn and mingled with the soft rustle of the wind through the budding trees. He liked that she didn't feel the need to fill every silence with talk. Not everybody understood the beauty of silence.

". . . you would actually let some son of a bitch go free because his Miranda rights weren't . . ."

". . . the law's the law . . . our constitutional rights are precious . . ."

". . . maybe it's time to rethink the entire penal system . . ."

Next to him, Kate made a face. "I feel like I'm channeling Fox News."

"We could walk around back and look at the stream."

She hesitated and his heart sank. So there *was* something going on between Kate and the angry guy.

"Or not," he said. "It's up to you."

"It's an awkward situation," she said after a long pause. "Is it?"

"Not because of you—" She stopped and looked at him. "Okay, a little because of you but mostly because my heart attack seems to have triggered some . . ." She hesitated, searching for the right word.

"Some unexpected emotions."

"Paul and I have been friends since grade school. He's Gwynn's godfather. We've been there for each other through divorce and everything else life threw our way, but we've never been romantic."

He nodded. "I get it."

"I know this is only temporary," she said. "I had a heart attack and he's feeling his mortality but right now he thinks he's in love with me and I don't want to hurt him." She stopped for breath this time. "Too much information. Sorry. I'm usually not this forthcoming with strangers."

"We're not strangers," he pointed out.

She wrapped her arms around her chest and gazed up at the night sky. "We're pretty close to it. I don't know if you're married—"

"I'm not."

"—or gay—"

"I'm not."

"—or where you live."

"Rocky Hill."

"The Old Grist Mill was quite a schlep for you."

He did a quick calculation in his head. "You're not exactly close to home yourself."

"Why did you come here?" she asked. "I mean, how on earth did you end up at a steak place an hour and a half away from home?"

"It's Scott's favorite place. He grew up two towns over." Turnabout was fair play. "How did you end up here?" He executed a perfect Mr. Spock eyebrow lift. "A steak place?"

"I know, I know." Her sense of humor was obviously

intact. "Not exactly where you'd expect to find a cardiac patient one week out, is it?"

"Not exactly."

"Paul's idea. He wanted someplace—" She stopped. "You can figure it out, right?"

"Romantic."

"Yep." She gestured toward the inn nestled in a stand of oaks and maples. "Nothing says romance like candle-light and dead cows."

He threw back his head and laughed loudly enough to stop conversation across the parking lot. "You're the second person in the last twenty minutes to reference dead cows. Glad we talked after I finished the porterhouse."

"So Episcopalians like their beef, do they?"

"Some of us do."

She nodded. "Good to know."

Was this what happy felt like? He used to be good at being happy. He wouldn't mind trying it again.

"It seems we're destined to keep running into each other, doesn't it?"

"I don't mind," he said. "Do you?"

"No," she said, "I don't mind at all."

"Some people would call this the hand of God at work."

"Or the hand of fate."

"I'm a God's-plan kind of guy."

"I kind of figured that out, Father Mark Kerry."

"And you're a hand-of-fate kind of woman?"

"Twelve years at St. Aloysius will do that to you."

"Twelve years in the same school? This isn't *Little House on the Prairie* territory."

She swatted him lightly on the arm. "St. Aloysius provided a quality education from kindergarten through senior year of high school. Once they got you, you stayed got." She shot him a sly look. "At least until you graduated."

He had a score of questions he wanted to ask her, but

this wasn't the time or the place and, quite frankly, he wasn't sure he wouldn't be crossing some invisible social boundary. Silence was a good substitute. A companionable silence, even better. He had never been with someone like her before. It didn't matter if they were laughing, talking, or looking up at the stars: he felt fully connected to her just the same.

"Looks like court adjourned for the night," she whispered as Scott, Marcy, and the angry guy strolled across the parking lot toward them. "Listen, I didn't mean to railroad you into lunch on Tuesday. If you want to cancel, I promise there won't be any hard feelings."

"Do you want me to cancel?"

"No," she said. "Do you want to cancel?"

"I don't want to cancel."

"Then I guess it's settled."

"Good."

"One o'clock at my house."

"I'll be there."

"I'm counting on it."

"Okay, you two, what was all the whispering about?" Marcy teased. "You were thick as thieves over here."

"Mark is coming over for lunch this week and we were confirming the day and time." She said it easily and naturally as if that was all that had been going on between them.

Then again maybe it was. Maybe he'd gotten it all wrong and the sparks he saw arcing between them in the early spring darkness were all in his imagination, like the memory of love.

* * *

"Looks like Maeve left the porch light on for you," Paul said as he turned in to Kate's driveway. "I feel like it's senior year all over again."

Kate was silent as memories of that tumultuous year rose up before her.

"Bad choice of years," he said. "Sorry."

Senior year of high school was supposed to be about college applications and prom dresses, not morning sickness and maternity bras.

"At least it had a happy ending," she said, wishing she could get this crying thing under control. "I had a beautiful baby girl to show for it." And a seventeen-year-old husband who was man enough to shoulder his half of the burden and more. "When I look back I understand why Maeve was half out of her mind with worry. It could have been a train wreck."

Paul nodded in the darkness. "We didn't know what we didn't know. We thought we had life by the balls."

"I don't know if I'd go that far." Sixteen and pregnant was hardly a position of power for any girl. "I was pretty uncertain about the future."

"You? I never saw anyone more determined to make her way in the world than you."

"Are we talking about the same girl?" She remembered herself as a needy, insecure teenager who didn't know which end was up.

"You're strong, Kate. You always have been. There was never any doubt that you'd find a way to be successful."

"Thanks," she said. "I think."

He groaned and let his head fall back against the head rest. "What I'm trying to say is we all did well for ourselves. We all came from the same background and we all managed to climb a few rungs higher on the ladder."

"All that because my mother left the porch light on?" she teased. "You're worse than Proust."

"You can invite me in for coffee," he said. "We haven't had a chance to talk yet."

"Paul, I hope you don't mind if I beg off tonight. I'm not quite up to full speed yet."

He wasn't a stupid man. He knew what she wasn't saying. "I fucked it up, didn't I?"

She took his hand and gave it a quick squeeze. "You couldn't if you tried."

"He's all wrong for you," he said as they walked to the front door.

She loved her friend too much to pretend she didn't understand.

*   *   *

TO: kate@frenchkiss.biz
FROM: mark.kerry@mklj.net
SUBJECT: Episcopalians

. . . like steak, plaid, golf, sailboats, sunsets, the Rolling Stones but not the Beatles, old cowboy movies, the History Channel, big dogs who slobber, kids who don't, women with auburn hair and hazel eyes

And the Grateful Dead.

* * * * * *

TO: mark.kerry@mklj.net
FROM: kate@frenchkiss.biz
SUBJECT: RE: Lapsed Catholics

. . . like tuna sandwiches, Irish lace, bowling, rowboats, sunrises, the Beatles but not the Stones, little dogs with impeccable manners, kids without, men who drive beat-up blue Hondas

But not the Grateful Dead.

* * * * * *

TO: kate@frenchkiss.biz
FROM: mark.kerry@mklj.net
SUBJECT: RE: Lapsed Catholics

I can deal with bowling, rowboats, and little dogs but
not liking the Dead?
Tell me you're kidding.

* * * * * *

TO: mark.kerry@mklj.net
FROM: kate@frenchkiss.biz
SUBJECT: RE: Lapsed Catholics

Sorry. I'm not kidding. Never liked them. Never will.
How do you feel about Blondie?

* * * * * *

TO: kate@frenchkiss.biz
FROM: mark.kerry@mklj.net
SUBJECT: RE: Lapsed Catholics

Overrated.
B-52's?

* * * * * *

TO: mark.kerry@mklj.net
FROM: kate@frenchkiss.biz
SUBJECT: RE: Lapsed Catholics

I needed 911 again. YOU like the B-52's?!?!?!?!

* * * * * *

TO: kate@frenchkiss.biz
FROM: mark.kerry@mklj.net
SUBJECT: RE: Lapsed Catholics

Who doesn't like the B-52's? Don't tell me you were
Huey Lewis and the News.

* * * * * *

TO: mark.kerry@mklj.net
FROM: kate@frenchkiss.biz
SUBJECT: RE: Lapsed Catholics

How judgmental! Huey Lewis was a minor god. (No offense.)
Dealbreaker: Springsteen or Joel?

* * * * * *

TO: kate@frenchkiss.biz
FROM: mark.kerry@mklj.net
SUBJECT: RE: Lapsed Catholics

The Piano Man.

* * * * * *

TO: mark.kerry@mklj.net
FROM: kate@frenchkiss.biz
SUBJECT: RE: Lapsed Catholics

I like you anyway.

* * * * * *

TO: kate@frenchkiss.biz
FROM: mark.kerry@mklj.net
SUBJECT: RE: Lapsed Catholics

Sleep well, Kate.
Until Tuesday,

Mark

* * * * * *

TO: mark.kerry@mklj.net
FROM: kate@frenchkiss.biz
SUBJECT: RE: Lapsed Catholics

You too, Mark.
Until then,
Kate

Nine

"I'm going home today," Gwynn announced over breakfast the next morning. "Monday lunch is usually pretty busy and Aidan can use the help."

Kate managed to keep her mouth shut but it wasn't easy. Last Monday, just before the heart attack, her daughter had said the opposite was true.

"You can take my Miata," Kate offered. "I can't drive for another couple of weeks."

"I'd offer my VW," Maeve said, "but I have an appointment tomorrow in Paramus."

Gwynn beamed them both a happy smile. "Thanks, both of you, but Andrew is driving up to get me."

Kate focused on her egg-white omelet.

"When is he coming?" Maeve asked as she slathered raspberry preserves on a slice of unbuttered whole-wheat bread.

Gwynn looked at the microwave clock. "In about twenty minutes."

"He's welcome to stay for breakfast," Kate said. "Unless he actually likes his eggs with yolks in them."

"That's okay." Gwynn looked charmingly uncertain and more than a little in love. "He's been up since four. He had breakfast a long time ago."

"He can at least come in for coffee," Maeve said. "It's a long drive."

Paradise Point was two hours away from Coburn and that was without traffic.

"Coffee sounds good." Gwynn glanced over at her mother. "I really want you to meet him, Mom. I know you think he's—"

"I don't think anything, honey. I barely know him." The little white lie. Where would civilization be without it?

"Exactly! He's really nervous about you and Maeve and I thought maybe this would make the first time less scary."

"We're scary?" Kate looked over at her mother, who would probably get a bestseller out of this exchange. "Did you know we're scary?"

"Of course we're scary," Maeve said, reaching for another slice of toast. "Matriarchs are powerful figures who are meant to inspire awe."

"Gwynnie didn't say we're awesome," Kate corrected her, "she said we were scary."

"But scary in a good way," Gwynn said, then started to laugh. "You know what I mean."

"And what did you mean by 'first time'?" Kate asked as she polished off the last of her fake eggs. "We've met Andrew before."

"I mean, first time since I told you our news."

So there it was again. She had hoped the whole getting married thing would blow over like a spring storm, but no such luck. She had two options: she could ignore the situation and pretend it didn't exist (which was very tempting) or dive in with both feet and hope she remembered how to swim.

The old Kate would have pushed the matter into the bottom drawer of her file cabinet and ignored it the way she ignored most anything of a highly charged emotional nature. The new Kate, however, found she needed to know.

"What did your father have to say?"

Some of Gwynn's sparkle dimmed. "He was cool with it."

"Was he?"

"He didn't go ballistic, if that's what you mean."

"So he thinks you should wait."

Gwynn shot her mother a look. "You probably told him what to say."

"I didn't tell him anything."

"Right," Gwynne said. "Like you didn't get your whole agenda out there while I was arranging those stupid flowers."

"Your mother didn't say a word," Maeve said. "I was there and—"

"Thanks, but I don't need you to defend me, Maeve." Kate's temper was approaching the boiling point. "Your father makes up his own mind, Gwynn, and if he went ballistic, as you put it, then he went ballistic on his own. I had absolutely nothing to do with it."

"But he—"

"Your father was even more delighted than I was that you were going back to school for your master's. We love you, Gwynn, and we want the best for you." She wiped tears from her eyes with a quick swipe of her hand. Damn these stupid unpredictable emotions anyway. It was so much easier to make your point when you weren't sniveling like a schoolgirl.

"I think I know what's best for me." Gwynn's spine was every bit as strong as her mother's and grandmother's.

"Waiting tables at a dockside restaurant while your husband floats around on a fishing boat? I don't think so."

"You're a snob," Gwynn said. "I never realized it before, but you are."

"I resent that."

"Gwynn has a point," Maeve said. "You are a bit of a snob, sweetie, just like your father was."

"I'll have to take your word for it," Kate shot back, "since I never met the gentleman." Her father, the oldest son of a well-known senator, split with Maeve a few weeks before Kate's birth and wasn't heard from again.

"This is what always happens," Gwynn shouted over the din. "We're supposed to be talking about me, about *my* life, and somehow you two always manage to bring it back to your problems."

"Problems?" Maeve looked shocked. "We don't have problems, do we, Kate?"

"Problems?" Kate asked, wide-eyed. "Us?"

Thank God, even Gwynn laughed.

"All Andrew wants to do is come in for a minute and say hi." Gwynn hesitated. "And to give you some flowers." She took a deep shuddery breath Kate could hear from six feet away. "He wanted to visit you in the hospital but he would have had to turn down a three-day trip and we really need the money."

"You don't have to explain, honey."

"Yes, I do." Tears streamed freely down her daughter's cheeks but Gwynn didn't seem to notice. "This is important to me, Mom, and it's important to Andrew. He knows he isn't exactly what you've been dreaming of for me. Don't make it any harder, okay?"

"I won't," Kate promised, enveloping Gwynn in her arms. "You don't have to worry."

I'll be worrying enough for all of us.

Pinecrest Village Assisted Living—the same day

For the last eighteen months Mark had been going steady with a woman named Charlotte Petruzzo, a ninety-something-year-old widow with dyed auburn hair and a sense of humor that nothing life threw at her had been able to suppress.

It had been his privilege and honor to sit with her two afternoons a week and talk to her about everything from God and the probability of heaven to her great-grandchildren's exploits to why she didn't believe in term limits.

"Where is she?" he asked Charlotte's next-door neighbor, a spry octogenarian named Max Remar who was a legend among the widows of Pinecrest. "I knocked and there's no answer."

"She's in the hospital wing," Max said around his enormous unlit Cuban cigar. "Had trouble breathing last night and pressed the Life Alert button. You shoulda seen this place. Looked like a movie set."

"How is she?"

Max made a so-so gesture with his hand. "She's ninety-seven. How's she gonna be?"

"Ninety-seven?" Mark chuckled. "She told me she was ninety-two."

"Don't tell her I told you. She'll stop sharing her amaretti with me."

"I'm a priest," Mark said. "I'll consider it privileged information."

The hospital wing was a low white building situated near an artificial pond on the southwest corner of the Pinecrest complex. It was equipped to handle minor surgical procedures and a small number of long-term convalescent cases, but more serious problems were dispatched to the Medical Center at Princeton. He turned off his cell and pushed through the front door.

"Mrs. Petruzzo is in 1-D," the head nurse told Mark a few minutes later.

"How is she doing?"

"She's ninety-seven," the nurse said with a bittersweet smile. "I'm afraid it's finally caught up to her."

He knew what that meant and it made him profoundly sad.

"Can I visit with her?"

"She'd be furious if you didn't."

Charlotte looked the same as always. Impeccably groomed. Eyes bright with curiosity. She was decked out in her finest embroidered silk robe from her years in China with her late husband. Her gnarled fingers glittered with gold and silver rings heavy with jewels in every color of the rainbow.

But something had changed. He knew it the second he walked into the room.

"You're late," she said as he kissed her Estée-Laudered cheek.

"Next time you move, make sure you send out a change-of-address card."

She laughed heartily, but it seemed to drain her of energy. She rested her head back against her pillow and closed her eyes for a moment.

"So pull up a chair and stay a while," she said. "I want to hear all about your weekend. Did you find your mystery woman?"

Usually he listened while Charlotte told him tales from a life well lived but today her question opened the floodgates and he heard himself telling her everything.

"That explains it," Charlotte said when he finished. "I knew something was different the second you walked in the room. You have that glow."

"Men don't glow."

"Oh, they glow," she said with a knowing laugh, "but

you have to be very old before you can spot it. Imagine what the young ones could do with that knowledge. Society would be turned on its head!"

Had she been this vital in her prime, this wise and wonderful, or was this all part of God's plan to save the best for last?

"You had yourself a weekend too, Charlotte." He met her eyes. "I knew something was different the second I walked into the room."

She laughed and pointed an index finger at him. "I always said you were pretty funny for a priest."

"Seeing as how your average priest is a real stand-up comic."

She made a broad gesture that encompassed herself, the hospital bed, the room. "I imagine you have this all figured out."

"Maybe, but I'd rather hear it from you."

"I think it's time."

He nodded. "That's possible."

"I have this sense of—" She stopped for a moment, then shook her head. "I wish I could explain the feeling to you."

"Completion?"

"Yes! That's it. Completion. As if I've done what I was meant to do and it's time to turn the page."

"How does that make you feel?"

"A little disappointed," she said. "I still had hopes that Sean Connery would find his way to Pinecrest."

It was an old joke but one that still made them both laugh.

"Have you spoken with your doctor?"

"What can he say that I don't already know? I'm old. I've lived a long, full life. Sooner or later God calls you home."

"You sound like you've made your peace with it."

Her eyes flashed with remembered fire. "I'm not saying I want to go tomorrow," she reminded him, "or even next week, but I will be going before too long. I don't want you to be surprised."

He nodded, but the truth was that he was always surprised. Even though his faith was firmly rooted in a belief in the hereafter, he was never ready to see one of his own say good-bye. For all of his education, all of his training, he had yet to find a way to gracefully accept death as a fact of life.

"When do you leave us for the north woods?"

"The Thursday before Memorial Day."

She nodded. "Good. I'll still be here so I can give you a proper sendoff."

"Balloons and a brass band?"

"And a parade."

"I'm going to hold you to that, Charlotte."

"You've been in my prayers," she said. "I hope going home again will make you happy."

"I need to go back," he said. "I have some debts to repay."

"Or maybe you have some ghosts to put to rest."

"Could be."

"Quite a few of us had hoped you would change your mind and stay here in the Garden State."

He had two offers on the table from New Jersey parishes in search of a permanent rector, but he had committed himself to his old parish in New Hampshire.

"I'm going to miss my friends," he said. "It's been a good few years down here." He could have made a life for himself here if his old congregation hadn't asked him back.

"Seems a shame to pack and move right after you found someone interesting."

"Don't read more into my weekend than was there.

I talked to a woman in a parking lot. That's all that really happened."

"Are you going to see her again?"

"She invited me to lunch tomorrow." He raised his hand at the look of delight on Charlotte's face. "A thank-you lunch."

"You're in my prayers every night," she said. "You deserve some happiness."

"Your prayers have been helping. I think I'm finally on the right road, Charlotte." He took her hands in his. "Let's take this chance to pray together." Charlotte bowed her head and he began, "Almighty God, we entrust all who are dear to us to Your never-failing care and love, for this life and the life to come, knowing that You are doing for them better things than we can desire or pray for; through Jesus Christ our Lord. Amen."

And then he added one more silent prayer to God, asking that He not take Charlotte until she was ready to go.

* * *

Mark turned his cell back on as soon as he cleared the hospital unit. The voice mail alert sounded immediately.

Three calls. All from Maggy Boyd.

"Where have you been? Did you forget to turn on your phone?"

"I was on a hospital visit. What's up?"

"A bump in the road," she said. "Nothing major." He heard the hesitation in her voice. "At least I don't think it is but you need to know that Bishop Clennon hasn't signed off yet on your contract."

"Why not?"

"He has some . . . questions."

"Come on, Maggy. You've always been straight with me. It's about the drinking, isn't it?"

"Yes," she said. "They had a problem down in Laconia

with a rector that ended up in an ugly court case last year. I guess he's feeling a little skittish."

"If he has questions, why didn't he ask them during the negotiation?"

"I don't have an answer for that, Mark."

This wasn't about his drinking at all, he suddenly realized. This was about something else entirely. "He's found another candidate, hasn't he?"

He heard her sigh. "That's the talk, yes." A young, homegrown family man whose only baggage was a diaper bag and a laptop case.

"So what can I do about it?"

"Not much," she said. "The vestry is getting together tonight and we'll marshal our forces, but I have to tell you that you have competition."

He tried to force a laugh, but it wasn't easy. "I hope I can back out of the house sale."

Maggy's response was one word, definitely unprintable.

"E-mail me tonight and let me know how it went."

"I'm really sorry, Mark," she said. "None of us saw this coming.

"We'll win him over," Maggy promised. "You've always been the right man for this job. Nothing can change that. Just hang tight a little longer."

He didn't have a choice. It was in God's—and Bishop Clennon's—hands now.

Ten

"I'd say it went pretty well, all things considered." Maeve tossed a red onion into the shopping cart and reached for a bunch of seedless white grapes.

Kate, who had been inspecting the Fuji apples with the eye of a nuclear scientist, shrugged. "I never said Andrew wasn't a nice guy."

Andrew Dempsey drove a pickup truck that made Mark Kerry's beat-up Honda look like a Lexus. He wasn't much taller than Gwynn but he made up for it with an impressive arrangement of muscle. His hair was sandy brown, bleached blond in places by sun and salt water, and his eyes were the faded blue that seemed to be the province of sailors and fliers. He came bearing flowers and a box of bakery cookies tied up with red and white string.

He was awkward and painfully shy and left most of the real talking to Gwynn, who had been more than happy to fill in the silences with a résumé of his wonderfulness.

All in all, it had been the longest eleven minutes of Kate's life. She would have breathed a long loud sigh of relief when they drove away in that brine-seeped pickup truck if she hadn't been bawling her eyes out instead.

They had meds to keep her mending heart under control. Why couldn't they invent something that would help her rule in these unfamiliar, pesky emotions?

"I think this might be the real thing," Maeve said.

That caught Kate's attention.

"The real thing? I'll believe it's the real thing when she moves into his place near the docks and sees all of her dreams washed out to sea with the tide."

"Gwynn isn't afraid of hard work."

Kate arched a brow in her mother's direction. "Gwynn still brings home her laundry. She has trouble working four days straight at O'Malley's without calling in sick so she can catch up on her soaps." Both Gwynn and Andrew were in for a shock.

"I think you'll be surprised," Maeve said. "You and I are both hard workers. I can't believe that particular apple fell very far from our trees."

"Sometimes I think that apple fell from a tree outside the Gap at Short Hills Mall."

"I'll admit Andrew doesn't look like a Short Hills type," Maeve said, "but those flowers were a very sweet gesture."

Kate didn't want to feel tenderness toward the rough-edged young fisherman who had apparently claimed her daughter's heart. "It was either that or a bucket of steamers. He made the right choice."

"Did you see the way he looked at her?" Maeve sighed as she dropped a bunch of grapes into a plastic bag. "It's been a long while since anybody looked at me that way."

Kate rolled her eyes. "Nobody has ever looked at me that way and I'm still managing to walk upright."

"Oh, really?" Her mother added some broccoli crowns, radishes, and a bag of baby greens to the shopping cart. "I'd say your new friend came very close the other day."

She turned away and smiled into a display of insipid hothouse tomatoes that were a crime against the Garden State. "Mom, you always did see what you wanted to see."

"I know you're smiling," Maeve said.

"How can you know that? My back is turned."

"I'm your mother. You can't fool me, honey. I saw the look on your face when you got home last night and I know Paul wasn't responsible. Thirty minutes in the parking lot with Mark lit a flame that thirty years of Paul's friendship never could."

"No wonder your books sell like hotcakes," Kate said dryly. "You really do have a way with words."

"Sexual chemistry is a wondrous thing," Maeve said as they strolled toward the dairy department. "Especially when it's forbidden."

"Okay, now you've gone too far."

"My little puritan." Maeve laughed. "Admit it: didn't you get just the tiniest thrill when you saw that clerical collar?"

"Mom!" She glanced around, praying none of her neighbors were within earshot. "I was *horrified* when I saw that collar. I spent twelve years in Catholic school. If there's one thing I know, it's that priests are off-limits."

"So isn't it lucky that he's not Catholic."

"It doesn't matter a bit to me if he's a practicing Druid. I'm not interested in him that way at all."

With that she burst into tears over a pyramid of low-fat cottage cheese with pineapple and pretty much confirmed every suspicion Maeve had.

Rocky Hill—Monday evening

One of the things Mark had learned during this five-year odyssey back to a healthy, productive life was that he had a major problem with change.

Life couldn't be trusted. It threw curveballs at you when your back was turned, then laughed when you tried to pull yourself up again. Nothing stayed the same and the best thing you could do was keep moving forward.

How many people had he dropped that load of crap on over the years? *Stay strong. Things will work out in the long run. It all happens for the best.*

Some of the biggest lies known to humankind.

The truth was that life didn't always work out the way you thought it should. You could do all the right things and still end up with your heart broken and your soul in pieces. It was what you did about it that mattered.

Booze didn't work. He knew that for a fact. The pain still managed to find its way through the fog of vodka and whiskey. It managed to find its way into his dreams.

He probably would have spiraled down into tragedy before the first anniversary of Suzanne's death if his bishop and two parishioners hadn't staged an intervention and pushed him in the direction of help.

His faith had taken a beating during her illness. It took getting sober to reawaken his soul and remind him that God had given him the tools to rebuild his life. Faith gave him a stronger spine, a deeper resolve, the assurance that there was a plan hidden deep within the chaos and all he had to do was try a little harder, pray a little longer, and God would help him find his way to the finish line.

He had gone to a meeting tonight across the street from the Medical Center at Princeton because, for him, change was also a trigger for old behaviors. Charlotte Petruzzo's hospitalization coupled with Maggy Boyd's phone call awakened old feelings in him, bad ones, the kind of feelings that could send a man looking for old friends in dangerous places. It helped to talk about it with people who understood; it helped to put ego aside and work the program the way it was meant to be worked.

Not as easy as it sounded.

He rolled up the gravel driveway and shut off the engine. The house was dark and quiet, the SOLD sign Day-Glo bright in the moonlight. He should have turned on a light before he left, maybe switched on a radio against the silence. Once he was settled up in New Hampshire, he would find himself a shelter dog and—

No point making plans just yet. Suddenly those plans were cast in shadows.

He slapped together a PBJ on squishy white bread and scarfed it over the sink. He washed it down with a quart of skim. He flipped through the mail, paid his electric bill, checked his machine for messages, stripped, and showered.

Unless he was in the mood to recaulk the tub, he had run out of ways to avoid switching on his laptop and downloading his e-mail.

TO: mark.kerry@mklj.net
FROM: annie-s@aol3.com
SUBJECT: Friday's meeting

God bless the Unitarians. We're set for Friday at their space. Sent a notice to the group. Hope everyone checks his/her e-mail between now and then.
See you then,
Ann

* * * * * *

TO: mark.kerry@mklj.net
FROM: marcy_n_scott@quickaccess.com
SUBJECT: great dinner, great conversation

We had a great time last night. So that was the woman you were looking for? Looks like you have

some competition. LOL. Wish you weren't leaving so soon. We'll squeeze in a bbq before you go, ok?
Love, Marcy & Scott

* * * * * *

TO: mark.kerry@mklj.net
FROM: mboyd@nh2day.net
SUBJECT: vestry meeting

Not much to report. We met for three hours. You have lots of support so that's good, but the bishop has the last word. If you can update your c.v. to showcase what you've been doing the last two years it would be a BIG help. We'll need it ASAP, like in the morning. You're young enough for an all-nighter, right? Wish I had something solid for you but I tried. Most of your congregation is behind you, Mark, but the new guy is definitely something special. If we fight hard enough I know we can bring Clennon back around.
Maggy

* * * * * *

TO: mboyd@nh2day.net
FROM: mark.kerry@mklj.net
SUBJECT: RE: vestry meeting

How about I give Clennon my updated c.v. in person? I could fly up tomorrow night and be in his office first thing Wednesday morning. You and the vestry have been fighting my battles for me. Time I got a little bloodied too.
Let me know, ok?
MK

* * * * * *

TO: mark.kerry@mklj.net
FROM: mboyd@nh2day.net
SUBJECT: RE: vestry meeting

GREAT IDEA. We'll make it happen. I'll phone you
when I have it nailed down. I think tonight calls for a
few extra prayers, don't you?
Maggy

He shut down the laptop, locked up the house, and
went to sleep.

Kate's house—the next morning

"You won't be here?" Kate popped out of her bedroom,
wet hair tumbling over her shoulders, and grabbed her
mother's sleeve. "You can't leave me here alone!"

"I'm taking advantage of the situation," Maeve said,
blue eyes twinkling, "and going out for a late lunch with
Amelia and Sunny. You'll be in good hands."

"I was counting on you being here with us," Kate said.
"You know, in case conversation falters."

"I don't think that will be a problem."

"Please!" Kate wasn't too old to beg. "If you're not
here it will look like I think this is a date or something."

"Isn't it?"

"Of course it isn't. This is a thank-you lunch, that's all.
I'm repaying a debt of gratitude."

"You could always write a check to his favorite charity, honey. That would cover it."

Maeve looked altogether too amused for Kate's taste.
"I already thought of that but he nixed the idea."

"Then I guess you'll have to feed him lunch."

"You're doing this on purpose, aren't you?" Kate flew

down the stairs at her mother's heels and had to stop at the bottom to catch her breath. "Wasn't this in one of your books? *Matchmaking Magic* or something?"

Maeve checked her hair in the hall mirror. "*Matchmaking and Magic,* but you were close, honey, and yes, you're right. I am doing this on purpose."

Her mother's admission knocked the wind from Kate's sails, and she sank down onto the bottom step and buried her face in her hands. "I thought you were supposed to be taking care of me while I get back on my feet, not torturing me."

"I talked it over with Gwynnie and we both agree this is the right thing to do."

"Wonderful. Now you two are talking about me behind my back."

"We've always talked about you behind your back," Maeve said, hunting around for her purse and car keys. "You just weren't paying attention."

"He's going to know you set this up."

"You're a forty-one-year-old woman. I don't think he expects you to need a chaperone."

"I'm a postcardiac patient. I need supervision."

"He's a trained EMT. You'll be in good hands."

"I still have to shower, blow-dry my hair, figure out what I'm going to wear and—how could I forget?—put together a fabulous lunch for the man who saved my life."

Maeve took Kate by the hand and led her into the kitchen. "I made the lunch," she said as she swung open the door to the fridge. "Sesame chicken on a bed of bok choy with julienned vegetables and a Thai-influenced dressing. Peach iced tea. Mango sorbet for after."

"This is so wonderful!" Kate peered into the fridge like a kid on Christmas morning. "I can't believe you did this for me, Mom."

Maeve sighed in pretend exasperation. "It's nothing to
cry about, honey. It's what mothers do. You know that."

It wasn't exactly something her mother had ever done
before, but Kate was too busy sniffling into a square of
Bounty to quibble. These random acts of kindness were
going to be her undoing.

"Finish blow-drying your hair," Maeve ordered. "I'm
going into town to see if Fran made those delicious brownies today. That sorbet might be a bit too precious for your
Father Mark."

The rest of the morning passed in a blur of expectant
primping. The last time Kate could remember putting so
much effort into her appearance was the night of the
St. Aloysius High School Christmas Festival during senior year. That was the night she and Ed made love for
the first time and, quite probably, the night Gwynn was
conceived.

She fiddled with the flowing sleeve of her deep peach
silk sweater. At least she knew one thing for sure: no babies would be conceived between the salad and the sorbet.
That crazy out-of-control feeling that had possessed her
Sunday night in the parking lot of The Old Grist Mill had
dissipated itself, for which she was deeply grateful. She
no longer worried that the sight of him on her doorstep
was going to fling her backward into romantic chaos and
hopeless longing. She might still be crying her eyes out at
the drop of a kindness, but her brief infatuation with romance seemed to have run its course.

Nobody needed to know she had fallen asleep last
night with the laptop on the pillow next to her just in case
he sent an e-mail or tried to IM his regrets at three in the
morning and needed an immediate response.

At twelve forty-five she walked into the living room
and pirouetted for Maeve. "How do I look?"

"Like a dream." Her mother looked up from her magazine and considered her. "You've always looked beautiful in that color."

"What about the skirt?" She did a half-turn and looked over her shoulder. "Does it make me look too fat?"

"It makes you look wonderful."

"Maybe it's too dressy for a Tuesday lunch. I'll be right back."

Five minutes later she was back downstairs in her most flattering pair of jeans, the gorgeous peach sweater, and ballet flats. She'd gathered her hair into a casual topknot, letting tendrils and waves fall where they might. Makeup, a little perfume, her favorite earrings, the ones that looked like captured sunlight.

"What do you think?" she asked Maeve, who was taste-testing the peach iced tea.

"You were right." Maeve nodded her approval. "That's absolutely perfect."

"I sound like Gwynn, don't I? What's happening to me?" She never wasted time debating outfits and hairstyles. Even as a teenager she had known what worked on her and what didn't and never turned to Maeve for help.

"Everything's all set," Maeve said, scanning the kitchen one last time. "I think I'll go."

"You can't go yet. He isn't here."

"It's eight minutes to one."

"What if he doesn't show up? I'll be here all by myself."

"I have my cell with me. If he doesn't show up, call me and I'll come right home."

Maeve's mind was made up and she was gone with five minutes to spare.

Kate was amazed by just how much worrying, fussing, and doubting a woman could cram into three hundred seconds. She questioned the lunch, her hair, her sweater, the sugar level of the iced tea, the existence of God, the old Latin mass, the flavor quotient of sesame seeds, Gwynn's choice of mate, and why she had ever thought inviting an Episcopal priest to lunch was such a great idea.

And then she heard the sound of an ancient Honda in her driveway and saw a tall, dark, and handsome man on her front porch and everything else fell away.

Eleven

He knew exactly what he was going to say when she opened the door. He had worked it out on the drive up to Coburn, practiced the timing while he waited for the florist to put some fussy shiny paper around the pot of showy flowers. Funny without being over the top. Warm without being smarmy. Neutral without being cold or distant. Writing an Easter Sunday sermon was easier, but finally he got it nailed.

He had the patter. He had the blooms. He even had a sunny day.

The whole thing was perfect, or would have been, except for the fact that the second she opened the door and he saw her standing there in a pair of jeans and a silky sweater, his brain short-circuited.

She looked fresh and young and as far as he could see she wasn't even wearing any makeup. Her hair was piled on top of her head but tendrils of shimmering auburn had escaped, framing her face with softness. She was exactly what God had been aiming for when he created Woman. Was she beautiful? He wasn't sure. The world's opinion didn't matter. The only thing he knew for certain was that he wouldn't change a thing.

She wasn't smiling. She stood there looking at him with the same expression of surprise that he imagined was on his face too. Surprise. Shock. That sense of recognition he had felt each time he saw her, as if everything that had ever happened to him in the past, every triumph, every mistake, every dream lost and then found again, had been preparation for this moment.

Somewhere on another street a car horn blared, breaking the spell they were falling under.

"You're right on time," she said with a wide and happy smile. "Come in."

"Traffic was light," he said, catching the intoxicating scent of her skin as he stepped into the hallway. "That shortcut you gave me was great."

He handed her the pot of flowers and her smile grew wider. "I love tulips," she said. "I'll replant the bulbs in the yard this autumn and have blooms next spring."

You would think he had won the Oscar when all he did was pick the right plant. "Something smells great," he said as they walked toward the back of the house. "Sesame?"

"I'm impressed," she said as they entered the kitchen. "I'm not sure I could have picked that out on my own."

"I lived over a Chinese restaurant when I was in seminary."

"Did you?" She opened the fridge and withdrew a large glass pitcher of something amber. "Maeve and I lived over a Hungarian restaurant when I was in sixth grade. I acquired a taste for chicken paprikash and violins that I can't seem to shake."

He suddenly noted that there were two plates on the counter, two glasses, two sets of silverware.

"Where is your mother?" he asked. "I thought she would be joining us."

"So did I." Kate opened a drawer and withdrew two freshly pressed linen napkins the color of summer sunshine. "She's off having lunch with two of her cronies."

"And your daughter?"

She turned away from him slightly as she reached for the tray leaning against the counter. "She went back to work yesterday."

"So it's just us."

"Yes," she said, "it's just us."

"Good." Great time for his internal censor to take a hike. She either hadn't heard him or was kind enough to pretend she hadn't. He needed all the help he could get to keep from saying something so ridiculous he would have to leave the state six weeks early just to save face.

"I read Maeve the riot act. I was afraid you'd think—" She swallowed the rest of her sentence. "Believe it or not, I used to be an intelligent, sophisticated woman." She pointed to herself with a broad, almost comical sweep of her hand. "This really isn't me."

"I rehearsed a speech on the drive up here."

"You did not!"

"I was practicing it in the florist shop. The clerk thought I was a head case."

"Isn't this ridiculous?" she said, pouring them each a glass of whatever it was in that icy pitcher. "We're acting like we just met. We're old friends."

"Eight days and counting." He took the glass from her. "Peach iced tea?"

"Don't tell me: you lived above a tea shop when you were in college."

"I saw the empty cans of peach nectar."

"I wish it were champagne," she said, "but alcohol is off-limits to me right now. Actually, if you'd like champagne we have a split in the fridge that I'd be happy to open for you."

"Alcohol is off-limits to me too," he said. "And not just right now."

She nodded, but she didn't ask questions and this wasn't the time to volunteer his life story. She poured them each a goblet of peach iced tea.

"Cent'anni," he said. "One hundred years."

"Cent'anni," she said, and then he watched, amazed, as she burst into tears.

He put down his glass and rounded the counter to where she stood sobbing into a yellow napkin. "Was it something I said?"

She shook her head and struggled to pull herself together. "Don't pay any attention to me."

As if that were possible.

She managed a rueful smile. "I know it's hard to believe, but the real me only cries at christenings."

He handed her a fresh napkin, which she accepted gratefully. "Nothing you can do except ride it out. It's part of the process."

"Well, I'm not too crazy about the process. I'm known as a hardheaded businesswoman. I have my reputation to consider."

"Businesswomen don't cry?"

"Not in the dairy aisle at ShopRite they don't. I made a holy show of myself yesterday over a display of low-fat cottage cheese. I'm going to have to change markets if this keeps up."

She said it with a self-mocking laugh in her voice that was as telling as it was endearing.

"Are you usually this hard on yourself?"

"You have a degree in psychology as well as theology?"

"Just an observation."

"It's absolutely gorgeous outside," she said, gesturing

toward the French doors. "How would you feel about eating on the patio?"

Which pretty much answered his question.

* * *

Kate didn't know what she would have done if he hadn't agreed to lunch on the patio. All she did know was that the room had grown too small for the emotions swirling about like mini-twisters. If they stayed in that room much longer, anything could happen.

He saw her too clearly. Most people thought she sailed through life on a wave of self-confidence, but he knew otherwise.

He was one of those rare men who pitched in without waiting to be asked. He carried plates and platters and pitchers and set them up on the table while she started the coffee, dug up the dessert dishes, and sneaked into the bathroom to check her hair and makeup.

Finally they were seated opposite each other at her glass-topped table. The sun was warm for early spring and the skies were deep blue and cloudless. Even nature was on their side.

"Springtime in New Jersey," she said with a theatrical sigh. "It doesn't get much better than this."

"You're right." His gaze roved the expanse of garden and lawn stretched out before them. "And I thought nobody did it better than we did in New Hampshire."

"You're from New Hampshire originally?" So that explained the vaguely Yankee accent she had detected.

"Born and raised so far north we were honorary Canadians."

She laughed. "I used to spend time around Laconia. It's one of my favorite places in the world."

"Vermont gets all the hype," he said, "but we deliver the goods."

" 'Live free or die.' " She quoted the state motto. "It's pretty hard to beat that sentiment." She gestured toward their lunch. "New Jersey's bounty. Enjoy!"

He hesitated for a fraction of a second, just long enough for her to notice, before he picked up his fork.

"Is something wrong?" she asked. "Do you need salt?"

"Everything's fine."

Then it dawned on her. "Did you want to say grace?"

His smile was easy and unembarrassed. "I just did but if you'd like to join me, I'd be happy to say it again."

"That's okay," she said, reaching for her glass of iced tea. "I'm fine."

He nodded and speared a piece of chicken with his fork.

"What I mean is, I don't usually say grace."

He popped the piece of chicken into his mouth. "No problem."

"I don't have anything against saying grace," she went on, "it's just that it isn't part of my routine."

"You don't owe me an explanation, Kate. It's fine."

She put her cards and her glass of iced tea down on the table. "I haven't been to church since nineteen ninety-three and the last time I said grace I was wearing a St. Aloysius uniform and studying for the SATs." What on earth was wrong with her? Talk about too much information.

"Roman Catholic?"

"Yes, and the word *lapsed* doesn't begin to describe it."

"I'm not wearing the collar today," he said. "I'm not here to judge you."

She fiddled with her dessert spoon. "I don't even know why I told you all of this. It just popped out when I realized you were saying grace."

"Religion is a touchy issue in our society. Most of us would rather talk about our sex lives than our religious beliefs."

He smiled and her discomfort melted away.

"I thought money was the touchy issue in our society," she said, reaching again for her iced tea.

He shook his head and speared some bok choy. "Believe me, religion has it beat. We're becoming a largely secular society and that puts people of faith on the other side of a cultural divide."

"Separation of church and state," she reminded him. "That's a good thing."

"Agreed, but that isn't what I'm talking about. Religion makes a lot of people uneasy." He gestured toward himself. "That's why I'm not wearing my collar today."

"Because it would have made me uncomfortable? I don't think it's possible to be more uncomfortable than I am right now."

"Then let's change the subject." He leaned across the table. "So who did you vote for in the last election?"

And just like that the tension between them vanished and they were back where they had been a few minutes ago: a man and a woman sharing lunch and laughter beneath a glorious New Jersey sky.

"You're a great cook," he said as he polished off the salad. "This is world-class."

"Thanks, but I can't take credit for any of it. Maeve put it all together for us. She's been very solicitous since my heart attack."

"Mothers are like that."

She laughed. "Not my mother. Maeve had her own theories on parenting and they didn't exactly follow the Donna Reed paradigm."

"She's a fascinating woman." He met her eyes. "I've read her books."

"You have not!" Maeve wrote about love and sex and romance, occasionally in graphic terms.

"She's good," he said. "She's honest and she's helpful. What's not to like?"

" 'What's not to like?' " She started to laugh. "Are you sure you weren't born here?"

"Positive." He drained his iced tea, then poured them each some more from the pitcher. "So what *was* she like as a mother?"

"Loving," she said, pushing her sesame chicken from one side of the plate to the other. "Caught up in her own dramas much of the time." She met his eyes. "Maeve is one of those women who fall in love easily and often. Unfortunately she's also one of those women who believe in marriage, which meant I had a lot of stepfathers."

"That must have been hard for you."

"It wasn't easy," she admitted, "but she had good taste in men. They were all extremely nice guys. I just wish we'd let one of them stick around long enough to unpack."

"So you moved around a lot."

"No, she made them move around a lot."

They locked eyes and burst into loud, raucous laughter that seemed to come from nowhere.

"Is your father still alive?" he asked as he helped her carry their empty plates into the kitchen. "I have this mental picture of an academic type with leather patches on the elbows of his tweed sport coat."

"You're close. He was the son of a famous senator from Rhode Island. They split up before I was born." She opened the door to the dishwasher and started loading plates inside. "He died when I was twenty-six."

He handed her the knives and forks. "I'm sorry."

"It would have been nice to have a chance to get to know him but—" She shrugged and closed the dishwasher door. "Your family is what it is and there's nothing you can do about it." She handed him the dessert plates, the bakery box, and the icy serving bowl piled high with mango sorbet. "How about you? Any senators hiding in your closet?"

He waited while she put the coffeepot, two cups and saucers, and a pitcher of milk on a tray. "No senators," he said, "but we do have a couple of Episcopal priests lurking in there."

"So you went into the family business." She led the way back out to the patio. The warm sun felt like an embrace.

"I never thought of it that way, but I guess I did."

"You never thought of it that way?" She arranged everything on the glass-topped table and leaned the empty tray against the house. "Most families don't have multiple clergy members gathering around the Thanksgiving Day dinner table."

"My parents were dairy farmers who only went to church for christenings, funerals, and the occasional wedding. They weren't exactly thrilled when I said I was going into the seminary."

"When I was little, the nuns talked a lot about hearing the call. I remember walking to school and praying God wouldn't tap me on the shoulder and tell me I had to join the convent."

"That's not how it works."

"I know that now," she said as she poured him a cup of coffee, "but when you're seven years old, anything seems possible."

"So are you asking me if God tapped me on the shoulder and gave me a one-way ticket to the seminary?"

"Yes," she said, sliding his cup and saucer toward him. "That's exactly what I'm asking." Why pull her punches? The odds were pretty good that they would never see each other again. They could afford to be honest.

"I can't remember a time when I didn't know that I would be a priest."

"No offense, but you don't exactly seem like your average holy man. You were wearing a Grateful Dead T-shirt the day we met. You drive a truly awful powder blue car.

And, to be completely frank here, I don't think I've heard you say anything holy or spiritual yet."

"Maybe you haven't been listening."

"Every time I think I have you figured out, you say something like that and I have to start from scratch."

He served her a small crystal bowl of mango sorbet and slid it toward her. "You've been trying to figure me out?"

"You're very mysterious," she said. "A New Hampshire priest churchless in central New Jersey. I Googled you but couldn't find out a single thing."

She offered him the sumptuous double-chocolate brownies Maeve had brought back from the bakery. He took two. She liked a man who liked chocolate.

"I Googled you too," he said. "There were fifty-two mentions of Kate French and/or French Kiss last year alone."

She smiled and took a spoonful of sorbet. "We had a good year."

"Now I see how those documents figure into the equation."

"The eighteenth century, mainly the Colonial through Revolutionary War period, is my specialty," she said. "Clothes, household items, ephemera. Unfortunately the good stuff is getting harder to find around here. I had to go all the way to England for the documents you saved for me." She had a new appointment with Professor Armitage set up in two weeks.

He flashed her a surprisingly wicked grin. "Did the ghost of George Washington tap you on the shoulder and say, 'Thou shalt deal in antiques'?"

She threatened him with a spoonful of mango sorbet. "The senator's son left me some money when he died. His second family contested the will but his and Maeve's marriage had been legal and binding and I was among his legitimate issue." She popped the sorbet into her mouth, savored the smooth sweetness, then swallowed. "I bought this carriage house and then I bought a half-interest in the antiques shop where I'd been working. Two years later I bought out the owner."

"What about Gwynn's father?"

"Ed and I married in high school." She met his eyes. "Yes, for the reason you think. We loved each other as friends but we were never in love the way a married couple should be. We divorced when Gwynn was ten years old. He remarried a few months later and is very happy living in Pennsylvania with Marie and their kids."

"You never married again?"

"No."

"Ever come close?"

"Not even remotely close."

"Ever wish you had?"

"Not even remotely." She pretended to study him carefully. "Now you look like the marrying kind to me. You said you aren't married now but that leaves—what? Thirty-five or forty years unaccounted for."

"Suzanne died five years ago." The words were stark, his emotions palpable.

"I'm sorry." She wanted to take his hand, but suddenly the distance between them seemed vast and uncharted. "I was trying to be funny and I—"

He shook his head. "We were trying to get pregnant and it wasn't working. Finally we drove down to Boston to see a fertility specialist. They ran the usual tests on me and everything was okay. They ran a few preliminaries on Suzanne and called us back in. Eight months later she was gone."

She had no right to cry for his dead wife, but the tears came anyway. So did the nerve to reach across the wide expanse between them and take his hand.

"But you're okay now."

"I take it day to day but yes, I'm okay."

"I'm glad."

"I almost told you the whole story when you asked about making a donation to my congregation."

"You don't owe me any explanations, Mark."

"I know that. I want to tell you."

She listened. He talked.

She talked. He listened.

Paul phoned her cell number, ostensibly to see how she was doing, but she knew he was checking up on her lunch with Mark. Maeve phoned around three o'clock to make sure everything was going well. Mark fielded two calls from his real estate agent, and one from a colleague in New Hampshire who delivered news that clearly made him unhappy.

The sun reached its peak and began the slow downhill slide toward late afternoon. The flow of conversation dwindled down to an occasional murmur. Light cloud cover moved in, dropping the temperature, and they moved inside to the sunroom adjacent to the kitchen.

"A glider," he said with delight. "I haven't seen one of these in years."

"I thought every front porch in New England had one of these."

"Not that I've noticed."

"Sit down," she said. "You'll like it."

"I should go. You've had a long day."

"Doing what?" she said with a laugh. "My mother made lunch. You served most of it. All I've done is drink iced tea and talk."

"And listen."

"You listened too."

"I don't usually open up like that," he said with an embarrassed shrug. "I don't know what that was all about."

"Neither do I." She was painfully aware of her voice, the sound of her breathing, the rhythm of her heartbeat. "I told you things my mother doesn't even know about."

They were standing inches apart, so close she could feel the warmth of his skin and inhale the fresh-mowed grass smell that clung to his clothes from the hours they had spent outside.

He took her hands and her eyes filled instantly with tears. "Allergies," she said, ducking her head. "Springtime is lethal."

And it was, in many ways. Springtime was rife with danger. A woman might do anything on a warm spring day with the right man.

Except this wasn't the right man. She had better keep reminding herself of that very important fact. Men didn't get any more wrong than a widowed recovering alcoholic who happened to be an Episcopal priest on his way back to resume his old life in New Hampshire, more than three hundred miles away.

You would have to be crazy to let your guard down around a man like that.

"This is crazy," she said as they fell into each other's arms.

"Completely nuts," he agreed as they tumbled onto the glider.

They were so close their breath mingled in the whisper of air between them.

"You'll only be here another six weeks," she said, tracing the contours of his face with her fingers, memorizing the planes and angles, the shadowy stubble darkening his cheek and jaw. "There's no point to starting anything."

"No point at all."

He pressed a kiss to the hollow of her throat and if she hadn't been sitting already she would have melted into the ground.

"We both know it would have to end when you leave for New Hampshire."

"Your life is here in New Jersey."

"Absolutely," she said. "My home, my family, my work. Everything."

"And my future is up in New Hampshire."

"A second chance," she said, kissing the strong curve of his jaw. "Your second chance to make things right." She got it. She even understood. But she didn't have to like it.

His mouth found the nape of her neck, the tiny pulse that was beating crazily in her right temple. She felt as if he were setting off tiny explosive charges everywhere his lips touched.

His lips touched her ear. "I wanted to do this the first moment I saw you."

She shivered at the sensations rippling through her. "I saw you leaning against your car and I almost tripped over my own feet."

His thumbs grazed either side of her mouth. She was finding it harder to breathe with each second that passed.

"I can't make any promises, Kate. I've already made them to my old congregation."

"I don't believe in promises," she whispered, her lips soft against his. "This is enough for me."

The kiss was as natural as breathing, as intoxicating as champagne. Her mouth opened beneath his and she gasped at the feel of him, the way he tasted of chocolate and mango and heat. She felt dizzy, knocked off center, and she clung to his shoulders so she wouldn't slide off the face of the earth and into some vast unknowable universe of shooting stars and fireworks and whispered warnings that some things are too good to be true.

He kissed her as if kissing were an end in itself, as if he loved the feel of her mouth beneath his, the sounds she made deep in her throat, the way she arched against him, trying to crawl inside his skin and stay there.

They broke apart, breathless and dazed, and looked into each other's eyes for an eternity as if they couldn't quite believe this was really happening.

"A big mistake," she said. "It's moving too fast."

"Tell me to go and I will," he said. "It's not too late."

But it was too late and they both knew it. They were already in over their heads.

Twelve

The rules were simple: they would enjoy each other's company and say good-bye without regret the day he left for New Hampshire. Neither one knew exactly where the next six weeks would take them but it was impossible to deny the fact that they had been brought together by a force, or forces, greater than either one of them.

They kissed on the glider until they heard the sound of Maeve's car in the driveway and leaped apart like guilty teenagers. Kate's mouth was swollen and red from his kisses and he had to stay seated when Maeve walked into the room until his erection caught up with the change of activity.

Maeve was a smart woman who made her living exploring the chemistry between men and women. She had probably known this was going to happen before he and Kate did, but she didn't let on. Only the happy sparkle in her eyes gave her away.

Kate walked him out to his car, where they held hands in the gathering darkness.

"You're asleep on your feet," he finally pointed out when she dozed off against his shoulder. "Go inside."

"This is too easy," she said. "Isn't this sort of thing supposed to be fraught with anxiety?"

"I don't know," he said. "Nothing like this has ever happened to me before."

She hid a small yawn behind her hand and looked up at him. "You mean you don't cruise shopping mall parking lots looking for lapsed Catholics to save?"

"Only you."

That wasn't what he had meant to say. The words seemed to have a will of their own and he wished he could push a button and erase the tape.

She lowered her head and he didn't have to ask her if she was crying. He knew she was. Maybe this whole thing wasn't such a good idea. She was one week out from a cardiac incident, in a highly vulnerable and emotional state of mind. Her decision-making capabilities might not be at their peak. The problem was he couldn't have turned away from her if he tried. The sense of inevitability that had surrounded them from the start was too powerful to be denied.

She surreptitiously wiped her eyes on the sleeve of her pretty sweater, then looked up at him again. "I'm scared out of my mind," she said.

"So am I."

"Maybe we're making a terrible mistake."

"Could be."

"We've only known each other a week. It isn't possible to feel this way after only a week."

"But we do."

"I know," she said, "and that's why I'm scared out of my mind."

They agreed they could always slow things down, retreat to their separate corners and wait for the romantic fog that had enveloped both of them to lift, but the fact that they couldn't stop kissing while they discussed the matter undermined their hardheaded determination.

"What are we worried about?" Kate leaned in the open driver's-side window of his car and touched a hand to his cheek. "We keep forgetting that we have a built-in six-week shelf life and when it rolls around you'll be three hundred miles away and that, Father Kerry, will be that."

Three hundred miles sounded like a great distance, but at that moment he knew he would walk it barefoot during a snowstorm to see her again.

Three thousand miles wouldn't be far enough to keep him away.

*   *   *

Kate was lying on top of her bed, staring at the ceiling and trying very hard not to think about Mark and the spectacular afternoon they had just shared. She had already replayed it in her mind at least ten times, from the moment she heard his car crunching its way up the drive to the sight of his taillights disappearing down Indigo Lane. She remembered every word, every sentence, every smile, every laugh . . . every kiss.

Oh God, those kisses! He was a spectacular kisser, a world-class kisser who could turn the innocent pastime into an erotic Olympic event. No doubt he had been blessed with above-average equipment for the job: a gorgeous mouth, full lips, the faintest scratch of stubble along his cheek and jaw (just enough to keep it interesting), but it was what he did with all of that wonderfulness that turned kissing into something more.

He kissed as if he had all the time in the world, as if kissing had been his goal right from the start. She wasn't a young girl. She had been married for ten years. She had dated her share of Mr. Wrongs. She knew the difference between a man who kissed because it was expected and a man who kissed because he was sensual right down to the center of his being, and there was no doubt where Mark Kerry fit in.

"Are you okay in here?" Maeve appeared in the doorway wearing one of her flowing New Agey outfits with a Betty Crocker apron tied around her still-slim waist. "I taped *American Idol* for you, if you're interested."

"Just tired," Kate said, leaning up on her elbow and smiling at her mother. "It was a long day."

"You noticed that I'm not asking any intrusive questions, didn't you?" Maeve sat on the edge of the bed. She smelled like a combination of Obsession and cinnamon.

"I noticed."

"It's not easy," Maeve said, "not after seeing the way you two kissed out there by his car."

"You spied on me?"

"It isn't often I get to watch sexual chemistry turn into a budding romance right before my eyes. I think of it as research."

"Well, don't get your hopes up. He'll be moving back to New Hampshire at the end of May."

Maeve considered her words for a moment. "A lot can happen in six weeks. Plans can change. He might decide to stay. You might decide to go. You never know how it will all play out."

"Yes, we do," Kate said. She could hear the faint glimmer of her old self behind the words. "Whatever this is, it comes with an expiration date."

"Don't you mean safety net?"

"Nothing wrong with knowing your limitations, right?"

Her mother leaned over and pressed a kiss to her forehead. "And there's nothing wrong with stretching your wings."

Maeve went back downstairs to make some phone calls.

Kate stared up at the ceiling a while longer, then propped herself against the pillows and switched on her laptop.

TO: kate@frenchkiss.biz
FROM: gwynnbann@njshorefun.net
SUBJECT: this'n'that

Weren't Andrew's flowers *beautiful*? He picked out every single one himself. His e-mail is bigfish@three milelimit.biz in case you want to drop him a note or something. I kind of thought you'd have done it by now. BTW I forgot to give you my new address. We're moving my stuff over to Andrew's tomorrow but I'll keep checking the old place for mail. Anyway, here it is:

    Gwynn Bannister
    c/o Three Mile Limit Fishing and Whale Watches
    23 Dockside Plaza
    Paradise Point, NJ (I can't remember the zip)
My cell #'s the same and I gave Gran Andrew's number.

How are you feeling? Gran said you have a dr's appt tomorrow. I'll say a prayer for you at morning mass.

xoxoxoxo gwynnie

Where were her glasses when she needed them? Kate leaned closer to the screen of her laptop and peered at the string of words as if she were trying to decipher the Rosetta Stone. There it was again. She hadn't imagined it. "I'll say a prayer for you at morning mass." Since when? Was Andrew a Roman Catholic?

And wait a second. What was that about a doctor's appointment? She didn't have a doctor's appointment tomorrow, did she? She clicked over to her organizer and couldn't find anything for Wednesday. She got up and walked to the top of the stairs and hollered to Maeve, who hollered back that yes, she did have an eleven o'clock with Dr. Lombardi and it was a must-keep appointment.

"Damn," she whispered. Now she would have to cancel her plans with Mark. She was supposed to be incorporating mild physical exercise into her daily routine and he had suggested a trip to Spring Lake and a walk on the beach. The weather was supposed to be every bit as perfect as it had been today, and the thought of strolling along the water's edge hand-in-hand with him was enough to elevate her heart rate without her moving a muscle.

Maybe they could postpone it until later in the day. She clicked over to her instant-messaging program.

KATEFRENCH: Are you online, Mark?
KATEFRENCH: Mark? Are you there?
FATHERMARK: I thought you'd be asleep by now.
KATEFRENCH: It's not even ten o'clock yet!
FATHERMARK: So you're a night owl?
KATEFRENCH: Given the chance. You?
FATHERMARK: Day person. I'm catching up on msgs.
KATEFRENCH: Guess there's not a big demand for ten p.m. masses and midnight church buffets!
FATHERMARK: I was just about to e-mail you. Something's come up and I have to cancel tomorrow.

No fair crying, Kate. You were about to cancel on him!

FATHERMARK: Kate? Are you still there?
FATHERMARK: Kate?
KATEFRENCH: I'm here. I was about to tell you that I had to cancel tomorrow.
KATEFRENCH: I forgot my appointment with Dr. Lombardi.

KATEFRENCH: Thursday's okay though.
FATHERMARK: Thursday? I'm not sure I'll be back in
    time.

Back in time? What was he talking about?

KATEFRENCH: No problem. I understand. Things
    happen.

Actually she didn't understand. Not even a little bit.
Three hours ago they had been wrapped in each other's
arms kissing as if they were on the *Titanic* and they had
run out of lifeboats. Who needed a six-week shelf life
when the man in question couldn't make it six hours
without looking for an escape hatch.

If this was the flip side of all the wildly romantic feelings she'd been dealing with the last few days, thanks but
no thanks. Life was a lot less complicated without them.

She waited for him to type in a series of lame excuses
but the cursor just sat there flickering at her.

Where was he? How dare he drop a bomb in her lap
and disappear.

KATEFRENCH: Mark?
KATEFRENCH: Mark, are you there?
KATEFRENCH: My cell's ringing. Gotta go.

"Hello, Kate."

Who would have thought clergy could be so sneaky.

She wasn't going to give him the satisfaction. "Who is
this?"

"It's Mark. I think this is too important for IM."

Oh great. This didn't bode well. If he was having second thoughts, she would just as soon he had them online

than on the phone. She could do without a fake apology meant to soothe his conscience.

"You don't understand." He had a great phone voice, a little angry, a whole lot sexy. "I—"

"You've had a change of plans. You already told me that."

"You had a change of plans too."

"I have a doctor's appointment. I'm not trying to back out."

"I'm flying up to New Hampshire in the morning," he said in what she assumed was his pulpit voice, direct and commanding. "We've run into problems and I have to plead my case to the bishop. It was my suggestion. I should have thought about it before we made plans."

"Problems?"

"He isn't sure how he feels about handing over a congregation to a recovering alcoholic."

"Shouldn't he have had the second thoughts before they sent you a contract to sign?"

"That's my thinking too." He explained that the bishop had made his decision based on his earlier track record and the enthusiastic support of his congregation.

"So you might not get the position after all?"

"It better not come to that," he said, trying to laugh. "I sold my house."

"What are you going to do?"

"Fly up to New Hampshire, like I said, and meet with Bishop Clennon. The rest is up to him."

"I hope it works out."

"So do I. The house is sold and I'm not looking forward to sleeping in my car."

"I've seen the car," she said, doing her part to lighten the gloomy mood. "I wouldn't look forward to it either."

"What time is your doctor's appointment tomorrow?"

"Eleven."

"I'll say a prayer for you."

"When is your appointment with the bishop?"

"Two p.m."

"I'll hold a good thought."

In the blink of an eye their brand-new, six-week-expiration-date romance was already in danger of morphing into something messier and more open-ended, a little bit closer to real life.

Which was something she absolutely positively didn't want any part of.

Thirteen

"Yo, Father." The security agent motioned toward Mark. "Step aside, please, for further attention."

They wanded him, ran him through the magnetometer two more times, and were considering a body cavity search when he was finally waved through just in time to make his plane.

So far it hadn't been his greatest morning. He stopped off at Pinecrest to see Charlotte, but she had had a bad night and was sleeping. He scribbled a note for her and left it on her nightstand and was halfway out the door when a nurse flagged Mark down to say that Mr. Kelsey in 7-G had been asking for him.

"He's not doing too well," the nurse said. "I know a quick visit would make all the difference."

He hadn't chosen this vocation so he could turn away from the people who needed him most.

He made it to Newark Liberty with little time to spare. Thanks to that holdup at the security checkpoint he was the last passenger to board.

"Looks like God's on your side," the flight attendant said as she waved him to the last available seat in coach. "We were just about to close up shop here."

The flight was uneventful. It landed on time at Logan, where he changed planes, boarding a puddle-jumper that would take him into Greenwood, where Maggy Boyd would be waiting for him in the parking lot.

He checked his watch after takeoff. Eleven-twenty. Kate was probably sitting in a drafty examination room, wired up to an EKG, waiting for her doctor to give her the requisite eleven minutes of expert attention. He conjured up her smile, her beautiful hazel eyes, her laughter, and asked God to bless her with good health and joy.

Their last conversation still had him off balance. She hadn't been very happy when he told her he had to cancel their Spring Lake plans, but that was nothing compared to how she sounded when he told her why. She hadn't been kidding when she said she was fine with the six-week limit on their romance. He wouldn't have minded a shade less enthusiasm.

Maggy was waiting for him in the parking lot as promised. She was wearing a bright red sweater he could see from across the airfield. She waved wildly when she spotted him, and he felt the usual combination of happiness and guilt.

"Wow!" she said as he approached. "You look great."

"And you look even better," he said, and she did. There was a glow about Maggy that hadn't been there the last time he saw her. "Did you change your hair or something?"

Her smile was full of secrets. "Or something."

He tossed his briefcase into the backseat of her Jeep, then climbed in next to her. "You didn't have to play chauffeur, Mag. I could've rented a car for the day."

She shrugged off his thanks. "This'll give us a chance to catch up."

Catch up? What was there to catch up on? They had talked or e-mailed every day for the last two months of negotiations. He found it hard to believe there was anything left to be said.

"You're meeting the bishop at two," she said as they entered the highway north. "That probably won't last more than an hour. I figured we could have dinner in town with the vestry and a few friends. They want to show their support."

He had held out the hope that he'd be able to make the return flight that night, but that wasn't going to happen.

"What do you think my odds are with Clennon?" He and Maggy had always been able to get straight to the heart of things.

"Fifty-fifty," she said bluntly, glaring at a driver passing on the right. "He's been listening to horror stories from other parishes. That's why this meeting is a good thing. He didn't know you—" She stopped and shook her head. "You know."

"Before Suzanne died."

She met his eyes for a moment, then looked back at the road. "When times were good."

"Same thing, Mags."

"I guess it is." She brightened. "I've gotta tell you, I don't think I've ever seen you look so good. Have you started running or something?"

"Roofing," he said, laughing at the look on her face. "My next-door neighbor's a roofer and when he heard I did roofs in seminary, he hired me on as a part-timer. It's better than pumping iron in a gym."

"I'll have to look into it." She gestured toward her posterior. "Damn computers. All I do is sit."

"Whatever you're doing, Mags, it works."

She took a deep breath and he braced himself for bad news. "I met someone."

He wasn't sure he'd heard right. He swiveled toward her. "What?"

"He took over Harry's veterinary practice just before Thanksgiving. I think you met him."

"The tall skinny guy with glasses?"

"I prefer to think of him as lanky and intellectual, but yeah. That's Sam."

"And you're seeing this Sam guy?"

"Actually we're engaged." She flashed him her bare left ring finger. "No ring. We're putting the money toward a down payment on a house." She looked at him again and laughed. "Well, say something, you fool. This is big news."

He knew all the right things to say, but he had trouble saying them in the right order. This was exactly what he had prayed for, but it didn't feel the way he had thought it would.

"I finally woke up," she said as she exited the parkway and headed east toward Greenwood. "I know you knew how I felt about you and I spent a lot of years trying to convince myself that kindness and love were the same thing. You can breathe a big sigh of relief now, my friend."

"Sam's a lucky guy."

"We're both lucky," she said. "I'm thirty-eight years old, Mark, and I have to tell you I didn't think it was ever going to happen for me."

"I hope I never led you to think that—"

"Oh no!" She sounded horrified. "You didn't lead me on, if that's what you're thinking. I knew Suzanne was the love of your life and I knew you saw me only as a friend but—" She shrugged. "What can I tell you? Love doesn't always make sense. Sometimes you have to beat it with a stick before you can make it do what you want."

Sometimes the best thing a man could do was keep his mouth shut and just listen.

* * *

"You're a model patient," Dr. Lombardi said, after reading the results of her echo and blood work. "Textbook
case."

"Can I have another tissue, please?"

He slid the box across his desk toward her and smiled.

"You were right about the emotions," she said, sniffling loudly. "I'm crying at trash bag commercials."

"It's not uncommon. I promise you it'll pass."

"And I seem to be forming . . . attachments to people
very easily."

"Your emotional responses are heightened right now.
It's to be expected."

"The thing is, I think I like it."

"It won't last," he warned her. "It's all part of the healing process, Kate. Don't go making any major decisions
the next few weeks. No sense making life any more complicated than it needs to be."

He was a man of science. What did he know about the
world of emotions?

She changed the subject. "You want me to walk at
least an hour a day. What if I walked to my antique shop
and back every morning? It would be a good start."

"And I suppose you'd like to stop in and make sure
your employees are keeping things running smoothly."

"What a great idea!" she said, laughing. "I promise I
won't stay more than an hour." Maybe two, but he didn't
have to know that.

"One hour."

"But—"

"We're not negotiating terms, Kate. One hour in the
shop and that's all. I want you to take it slow for two more
weeks. No driving yet. We'll cut down the visiting nurse
to twice a week." He consulted the list in front of him.

"We'll schedule a stress test for the end of the month and then you'll be able to resume a normal sex life."

A normal sex life? She almost laughed. It had been so long since she had any sex life at all, normal or otherwise, that the memory was lost in the dim recesses of her personal history.

Her passionate afternoon in Mark's arms was the most exciting thing to happen to her in longer than she would admit to anyone.

Maeve was waiting for her in the hospital coffee shop. She looked up from her laptop at the sound of Kate's heels clicking across the tiled floor.

"I don't know why you didn't let me come with you," her mother said as she saved her work and shut down. "A patient should always have her advocate with her to take notes and ask things the patient might forget."

"A geriatric patient maybe," Kate said. "There's nothing wrong with my memory."

"It's a known fact that patients tend to hear what they want to hear. Pertinent information often slips between the cracks."

She raised her hands palms out in surrender. "Mom, please! I'm fine. Lombardi says I'm a textbook case. Everything's progressing right on schedule."

"Did he adjust the Lipitor? What about the Procardia? Any dietary changes we need to incorporate? You're not exercising enough. You really should get out there every day."

"If you don't knock it off, I'm going to order bacon and eggs and English muffins drenched in butter."

Maeve pretended to shudder. "I'm going in with you next time, Kate. Somebody needs to know exactly what's going on."

"When did you become this maternal?" Kate asked as they walked across the courtyard to the parking garage. "I don't remember all this fussing over me when I was a kid."

"You wouldn't allow it," Maeve said, as she pulled her car keys from the pocket of her hand-knit sweater. "Even as a baby, you pushed me away whenever I fussed over you too much. You've always needed your space and you taught me to respect that."

"I was a baby," she said. "I can't believe my likes and dislikes were that well developed."

Maeve laughed as she unlocked the car doors with a beep from her keypad. "I remember sitting in the pediatrician's office, sobbing my eyes out because I couldn't seem to figure out what would make you happy on any given day."

"Gwynnie was a breeze," Kate said, smiling at the memory. "She loved everything and everybody."

"I always said Gwynnie took after me."

Those stupid ridiculous tears spilled over again. "You've been so wonderful to me, Mom. I don't know how I would have managed without you here."

"I have complete faith in you, honey. You would have found a way. I'm just glad I could be here to take care of you."

"I wish I could drive. Bet you never thought you'd be driving carpool for your forty-one-year-old daughter."

"No, I can't say I ever did." Maeve paid the parking fee and exited the garage. "Although it's given me an idea for a new series of self-help books for mothers and daughters of a certain age."

Kate clapped her hands over her ears. "If a red lace thong figures into it, I don't want to hear the details."

They bantered amiably on the drive home. Maeve swung by town, where they stocked up on supplies at ShopRite and refilled Kate's prescriptions. Kate grumbled about the number of pills required. "I used to be a multivitamin and extra C girl," she said. "I hate taking all these meds."

"Too bad," Maeve said cheerfully. "If that's your only problem, you are a very lucky girl."

"How about I make lunch?" Kate suggested as they loaded groceries into the trunk of Maeve's VW and headed for home. "I've been craving salad Niçoise for days now."

"Do we have tuna in the house?"

"Couldn't live without it," Kate said. "And I think there're some fresh string beans in the crisper."

"Why don't you take a nap when we get home? I wouldn't mind preparing the salad."

"I'm not tired," Kate protested. "I've missed puttering around the kitchen."

"You sound like you've been on the mend for months instead of days."

"You know me, Mom. I don't do leisure time well at all."

"Weren't you and your Father McDreamy supposed to go somewhere today?"

"You really have to stop with the McDreamy," she said. "You sound like Gwynn." She explained about his sudden trip up to New Hampshire and realized it was almost time for his meeting with the bishop. *I didn't forget, Mark. I'm holding a good thought.*

"What did I tell you!" Maeve all but clapped her hands together in delight. "Even the best-laid plans can turn on a dime."

"Oh great," Kate said with a groan. "That's Paul's car in the driveway, isn't it?" A sleek black Mercedes with New York plates. "He doesn't know how to use a phone?"

"You expect your best friend to rely on ceremony?"

"Yes," she said. Especially when the best friend in question was now pushing for something more. She loved Paul dearly and didn't want to see a decades-long friendship go up in smoke because she couldn't return his romantic feelings. "Don't ask him to stay for lunch," she warned her mother. "I don't want to encourage this dropping-in-unexpectedly thing."

"Of course we're asking him to stay for lunch. Don't be ridiculous."

He leaped to his feet as they pulled into the driveway next to him. "I would've called," he said as he crossed the front yard toward them, "but my cell went dead."

"A likely story," Kate said as they kissed cheeks. "Aren't you supposed to be in Manhattan where you belong, Grantham?"

"A tongue like a viper," Maeve said, giving Paul's cheek a kiss. "I don't know where she gets it from."

"Make yourself useful," Kate said. "We have groceries to unload."

Maeve said something highly annoying about how nice it was to have a man's help, but then Maeve had the habit of flinging compliments around like rice at a wedding. Kate knew better than to take her seriously, but Paul, who had been around long enough to know better, lapped up the remarks.

"What are you doing here?" she repeated as he schlepped packages around back to the kitchen. "I thought you were gainfully employed."

"I had a breakfast meeting in Philadelphia," he said, putting the packages down on the counter. "I thought I'd take you and Maeve out to lunch."

"If you'd called, you would've known I had a doctor's appointment."

"Dead cell phone, remember?"

"You could have used a pay phone. I think there are still a few left on the planet."

"From my car?"

"Paul—" She stopped as Maeve walked into the room. Maeve looked at Kate, then glanced toward Paul, whose back was turned to her. "I forgot to stop by the bank," she said smoothly. "I'll be back in fifteen minutes."

"I love your mother," Paul said as Maeve backed down the driveway. "She always knows the right thing to say."

There was no denying that Maeve French had her moments, but this was one time when Kate wished she had stayed around.

"You're here to pick up where you left off on Sunday, aren't you?"

"In a way."

She groaned and started unpacking the grocery bags. "I had more fun at the doctor's office."

"I want to apologize."

She put the skim milk into the fridge and rummaged through the crisper for string beans. "I'm listening."

"I apologize."

"That's it?"

"Pretty much."

She shot him a look as she tossed the bag of string beans onto the counter. "You could have e-mailed that and saved gas."

"Cut me some slack, French. I'm trying to make amends."

"So you've regained your sanity." She pulled a can of tuna from the cabinet near the sink. "I was worried about you there for a while, friend."

He stepped into her line of vision. "I still love you, Kate, if that's what you mean."

"I should've quit while I was ahead."

"But I'm not going to push it."

She put the can of tuna on the counter next to the string beans. "You're not?"

He shook his head. "I saw you with the holy man Sunday night. I can't compete with what was going on there."

"Nothing was going on."

"Don't bullshit me, old friend." His choice of words caught her attention. Paul rarely used vulgarity to make a point, but when he did, you listened. "I might not have liked what I saw, but I'm not blind."

She couldn't deny it. What was more, she didn't want to. "I'm as surprised as you are."

"You and a priest." They locked eyes and there was nothing to do but laugh. "You two were shooting off more fireworks than Macy's on the Fourth of July."

She stopped laughing. "Well, those fireworks will put themselves out at the end of May."

The look on his face was priceless. "I know you're anal, but even you wouldn't put that sort of thing in your day planner."

"It's in his." She gave him a condensed version of Mark's return to New Hampshire in six weeks.

"What if he changes his mind?" Paul asked. "What would you do then?"

"Can't happen. That's his home. He's going back where he belongs."

"What if he asks you to go with him?"

"Paul," she said, raising her hands in surrender. "This is getting ridiculous. Let's change the subject."

"Okay," Paul said, "Lisa called last night. We talked for an hour."

"I like Lisa," she said, hearing text and subtext. "You should reschedule that trip to Barbados."

He met her eyes. "Maybe," he said. "We'll see how things play out."

"I think they're going to play out fine."

"Lisa isn't you."

"No, she isn't," she said. "She's my daughter's age."

An exaggeration, but not by much.

"Yeah?" He looked at her. "I hadn't noticed."

Which made them laugh for the second time.

She opened the fridge, grabbed two Snapples, then tossed him one. "Sunroom or yard?"

"Yard."

She led him across the shaggy grass to the park bench she'd purchased at a renovator's yard sale in Greenwich ages ago.

"You could use a man around the house," he said, leaning back and stretching his legs out in front of him. "It looks like the pampas back here."

"What I could use is a lawn tractor," she corrected him.

He took a swig of his drink. "Jill got married over the weekend."

They both fell so silent she thought she could hear the grass grow. "Your Jill?" she finally asked. A stupid, stupid question but it was the best she could do.

"Jake's Jill," he said.

"Don't tell me she married someone named Jake."

"Doctor Jake McDowell, cardiologist to Princeton's best and brightest."

"The kids didn't say anything?" Kids talked. Especially about their parents' choice of companions. Hard to believe his ex-wife's remarriage could come as a surprise when they shared four children in common.

"They eloped," he said. "The kids were staying with Jill's parents. They had a long weekend and flew off to Vegas."

"How are the kids taking it?"

"They love the schmuck," Paul said. "They think it's great."

"How does the schmuck feel about them?"

"It's a fucking love fest."

She reached for his hand and gave it a squeeze. "So be happy for them."

"I thought I would be," he said. "Turns out it's not so

easy." He took another swig of Snapple. "How did you feel when Ed and Marie married?"

"I was happy for them."

"That's it?" He gave her a curious look.

"Okay, I was relieved," she said. "Seeing him happily married made me feel less guilty about the divorce."

"I was there," he reminded her. "Your divorce was a textbook case on how to separate and not leave wreckage behind."

"Thanks for the compliment, but I'm not sure I deserve any of the credit. It's easy to stay friends when that's all you were to begin with."

"You think I'm still in love with Jill."

"I think it's a possibility."

He was quiet for a long time. "I always thought we'd find our way back to each other." He forced a laugh and she squeezed his hand. "I was wrong."

There was nothing she could say. His over-the-top reaction to her heart attack suddenly made perfect sense. In the space of a few days he had lost (or nearly lost) two of the most important women in his life.

"So now what?" she asked when the silence grew too long for her comfort. "You're going to buy them a nice gift, aren't you?"

He looked at her like she was an alien dropped from a flying saucer into his midst. "You really don't have a romantic bone in your body, do you?"

"It's not my fault. It's all in the DNA."

The expression in his eyes changed. "Tell that to your priest."

"He's not my priest," she reminded him, "and even if he was, six weeks from now it's good-bye and good luck."

"Be careful," her best friend warned. "In the right hands, six weeks can be a lifetime."

Fourteen

What he remembered most about the day was Suzanne's smile. It seemed to follow him wherever he was, whoever he was talking to, whatever was happening around him; her smile was constant as the North Star guiding him home.

His parents were there, watching the proceedings with a mixture of pride and puzzlement, wondering what strange forces had led him along the path to an Episcopalian priesthood. They held hands. If he closed his eyes he could see them there in the first pew, following the proceedings with open hearts and minds. Three years later they would both be gone.

Suzanne's mother was there, beaming through her tears, as proud of his accomplishments as she was of her daughter's.

Family, friends, neighbors, they had all gathered to celebrate his induction as rector of St. Stephen's of Greenwood Episcopalian Church.

Maggy's father, Henry Boyd, was the first to speak.

Bishop Harrigan, we have come together today to welcome Mark Francis Kerry, who has been chosen to serve as rector of St. Stephen's. We believe that he is well qualified, and that he has been prayerfully and lawfully selected.

Bishop Harrigan turned to him and his baritone rang out across the crowded chapel.

Mark, do you, in the presence of this congregation, commit yourself to this new trust and responsibility?

I do.

Will you who witness this new beginning support and uphold Mark in this ministry?

We will.

Let us then offer our prayers to God, for all his people, for this congregation, and for Mark, their rector.

Amen.

Mark, take this water and help me baptize you in obedience to the Lord.

Amen.

Mark, receive this stole and be among us as a pastor and priest.

Amen.

Mark, receive this book, and be among us as a man of prayer.

Amen.

Mark, receive these keys, and let the doors of this place be open to all people.

Now he knew he wasn't dreaming. Blessing upon blessing was laid at his feet until he felt he was seeing a glimpse of heaven on earth.

But Suzanne's smile was the biggest blessing of them all. She loved him the way men dreamed of being loved, with her entire body, her entire soul. She was his friend and his companion, his partner in love and work, and one day soon she would be the mother of their children, their arrows into the future.

At one point he remembered stepping outside into the garden to catch his breath and realizing that at that single moment in time he had everything he wanted within reach. If God had chosen to take him home, he would have died a happy man.

Suzanne slipped outside too when he wasn't looking and wrapped her arms around his waist.

"They're looking for you," she said. "The vestry has put together a catered dinner at the club. Sarah Whitfield made her maple walnut ice cream just for you."

"The rectory is too small," he said, and she laughed. "When the babies start coming, we'll have to sleep on the front porch."

"We won't have to worry until at least our third," she said.

"The Carnahan place is up for sale. We could buy it and get started on those three kids."

"Shh." She pressed her lips against his back and he could feel her warmth. "We have plenty of time, Mark. An entire lifetime."

Greenwood, New Hampshire—today

Bishop Clennon flipped through the stack of papers on his desk, then looked across at Mark. "This is a handsome accumulation of recommendations. You should be proud."

"I am," he said, not pulling his punches. "I feel I've done some fine work the last two years."

The bishop leaned back in his padded leather seat. "Which raises the question: why are you looking to leave a situation that clearly means a great deal to you?"

So this is what the other shoe sounded like when it finally dropped.

"That's a complicated question."

"Indeed," said the bishop, "but the answer should be a simple one."

"It is," Mark said and opted for unvarnished truth. "The parishioners of St. Stephen were there for me during some very dark times. I'm glad to be able to help them out now when they need me."

"So you're repaying a debt."

"To some extent, yes, I am."

"There's more to ministering to a parish than the repayment of old debts."

"I know that. This was my old parish," he reminded the new bishop. "I understand the needs of the parishioners."

"Greenwood has changed in five years. Since the addition of the Maple Grove subdivision, the age of the average parishioner has gone from sixty to thirty-two. Young families with small children make up almost two-thirds of the Sunday worship. The other candidate is a young husband and father."

"And you're afraid that I won't understand their needs since I'm not a husband or father myself."

"We all bring specific gifts to the job, Mark. You proved that with your exemplary work in New Jersey."

"Compassion and understanding are more important than hands-on experience."

"That may well be true."

Bishop Clennon rose to his feet, signaling that the meeting had come to a conclusion.

"I appreciate your candor, Mark." He extended his hand across the vast expanse of polished mahogany. "I believe you've answered all of my questions."

Okay, then. Case closed.

"And I appreciate the opportunity to address them personally, Bishop Clennon."

"This has been a difficult decision for me to make," the bishop went on. "The other candidate is a perfect fit in many ways. Young, enthusiastic family man with a theologian wife."

Clennon clearly wasn't ready to commit to a forty-something widowed priest who led AA meetings in his spare time. Who could blame him? He would pick the young family man too if the decision were up to him.

"Due to budget considerations, this is a one-year assignment," the bishop went on, "but I'm sure you know that we fully hope this will be a long-term commitment to the congregation at Greenwood. Our choice must be willing to commit to a future here."

The contract would be renegotiated this time next year and possibly extended for another five years. The new rector would be given the keys to the same house he had shared with Suzanne, the same church secretary, almost the same vestry, a travel allowance, someone to help out with gardening and general upkeep of the house, and a future that looked a lot like his past in many ways.

They shook hands and Mark was reminded of the nature shows on Discovery Channel. Jungle law in ecclesiastical robes. Maintain eye contact at all times and never let 'em see you sweat.

The bishop walked him into the reception area, where a pair of assistants carried on church business at a frantic pace.

"When can I expect your decision?" Mark asked. He didn't remind the man that as of the end of May he would be homeless.

"Didn't I make myself clear?" Bishop Clennon extended his hand again. "I'll be countersigning your contract this afternoon." They clasped hands. "Welcome back, Father Kerry."

Coburn, New Jersey—French Kiss Antiques & Collectibles

Kate had Paul drop her off at the shop on his way back to Manhattan.

"You want me to hang around?" he volunteered. "I can drive you home."

"Thanks, but I'm walking," she said. "Doctor's orders."

"You sure?"

"Paul, I'm not an invalid. The more I do, the faster I'll be given the all clear to get back to work full-time."

He didn't look at all convinced, but too bad. He was her friend, not her keeper.

"Maeve said to call her if you change your mind," he said as he rolled to a stop in front of the store.

"If I change my mind, Sonia will run me home. It's not a problem, okay?"

Finally he ran out of excuses to linger and she waved him off down Main Street. For the first time in more than a week, she was out alone without adult supervision, and it felt spectacular.

She pushed open the door, grinning at the sound of bells and the scent of apples and vanilla. "Look sharp, everyone, the boss is back!"

Sonia let out a whoop and ran over to give her a huge hug. Liz popped out of the office where she kept track of the books and inventory, and burst into tears. Two customers she had never seen before exchanged glances and started edging toward the door.

Let them, she thought. For once in her life, she didn't care if all of their customers walked out. The fact that she was there, surrounded by her friends and colleagues, was more than enough.

"We sold the Seaweed & Shell pitcher," Sonia was saying, "and the oyster plates Dianne Howell brought in on consignment." The dollar figures were impressive.

"Wow," she said, nodding her approval. "It looks like you have everything under control."

"We try, boss," Sonia said, "but it's not the same without you."

"It's quieter," Liz said, and they broke up into laughter.

Kate spent a few minutes on her computer, checking on the last week's sales figures, stock, and wish lists. The boxes she had brought with her from her U.K. trip were stacked against the back wall of the common room. The trip seemed a lifetime ago. Without her lists in front of her, she couldn't remember what was in half of them. Why not open one box a day, enter the items into the inventory, then phone customers who might be interested in a sneak peek before the items went public.

"I'll start tomorrow morning," she told Sonia over a cup of hot tea in the shop's tiny kitchen. "I'm supposed to be out walking every day, so this will give me a destination."

Sonia jumped up and gathered her into a major bear hug. "You don't know how much we've missed you around here. Old Mrs. Covington came in yesterday and pitched a fit over some Limoges she said wasn't up to standard."

"Wait!" Kate said. "I know the rest: she wanted a forty percent discount and for us to pick up the state tax."

"I came this close to telling her to stick the Limoges where the sun don't shine, but I said to myself, 'Now what would Kate do?' and that wasn't it."

"Wise choice," Kate said with a mock shudder. "Good thing I'm back to keep an eye on you reprobates."

"You sure you don't want a lift home? I need to make a bank run, so I'm going out anyway."

"I'm only a half mile from home. I'll be fine."

"You have your cell?"

"My God, you're worse than my mother." She patted the pocket of her trousers. "Yes, I have my cell."

"Call me if you change your mind about the lift, okay?"

"I promise."

They all meant well, she knew that, but she breathed a huge sigh of relief when she escaped back out into the world.

"Hey, Katie!" Gigi from the café across the street waved to her from the front door. "Good to see you back!"

"Good to be back!" she called.

"I saw Paul dropping you off," Gigi shouted across the din of traffic. "Tell Mr. Big Shot not to be such a stranger."

"I'll pass it on, Gee."

"You look terrific, Ms. French!" Frank the mail carrier gave her a thumbs-up as he trudged down the street wheeling his cart. "We missed you."

"Thanks for the flowers, Frank. That was so nice of you."

"You gave us all a hell of a scare," he said. "My wife made me get my cholesterol checked pronto."

"Good," she said. "I'm glad to hear it!"

It was slow going as she made her way along Main Street. News traveled faster than the speed of light in a small town, and it seemed her medical adventure had been discussed in every shop, café, bookstore, and office on the street. A few asked about Gwynn. A couple asked about Ed. A handful were surprised to see that she was still alive.

But absolutely everyone wanted to know about the priest in shining armor who had saved her life. By the time she turned off Main Street onto the relative peace and quiet of Elm Road, she had decided she would make up flyers recounting the incident and post them on every tree, lamp-post, and bulletin board in town. In fact, maybe she should take out a full-page ad in the *Coburn Bugle* while she was at it. It would save her vocal cords and it might even be good for business.

She stopped in front of Lena Bradley's house and leaned against her ancient Chevy Blazer. Maybe she wasn't quite as all the way back as she had thought. She was a little out of breath and she wouldn't mind giving her heartbeat a chance to slow down. A dog barked somewhere in the distance. A school bus squeaked to a stop at the opposite corner. Her cell phone turned into Tina Turner.

"I'm standing in the one working cell area in all of northern New Hampshire, so we have to talk fast." It was Mark. "How did it go with the doctor?"

"Great," she said as her smile grew even wider. "I'm a textbook case. In fact, I'm outside right now, walking home alone from French Kiss."

He sent up a cheer that warmed her down to her toes.

"Did you have your meeting yet?" she asked. "I've had my fingers crossed all day and they're starting to cramp."

"Uncross them," he said, his words breaking up thanks to the iffy connection. "The contract's been signed and countersigned. I'm set."

She started crying at the news, but let him think they were tears of joy.

"So when do you come home?" she managed. "The state isn't the same without you."

"Tomorrow afternoon." Unfortunately he had a youth club meeting at five, AA at seven, and a hospice visit scheduled for nine at a patient's home.

He suggested a Friday morning run down to Spring Lake, but she told him about her plan to walk to work every morning, stay an hour or so, then walk home, all in the name of physical therapy. Not to mention her sanity.

They settled on Friday afternoon and the beach at Spring Lake.

"I better go," he said. "Maggy's finished what she was doing in the bank and we're headed over to Greenwood to meet with the vestry."

"Vestry? I'm going to need an Episcopalian–English dictionary if I keep hanging around with you."

"You'll catch on," he said. "Your twelve years in Catholic school give you a head start."

She started to make a flip remark about how her years at St. Aloysius had to be good for something but let the moment slide. Her lapsed Catholic stand-up routine was wearing thin, even for her.

"I want to hear more about this Maggy when I see you," she said. "I'm picturing a nubile young church-woman with designs on you."

"I'll tell her. Believe me, she'll love you for that."

Swell, Kate thought after they said good-bye. Maggy Whoever-the-Hell-She-Was would love her for that. She didn't like the thought of them talking about her all the way up there in maple syrup country. She pictured a buxom farm girl type in a plaid shirt tied under her breasts and the Yankee Trader version of Daisy Duke cutoffs. It wasn't a pretty picture, but it was a whole lot more attractive than the way she was feeling. Something ugly and green nipped at her side and she didn't like it one bit. She had never been jealous of anyone in her life and now here she was getting all bent out of shape over a woman she would never meet and a man she barely knew.

Greenwood, New Hampshire

They went from the bishop's office straight to the hospital where Maggy's father, Henry, was recovering from his second round of cancer surgery.

It was hard to see the once-robust farmer lying shrunken and frail in his hospital bed, and Mark was grateful for the training that enabled him to maintain his focus and composure.

They talked for a while about better days, and Mark gave his old friend a condensed version of his work in New Jersey.

"So why are you here?" Henry asked in his blunt fashion. "Not that I haven't been waiting for you to come back, but sounds like you built yourself a good thing down there."

"You sound like the bishop," Mark said. "He asked me the same thing."

"Times change, son. Sometimes the best thing you can do is let go and move on."

Mark wasn't sure if Henry meant the words for him or for himself.

"Don't listen to him," Maggy said as they crossed the parking lot to her car. "He's on medication. It makes him say crazy things."

He let her remark slide, but the old man's words had resonated deeply with him.

For months it had seemed as if he were barreling toward a future that no longer seemed to fit. Through the darkest periods when his drinking was most out of control, the thing that had held him together was knowing that one day he would go home again.

Who knew that his definition of home would change when he wasn't looking?

They made a turn onto Chapel Road and he muttered a word he hadn't used in a long time.

"Don't blame me," Maggy said as they pulled up in front of the rectory. "I'm not responsible for this crowd."

He stared at the crowd of cars, minivans, SUVs, and

bicycles parked along the street, in the driveway, and in one case on the front lawn. "Somebody must have told them."

"I mean, I told them you were coming up from New Jersey but I didn't tell them the bishop signed off on the contract. We just found that out, right?"

He gestured broadly at the crowd. "Somebody told them something, friend."

"Well, I might have mentioned you'd be stopping by this afternoon . . ."

A fair number of his old congregation had gathered in the meeting room attached to the rectory to support his return to Greenwood. Faces he hadn't seen since Suzanne's memorial service beamed at him from the windows, the front steps, clustered on the lawn like daffodils.

He felt humbled by their loyalty, deeply grateful for their forgiveness, but mostly he was flat-out speechless by the waves of affection flowing his way.

"See that woman over there?" Maggy whispered into his ear. "The aging redhead with an overbite? That's the one who tried to block your assignment."

He turned and looked toward the door. "Hannah Owens?"

"Shh. The witch can probably read lips. She and her buddies were trying to promote her cousin's son, a child fresh out of seminary. Just because he bought a house in that new development—"

"I was fresh out of seminary when I first came here," he reminded her.

"That was different."

"And I had a lot of friends and family supporting my assignment."

"Oh, be quiet," Maggy snapped, glaring at him. "You sound like you wish Billy Owens *had* gotten the job."

So now the competition had a name. "Bishop Clennon had good things to say about Billy Owens." Even if the bishop hadn't mentioned him by name.

"Oh, I guess he's all right," Maggy said with a dismissive wave of her hand, "but he isn't you."

So it went even deeper than he had realized. This Owens clearly had something going for him if even Maggy softened so quickly.

"I recognize why I might not be somebody's first choice."

She rolled her eyes. "Where's the righteous indignation? You're being entirely too reasonable for me."

She managed to temper her irritation long enough to introduce him to her Sam, who seemed to be a genuinely nice guy. He was happy for them, hopeful for their future, and maybe just the slightest bit relieved that he had been so easy to replace.

He left them whispering together and wandered over to admire the buffet. With just a few hours' notice the Women's Guild had put together mountains of chilled shrimp, platters of blanched vegetables, buffalo wings drenched in hot sauce, quesadillas topped with melted cheddar, pitchers of lemonade and iced tea, and chocolate desserts usually reserved for saints in heaven. He was suitably wowed.

The men of the congregation hadn't been idle either. The rectory windows had been replaced, a new air-conditioning system installed, fresh paint and wallpaper and sparkling-clean rugs on polished wooden floors. They had done all they could to transform the home he had shared with Suzanne into neutral territory, a place where a man could start over again.

He didn't have the heart to tell them that he saw her everywhere he looked. She stood by the kitchen window, gazing out across the vegetable garden. She waited at the top of the stairs, laughing as he locked the doors for the night. "Nothing bad ever happens in Greenwood," she said as she took his hand. "Don't you know that?"

Vangie Paulos sneaked up and enveloped him in a bear hug. "This is just like old times," she said, beaming up at him. "You don't know how long we've been praying for this day."

"Don't get too excited, Vangie." Tom Meyerson popped up beside them, faded blue eyes twinkling. "He's only visiting."

"I know, I know, but it will be the end of May before you know it and everything will be back the way it should be."

"You're looking great, Vangie," he said. "Retirement agrees with you."

"If you think I'm looking good, you should see my grandbaby Edie. She's twenty-two now and a teacher, has her own pension plan and everything. I'll have you to dinner one night. You can see for yourself."

He gave her a noncommittal smile and tried to find himself a neutral corner, meaning one without a single woman or matchmaking mother lurking behind a potted palm.

Everywhere he turned there was a familiar face, most of them friendly and welcoming; a few seemed wary and fearful that the priest in whom they were bestowing their faith would fail them the way he had in the past.

But as he looked at them an odd thought worked its way to the surface. What if they felt they owed him this chance? Loyalty worked both ways. They were good people with good hearts and sometimes good people made choices that weren't always in their best interest.

Maybe Billy Owens *was* the better choice for them. Maybe the young priest and his family were exactly what Greenwood needed, but they felt they owed Mark this chance to put things right.

Still, there was no point dwelling on it. The decision didn't belong to him; it belonged to Bishop Clennon and he had to trust that the bishop's reasons were sound.

The only thing required of him was that he give them the next year of his life with a full heart. With a little luck, the future would somehow take care of itself.

Fifteen

French Kiss—Friday morning

"Go home already," Sonia said. "You're making us crazy."

"Amen!" Liz pushed her glasses back up her nose. "Don't you have to primp for your new boyfriend or something?"

Kate felt herself blush deep red. "He's not my boyfriend."

"He's definitely an 'or something,'" Sonia said, "otherwise you need to see the doctor again for this nervous condition."

"I've been cooped up for more than a week," she reminded them. "I'm looking forward to walking on the beach and getting some sunshine."

Sonia and Liz exchanged knowing glances.

"Oh, knock that off," Kate grumbled. "You act like you've never seen me go out with a man before."

"I don't think we have," Sonia said.

"I'm sure we haven't," Liz said.

"Gary Halston."

"Gimme a break," said Sonia.

"Ralph Mahoney."

"Total loser," said Liz.

"Bernie from the bank."

"Gay," said Sonia.

"Lucas the importer from Napa."

"We have to give you that one," Liz conceded. "He was pretty hot."

Not to mention boring and self-absorbed. Was it any wonder she preferred her own company on Saturday nights? The last few years it had been HBO On Demand and a bowl of popcorn, and not once had she felt like she was missing out on anything.

"I went out with Paul just the other night."

"Paul Grantham doesn't count," Sonia said. "He's just a friend."

She opened her mouth to say, *That's what you think,* but managed to close it in the nick of time.

"What were you about to say?" Sonia asked. "Is there something going on with Paul?" Small towns never lost track of their favorite sons, no matter how far they roamed.

"Nothing's going on."

"I saw the way he looked at you when you got out of his car the other day. Something's changed."

"He's worried about me," she explained. "Same as you are."

"I think he's in love with you," Liz said. "I could hear it in his voice when he called yesterday."

"His ex-wife just got remarried and his best friend had a heart attack. You'd sound strange too."

"Poor sap," Sonia said. "He doesn't stand a chance with Father McDreamy in the picture."

Father McDreamy? "Not you too," Kate said with a loud groan. "Did Maeve put you up to that?"

"Have you taken a good look at that man?" Liz demanded. "What else would you call him?"

"How do you know what he looks like? You've never met him."

Sonia and Liz exchanged glances.

"What?" Kate demanded. "You both look guilty as hell."

Sonia jerked a thumb toward the computer at the far end of the room. "Google. How else do people find out anything?"

"I Googled him and came up empty." Oh no. She hadn't wanted to admit that.

Sonia and Liz exchanged a longer, more pointed look and Kate tossed an empty paper cup in their direction.

"Google Images," Liz said. "There were twelve of them."

"Thirteen," Sonia corrected her, "if you count the high school yearbook photo. Anybody could find them."

She darted toward the computer and they all but tackled her.

"You have a ten o'clock with Grace for a blowout," Sonia scolded. "Quite frankly, Kate, I don't think you can afford to miss it."

"Besides," Liz added, "what do you need pictures for when you're going to spend the day with the real thing?"

Good question, but not one she wanted to answer.

They hadn't spoken in two days. They hadn't seen each other in three. Was it possible that all of that wonderful magic, that sizzle and spark, had run its course and they would find themselves alone on the beach at Spring Lake with absolutely nothing to say and nothing to do except wonder what on earth they were doing there in the first place?

Not that she was nervous or anything.

Pinecrest Village

"Look at you, Father Mark!" Charlotte's eyes brightened when he walked into her hospital room. "Pretty snazzy!"

"No collar today?" One of the nurses looked up from the computer terminal where she was entering data. "You make a good civilian."

He had been fending off good-natured teasing since the guard ushered him onto the property.

"Jeans and a sweater," he said. "What's the big deal?"

"You tell him," Charlotte said to the pretty nurse. "You're younger. He'll believe you."

The nurse laughed and continued her work.

"You're looking well today," he said, leaning over to kiss Charlotte's whisper-soft cheek. "Whatever they're doing for you here, it's working."

She patted his cheek with a be-ringed hand. "The bishop signed the contract?"

He nodded and sat down in the chair next to her bed. "He signed. It's all set for the end of May."

"I knew he would."

"I didn't."

"I'll admit to harboring some selfish feelings, Father. I hate to see you leave us. You've become very important to many people. You'll be difficult to replace."

"We can all be replaced, Charlotte."

"God doesn't work that way," Charlotte said. "You're meant to go back up there and get—what is that word they use these days?"

"Closure," he said.

"That's it." Charlotte beamed. "You need closure and that's the only way you'll get it."

As always, she saw right through him to the heart of the matter.

"I'm not as happy about it as I thought I'd be." He told her about the trip, the impromptu party at the rectory. "It doesn't feel like home anymore."

"It hasn't been your home for a long time. That town must be filled with ghosts."

"You're a wise woman, Charlotte. You should be running therapy sessions."

She studied his outfit with a critical eye. "That blue sweater brings out your eyes. She'll like it."

He tried to play dumb but Charlotte was having none of it.

"You're seeing that red-haired woman today, aren't you?"

"Do you mean Kate?"

"I'm an old woman. Don't expect me to remember names. But you know exactly who I'm talking about, Father."

"You got me." *Busted by a nonagenarian.* "We're driving down to Spring Lake for lunch."

"Spring Lake!" Her sigh was young and positively girlish. "A perfect spot for romance."

"We're just friends, Charlotte."

He hadn't spoken to Kate in two days. They hadn't seen each other in three. Trying to understand the chemical attraction between a man and a woman was like trying to catch lightning in a bottle.

Then again, maybe it wasn't like lightning at all. Maybe it was more like a bad cold. No matter what you did or didn't do, the cold ran its course in seven days and you forgot it ever happened until the next cold came along.

Just because he couldn't get her out of his mind didn't mean she had spent more than twenty seconds thinking about him. She might have opened her eyes this morning and wondered why she had said yes to an afternoon on the beach with a homeward-bound priest from New Hampshire who didn't know his ass from his elbow when it came to romance.

"You're not a Roman Catholic," Charlotte reminded him. "You're allowed to go courting."

"Don't get your hopes up," he warned her. "This isn't going to go anywhere."

"Not with that attitude it isn't," she assured him. "Life is short, young man. We aren't here forever. Why are you wasting your God-given time?"

He didn't know a clergyman or -woman on the planet who could have said it any better than Charlotte Petruzzo.

The Hairport

"The usual, Kate?" Grace drew the wide-toothed comb through Kate's wet hair. "Or maybe a French braid would be nice. Something a little different."

Kate looked at her reflection in the mirror and didn't recognize the woman looking back. She looked younger, happier, filled with hope.

"Loose," she said, shaking her head. "Long and loose."

"Say hallelujah!" Grace tossed the comb in the air and caught it on the way down. "It's only taken three years and a hospital stay to make the woman see reason."

The banter was good-natured and she let it fly over, under, and around her while Grace wielded the big round brush and the alarmingly phallic-looking blow-dryer.

"So what time does he pick you up?" Grace rubbed a tiny bit of shine serum on her palms then slid her fingers through Kate's amazingly long and terrific-looking hair.

"Excuse me?"

"We all know Father McDreamy's taking you to the beach today."

"Which big-mouth friend or relative of mine told you that?"

Grace paused, blow-dryer dangling from her right hand, round brush from the left. "Susie," she called across the floor, "who told us about Kate and Father McDreamy?"

"Maeve told Helen at the bakery yesterday and Helen told Jack and Jack told me."

"I heard it from Sonia," a woman with a headful of foil volunteered. "I was browsing across the street and I asked how Katie was doing and she told me the whole story. It's *so* romantic!"

"I'm thinking of converting," Lee said as she touched up Claire Shuster's gray roots. "That man is the poster child for Episcopalianism."

"You all seem to know an awful lot about a man you've never seen," Kate said to their reflections in the mirror.

"Haven't seen him?" Grace laughed and they all joined in. "Katie, his picture's splashed on the front page of this week's *Coburn Bugle*."

"What?" She leaped up, sending a lapful of clips and combs flying. "Let me see!"

They had a foot-high stack of them near the reception desk.

PRIEST SAVES LIFE OF LOCAL WOMAN

The headline was set in big bold letters.

The story read like romantic fiction, even though every word the reporter wrote was absolutely true. But those pictures . . .

"Oh my God!" She winced and turned the paper face-down on the table. "Where did they get that hideous photo of me?" She looked like something that had been left in the sun too long.

"Two thousand four Fourth of July Sidewalk Sale," Lee said. "We all looked like gargoyles."

They couldn't find a bad photo of Mark to help level the playing field? It looked like a case of Beauty and the Beast with the roles reversed. Was he really that gorgeous? Good-looking, yes, but she hadn't realized he had quite this much going for him. She had been caught by the sadness in his eyes, the gentleness of his touch, the warmth of his mouth on hers . . .

Whoa, French. Get a grip.

"I have a good mind to sue those idiots at the *Bugle*," she said. "How can they write a story about what happened to me without asking me any questions?"

"Angelina and Brad are probably asking the same thing," Grace said to howls of laughter all around. "Now get back here, Kate, and let me finish making you gorgeous."

This entire thing had a life of its own. It had from the moment she inadvertently stole his parking space and set into motion a series of events that still had her head spinning.

She couldn't remember the last time she'd had this much fun. The teasing, the laughter, the feeling of being one of the girls. Okay, middle-aged girls, but the sentiment was still the same.

"You look fabulous," Lee said when Grace finished her magic. "Thirty, thirty-five max."

"You should wear it that way all the time," Foil Head Woman said. "You look like that girl on *Will and Grace*."

"No, she doesn't," the woman with the formerly gray roots said. "A young Susan Sarandon."

Either way she couldn't lose.

She got whistled at by a UPS driver and flirted with at the stoplight at Main and Elm by a man old enough to know better. By the time she reached her driveway she had decided she would wear her hair long and loose until she needed Depends.

Maeve was gathering up her books and papers and loading them into one of her many leather totes when Kate walked into the house. "What did I tell you, honey? Once a woman lets her hair down, there's no stopping her."

Maybe it was time to put one of her mother's favorite theories to the test.

* * *

Nothing had changed. She was waiting on the front porch when he got there and the second their eyes met he knew this was either the best or the worst thing that had ever happened to him.

This was how happy felt. Not how he remembered it feeling. Not how he wished it felt. This was the real deal—full-blown, full-bore, full-throttle happiness.

She ran across the yard toward him, her hair long and loose, shimmering red-gold in the sunlight, and if you ever wanted to know why he believed in God, there was your answer. There could be magic between people, the kind of magic that made you want to do better, be better, reach for the stars and grab a handful.

"You look great," Mark said as he held open the car door for Kate. "Did you change your hair or something?"

She gave him one of those looks women were born knowing how to deliver. "I'm wearing it down today."

"You should wear it that way all the time."

"Thanks." She made a show of eyeing his hair. "Yours looks pretty good too."

"I combed it today," he said. "Makes a big difference."

"I like the sweater. Is that part of your priestly uniform?"

"Your Catholic schoolgirl upbringing is showing. Priests don't have a uniform."

"You should be required to wear a collar at all times," she said as he started the engine. "How else can we tell you from the civilians?"

They joked back and forth, trading comments at the speed of light. There was an ease between them, a deeper sense of communication that usually developed over a period of years, not days. He felt more fully himself, more connected with the world, optimistic in ways that should have surprised him into silence.

He had trouble keeping his eyes on the road. She was so vibrant, so alive, so filled with passion and energy, that he wanted to pull over to the side of the road and—

He was wrong. Something *had* changed and it wasn't just her hairstyle.

He was in love.

Sixteen

Spring Lake was a tiny dot on the map of the Jersey shore that boasted 2.1 miles of wide, sandy beachfront and a crystal clear spring-fed lake near the center of town. The word *charming* had been invented to describe places like this.

He parked the beat-up blue Honda in front of one of the old beachfront hotels and they held hands as they dashed across the wide sun-swept street to the sandy shore.

"I'm going to miss this," he said as they started walking south along the water's edge.

"The beach?"

"New Jersey."

She laughed as they stepped around a swirling tide pool. "Now that's something you don't hear every day."

"I like it here."

"You were highly complimentary the other day, but don't spread it around." She shielded her eyes and looked up at him. "Besides, I thought New England was the place to be when the leaves start to turn."

"New Jersey has it beat."

She knew what he was really saying, what those simple words meant. Two weeks ago the significance might have gone right over her head, but not today. Not with the warm April sun on their shoulders, the breeze off the ocean in her hair, her hand clasped tightly in his, the ocean at their feet. This was high school with a 401(k) plan and he had declared himself seriously smitten.

"We're famous," she said as they nodded toward some fishermen standing hip deep in the icy water. "Front page of the *Coburn Bugle*."

"The *Coburn Bugle*?"

"Best and only weekly in Coburn, New Jersey, source of all news social, retail, political, and religious in town."

"You told a reporter about what happened?"

"If I had my way I wouldn't have told my mother." She had to laugh at the look on his face. "People talk. We're a gossipy small town."

"Do you have a copy?"

"I left one in your car. We can analyze it over lunch."

The wind kicked up and she shivered. He dropped her hand and draped an arm around her shoulders and she settled in closer to his side. Something close to pure contentment moved through her.

"No point to keeping a low profile anymore, then," he said.

"None that I can see."

"Once you hit the front page, you've been outed."

"Totally."

They stopped walking. He shifted. She adjusted. The companionable arm around her shoulders turned into something else. Something she had read about in books but never in a million years thought she would experience. A melting sensation that turned her limbs to ribbons of taffy left out in the sun.

You couldn't hide in full sun. Full sun exposed every line, every wrinkle, every secret flourishing in the shadows.

His arms didn't hold her in place. She could have slipped his embrace if she had wanted to. She was there because she couldn't think of anywhere else in the whole wide world where she would rather be.

"Six weeks isn't a long time," he said.

"I know," she said. "We'd be crazy to waste a minute more of it."

He placed a finger under her chin and tilted her face up to his and for once in her life she didn't want to duck her head or turn away or hide behind a wall of words. All she wanted was to kiss him.

A kiss would be enough.

She hadn't expected, hadn't dreamed that a kiss could be everything.

Their lips met and the world around her slipped out of focus. Perfect . . . better than perfect . . . his warm mouth . . . his strong hands . . . his long lean body pressed against hers . . . the yearning deep inside . . . she wanted . . . everything . . . she wanted everything and she wanted it now and she wanted it forever . . . could you build a world from a kiss . . . could a kiss last forever . . .

"We're attracting a crowd," he said when they broke apart, breathless, hearts thundering, both of them dazed and on fire from the inside out.

She blinked and peered over his shoulder as the world came back into focus. Three fishermen, rods resting on their shoulders, were watching them from about one hundred feet away. Two elderly women, bundled into sweaters and bright purple hats, stared intently from the boardwalk.

"I don't care," she said, starting to laugh.

"Me either." He kissed her again, hard and fierce, and she melted against him.

"You don't kiss like a priest," she murmured against his lips.

"How many priests have you kissed?"

"None," she said, "but I'll bet you don't kiss like any of them."

They moved slowly apart, each trying to regain their balance and reclaim some of the space that used to exist between them.

She wasn't sure that was possible anymore.

* * *

They found a luncheonette on a side street that was still serving lunch. The place was a haphazard affair, two buildings stitched together with a staple gun and some duct tape and bound by a baseball theme. Babe Ruth beamed down on the cash register up front. Lou Gehrig pointed the way toward the restrooms. Thurman Munson guarded the stack of well-worn menus while Willie Mays, Mickey Mantle, and Jackie Robinson watched over diners in the back room. A pair of Louisville Sluggers were crisscrossed over the nonworking fireplace like swords at a military wedding. The salt and pepper shakers were plastic baseballs with holes punched where the stitching would be. The menu featured hot dogs, hamburgers, French fries, and as much Coke as you could drink in one sitting. Dessert was something called a Cracker Jack Sundae.

"We'd better find somewhere else," he said as they scanned the ketchup-stained menu. "This place will put you back in the hospital."

"I love it here," she said as the strains of "Take Me out to the Ball Game" wafted through the frying oil–scented air.

"You're kidding, right?" He had a pretty good Mr. Spock eyebrow lift going.

"Nope. *This* is romantic." As far as she was concerned, it put The Old Grist Mill to shame.

"Who are you, Kate French?" he asked as he put the menu down on the table. "Every time I think I know what you're going to say, you say something else."

She grinned at him. "That last one surprised me too. Since the heart attack even *I* can't believe the things that are coming out of my mouth."

"That's not an uncommon complaint."

"So I've been told, but it's still disconcerting. You go through life believing you're one type of person and then suddenly—" she waved her hand in the air—"poof! You're somebody else."

"And what is the real you like?"

"For starters, I'm not spontaneous and I'm not romantic. I'm definitely not a lacy, flowery type of woman."

He shot her a look. "I saw evidence to the contrary."

She blushed as red as the lace thong he was talking about. "An aberration," she said. "I was just back from ten days in London. I needed to run a wash. That was all I had in my lingerie drawer."

"But you had it."

"It still had the tags on it. Maeve gave it to me as a fortieth birthday gift. She thought I needed to shake things up."

"It worked," he said with a wicked grin. "I'm still shook up."

She tossed a straw wrapper in his general direction. "You're deliberately misunderstanding me."

"Who says this isn't the real you?" he countered. "Maybe the real you had been waiting for an excuse to get into the mix."

"I don't think that's the way it works."

"People change," he said. "I see it all the time. We're changed by the things that happen to us. There would be no growth if we weren't."

"You must have minored in psychology."

"I'm just a student of human nature. We're supposed to be changed by life. Otherwise there's no point."

"Well, the doctors seem to have this one all figured out right down to the millisecond. According to Lombardi, you'll never know the real me because you'll be heading back up to New Hampshire right around the time I'll stop crying at television commercials."

"You haven't cried once since I picked you up."

"The day's young," she warned him. "Give me time."

He ordered a cheeseburger with the works and a chocolate milk shake. She ordered a bowl of Manhattan clam chowder and a glass of iced tea. The waitress disappeared into the kitchen with their orders and Kate dipped into her bag for a copy of the *Coburn Bugle*.

It was Mark's turn to be embarrassed.

"You're blushing!" she exclaimed. "Which is it: the comparison to superheroes or the 'Father McDreamy'?"

"McDreamy," he said, looking as if he wanted to change his name and phone number. "Where do they get crap like that anyway?"

"You don't watch a lot of television, do you?" She explained the *Grey's Anatomy* reference.

"You didn't tell them any of that, did you?"

"Read that article again. I'm not quoted anywhere. Do you really think I would call myself a middle-aged shop owner?"

The wicked grin reappeared. "Guess not."

They took turns reading florid passages to each other, laughing until they cried at the quotes given by Maeve and Gwynn and everyone she had ever spent more than thirty seconds with in her entire life.

"No good deed goes unpunished," Kate said as she folded up the newspaper and tucked it back into her bag.

"It could have been worse."

"How? If they'd published my weight and my blood work?"

"At least they didn't write about the thong."

"You're right. Maybe there really *is* a God." She paused. "That's a figure of speech, not my own particular point of view."

"You don't have to explain away every reference to God, Kate."

She nodded, relieved they didn't find the need to tap-dance around the issue.

"Here we go, folks." Their waitress set down their platters and pulled a ketchup bottle from the pocket of her apron. "Enjoy."

They dug in. There was nothing like a long walk in the sea air to sharpen the appetite. For a few minutes conversation was limited to "Pass the pepper" and "I need some more iced tea."

"This is a great burger," Mark said. "We're coming back here again."

"Great Manhattan clam too." Kate pushed her bowl toward him. "You should try some."

She handed him a spoonful. He gave her one of his pickles in exchange.

"Have you ever been to a church supper?" he asked, pausing to drink some milk shake.

"I went to the United Methodist Pancake Breakfast last year. Does that count?"

"Not unless there was a Jell-O mold and at least two varieties of three-bean salad on the premises."

She leaned forward, elbows on the table, chin propped in her hands. "You sound like you've been to your share of them."

"Seven hundred thirty-three," he said. "Give or take a

few. I've eaten or pretended to eat at least forty different types of casserole, one hundred different salads, and at least sixty-seven Jell-O suspensions."

"Why?"

"Because that's what you do when you're rector of a small parish."

"Eat a lot?"

"Eat a lot, talk a lot, listen a lot, pray a lot."

"It doesn't sound like a bad life."

"It's a very good life if it's what you're looking for."

"And you are."

He nodded. "I am."

She tried to imagine the life of a small-town New England priest and came up empty. She tried to imagine the life of a small-town New England priest's wife and started to laugh.

He looked at her with a question in his eyes.

"Sorry," she said. "I was trying to imagine how I'd fare as a preacher's wife and the image I came up with was pretty funny."

Talk about the wrong thing to say. She might as well have dropped a bomb in the middle of the Formica-topped table and screamed, "Incoming!" Where was her internal censor when she needed it?

"I didn't—" She regrouped, wondering if she should make a run for the door. "What I mean is, it had nothing to do with you. I was just—" She threw her hands into the air. "Just take me outside and shoot me. Please."

He didn't. Instead he started to laugh and, despite her humiliation, she found herself laughing too.

"You're not going to use that against me, are you?" she asked.

"You don't think I'm entitled to a little McDreamy payback?"

"Hey, don't blame me for that McDreamy tag. I was

minding my own business in a hospital room when they came up with it."

"Likely story," he said, and they were off and running.

Their banter was light as air, surprisingly silly, better than champagne. She felt completely herself with him, even if she couldn't begin to define who that new self was, and it was wonderful.

She finished her soup and listened as he told her about the trip to New Hampshire, his meeting with the bishop, the surprise get-together at the rectory, the ghosts that seemed to follow him everywhere but the porch.

"Don't tell me you slept on the porch the other night! You were in New Hampshire. April is *cold* in New Hampshire."

"Tell me about it." Mark poured more ketchup on his cheeseburger and rearranged the remaining pickle slices. He met her eyes. "And before you ask, I accepted Suzanne's death once and for all a few years ago."

Her female antennae had been primed to pick up signs of a widower's torch but there were none, just the faint echo of the love he'd had for his wife. "So what was it?"

He took his time before answering. "The sense of going backward," he said at last. "I thought it would feel like going home, but it didn't. The truth?"

She nodded. "Why stop now?"

"I'm not sure I belong there anymore."

Her eyes widened. "That's a heck of a thing to discover after you sell your house."

"I'm going back," he said quickly. "I'm not going to change my mind."

"You haven't closed on the sale," she reminded him. "You could still back out."

"And back out on St. Stephen's too?" He shook his head. "Can't do it. I owe them too much."

She tried to hide her relief with admiration for his

sense of commitment, but in her heart she knew the truth. She could cope with the emotions he stirred up inside her if she could be sure that six weeks from now he would be three hundred miles away.

"So what are you going to do?" She fished out a particularly juicy-looking piece of clam and popped it into her mouth. "You can't spend the next year sleeping on the porch."

"I'll probably rent a small house within walking distance of the rectory."

She fished around for some potatoes. "I don't know anything about the inner workings of a church, but won't the powers that be feel offended?"

"That's the problem," he said. "They've knocked themselves out to make me feel welcome but the rector's house is—" He stopped and shook his head. "Can't do it."

"You shouldn't have to."

"Too bad you aren't a vestry member."

"You'll work something out," she said. "I can't believe they would force you to live where you're unhappy."

"These are group decisions. I don't have a lot of influence over them."

"And I'm a self-employed only child," she said with a comical eye roll that made him laugh. "I don't do groups well at all."

"I'm the middle of five. Either you learned to function within a group or you got trampled."

"Any other clergy in the family?"

"Two uncles, but I'm the only one in the immediate family. My older brother's a farmer. He bought us out and took over our parents' dairy farm after they died. My older sister is a makeup artist in Hollywood. My younger brothers are both in law enforcement in Boston." He took a swig of soda. "How about your family?"

"My mother is a writer, a lecturer, and a practicing Wiccan."

She couldn't help but laugh as his jaw dropped to the table.

"Sorry, I should have warned you," she said. "Maeve has sampled just about every major religion and a few minor ones. I think she's still Wiccan but she seems to be leaning toward Buddhism again, so you never know."

"And here I thought she was your average Roman Catholic."

"She was," Kate said, "but the Church's lack of regard for women in the clergy infuriated her when she was a teenager and she's been searching for something ever since. She's really a very spiritual woman." She paused. "Unlike her daughter."

"Maeve should investigate Episcopalianism. We welcome women into the priesthood."

"You may live to regret the invitation," she said dryly. "My mother is all about the questions."

"I'm not afraid of questions."

Time to test that statement.

"When all is said and done, aren't all religions the same? Most people are looking for something or someone to blame when things go wrong or plead to when they're in need, and God is as good a target as any." She blotted her mouth with the edge of her paper napkin. "I save time and put the blame on myself." She put the napkin down. "You were supposed to laugh, Mark. That was a joke."

She couldn't read his expression, and it made her vaguely uneasy.

"So you don't believe in God?"

"I don't know what I believe." She told him about Father Boyle's hospital visit. "I felt something when he prayed," she admitted, "but I'm not sure if it was real or just a learned response after twelve years at St. Aloysius."

"Prayer can be a comfort."

"You can't pray if you don't know where your prayers are going."

"Maybe they don't have to go anywhere. Maybe it's enough that you say them out loud."

"You're good," she said. "I can see why they want you back. It's just that for me there's an emptiness in prayer. It seems like talking to myself."

"I understand."

"How could you possibly? Your whole life is structured around a belief system in a higher power."

"That doesn't mean I don't have doubts. After Suzanne died, I didn't believe in much of anything for a few years there."

"You stopped believing in God?"

"Some people take solace in their faith after a tragedy. It didn't work that way for me."

"Father Boyle told me that a heart attack frequently triggers a rebirth of religious feeling in patients." She motioned for him to lean closer. "Don't tell anyone but I wouldn't have minded if it had. Life is much easier for people who have that to lean on."

"Make it so."

"You're quoting Captain Picard?"

"Who?"

"I think we need to schedule some serious tube time to get you up to speed."

"No wonder you haven't been to church since nineteen ninety-three. You've been too busy watching television."

"So are we ready for dessert?" Their waitress started clearing away their dishes with swift, practiced motions.

"What's good?" Mark asked.

"Everything."

"As long as it isn't Jell-O," Kate said. "I've had enough Jell-O to last me a lifetime."

"Cracker Jack Sundae," their waitress suggested. "It doesn't get any better."

"We'll take it," Mark said.

"Two spoons," said Kate, "and could you make half of it with frozen yogurt instead of ice cream?"

"I can make it with cottage cheese if you want, but it won't taste as good."

"That's okay," Mark said. "We'll go with the yogurt."

"We'll do half and half," Kate said. "No reason you should give up your ice cream."

Their waitress looked from Kate to Mark. "Ball's in your court."

"I'll take one for the team. Make it yogurt."

Ah, romance! It was better than a dozen red roses.

Seventeen

They lingered over the Cracker Jack Sundae so long that their waitress deposited a dinner menu next to their check and suggested the chicken pot pie.

"She's tired of us," Mark said.

Kate grinned at him as she slung her bag over her shoulder. "Ya think?"

They stepped out into the late-afternoon sunshine and were about to clasp hands and poke around Main Street when Kate's shoulder bag started ringing.

"Oh damn." She slipped it off her shoulder and rummaged around for her cell. "I thought I'd turned it off."

It was Gwynn, sounding very young and surprisingly nervous.

"Gwynnie, can I call you later?"

"Gran told me you were with Father Mark," Gwynn said, her words tumbling all over themselves. "That's why I'm calling."

Mark walked a few steps away, pretending to inspect a window display of bait and tackle.

Kate prepared herself for the worst. "I should be the one calling you," Kate said. "What were you thinking, spouting all that silliness to the guy from the *Bugle*?"

"You didn't like it?" Gwynn sounded sincerely shocked. "I thought it was the coolest, most romantic thing I ever read."

"Gwynn, I—"

"Mom, I talked to Andrew and we want to give a dinner party for Father Mark."

"What?"

"We're going to give a dinner party for Father Mark. We're inviting Gran, Uncle Paul, Daddy, and Marie."

"What about your brothers and sister?"

"We don't have enough room."

"When do you plan to host this party?"

Gwynn covered the phone and Kate heard urgent whispers. "A week from tomorrow." More whispers. "Six p.m."

"Can I call you back?"

"I thought he was there with you. Can't you ask him now?"

"Hold on." She joined Mark in front of the bait shop window and filled him in. "Believe me, I'll understand if you say no."

"Yes."

"You're sure?"

"I wouldn't miss it."

"How about you go and I stay home?" She put the phone back up to her ear.

"I heard that," Gwynn said.

"It was a joke, honey. Think about it: Maeve, Paul, and your dad all in one room. I'll need a defibrillator."

She was relieved to hear Gwynn's laughter. "I thought you were talking about Andrew."

She had been, but she would cut out her tongue rather

than admit it to her daughter. "Mark said he would love to come to dinner, and so would I."

"Great!" Gwynn said. "Terrific! We're going out to Pathmark now so we can start stocking up. You should go home soon, Mom. You need to get your rest."

Kate turned off her cell and dropped it back into her tote bag. "She thinks I should go home and get some rest."

Mark draped his arm across her shoulders and they set off in the direction of the bookstore. "What do you think?"

"I think my daughter needs to stop worrying and get back to normal."

"Give her time. She went through a traumatic experience."

"Excuse me, but *I'm* the one who went through the traumatic experience."

"Your family isn't immune to the aftershocks."

"Want some more truth? I really don't want to go to Gwynn's for dinner."

"Why? Because your ex-husband is going to be there?"

"Ed isn't the problem. My daughter's fiancé is."

* * *

They walked from one end of the town to the other, stopping briefly in the bookstore so Kate could grab the latest Robert B. Parker and the new *Vogue Knitting*.

"I never thought she would marry this young," Kate said as they started back toward where they'd left the car. "She's been floating around for the last couple of years, bartending, waitressing, and finally she decides to go back to school and get her master's and then—" She stopped and shook her head. "A fisherman?"

"Some of the apostles were fishermen."

She rolled her eyes. "And they took a vow of poverty. Something to look forward to."

"I did the math. You married even younger."

"Whose side are you on anyway? I want somebody to agree that my daughter is making a huge mistake, that she's throwing away a great chance to study architecture to live in some little apartment by the docks with a guy who guts fish for a living."

He stopped and pulled her into his arms. "Our first fight?"

She resisted for a moment. He could feel her pulling away from him, physically and emotionally, but then she relaxed and rested her forehead against his shoulder.

"Not much of a fight," she said. "We can do a lot better than that."

"I overstepped. Gwynn's decisions aren't any of my business."

"They aren't my business either. I've tried very hard to let Gwynn make her own choices without interference, but this time I can't seem to keep my mouth shut."

"Maybe you should try harder."

He saw a flash of something in her eyes, but she didn't erupt this time. "She has no idea what it's like to do without. Maeve and I lived a hand-to-mouth existence much of the time. Gwynnie's idea of hardship is buying her jeans at Lord & Taylor instead of Saks."

"Give her a chance, Kate. She might surprise you."

"You don't know my daughter."

"I know her mother and if Gwynn's anything like you, she'll get it right."

He wished he could be there to see how it all turned out.

* * *

They picked up Thai food for dinner and ate it in the car, laughing as pieces of chicken slipped from their chopsticks and bounced across the cracked leather upholstery.

"You've got to love old cars," Mark said as a peapod went flying past him. "You couldn't do this in a Rolls."

"You're right," Kate said. "I think it might be against the law."

They were parked at the edge of the beach. Sunset had come and gone and the sky was starry and dark. Early Springsteen played softly from somewhere in the distance.

"Next time I'll pick the music," he said, handing her a bottle of water from the bag on the seat between them. "The Boss seems to have a monopoly on you Jersey girls."

"Billy Joel isn't allowed across the state line," she said, swilling down a huge gulp of Poland Spring. "Listening to him is a felony."

The banter was silly and they both knew it. They also knew that something was happening between them, something so far beyond wonderful that it was the one thing for which they had no words.

And God knew they had words for everything else.

She polished off her food and tossed the empty container into the paper bag on the seat. "That has to be the best Thai food I've ever had," she said with a deep sigh of contentment. "I wonder if they deliver to Coburn."

"So you like Thai food, Manhattan clam, and iced tea," he said. "What else?"

"You."

Oops. That hadn't been on her list of recommended talking points.

She shrugged with a combination of embarrassment and delight. "Okay. I said it and I'm not taking it back." She took another long drink of water. "That's the good thing about having a six-week limit. We can be totally honest with each other without long-term repercussions."

His expression didn't change but she sensed a subtle shift in the atmosphere between them.

"Why don't we forget about the six-week limit and enjoy the ride?"

"Sounds like a plan," she whispered as he pushed the bag onto the floor and slid closer to her.

The kissing was even more delicious than the Thai food.

"You taste like basil and ginger," she said.

"So do you."

It was like being a teenager again but better. They both knew the boundaries, and for that moment they were willing to play by the rules. Forty-one was better than sixteen. Forty-one understood this unexpected gift for the priceless blessing it was and knew how to enjoy every kiss, every touch, every second of exquisite longing for more.

"We fogged up the windows," he said when they finally broke apart, on fire and yearning for more than either one could give at the moment.

"I see why you like this car." She sat up and straightened her shirt, her hair, her messy and tangled emotions. "I'd forgotten why bench seats were so popular."

He cupped her face with his hands and drank deeply of her mouth. "There's no time limit on what I'm feeling."

She wanted to tell him that there was no time limit on her feelings either, that she had never felt so open, so vulnerable, so filled with love and hope, but she didn't know where or how to begin.

Or if she even wanted to start.

She tilted her head to the right. "Did you hear that?"

He shook his head. "I didn't hear anything."

She took his hand and placed it over her heart. "I think the walls of Jericho are tumbling down."

* * *

Maeve was sitting in the kitchen, sipping herbal tea and working at her laptop, when Kate got home. "Almost midnight," Maeve said, eyes twinkling. "Feel like talking?"

Kate kissed the top of her mother's head. "No," she said. "Okay?"

"Whatever you say, honey." The twinkle in her eyes grew brighter.

Maeve probably thought they'd rented a room somewhere and made love all afternoon while an emergency medical crew stood guard at the door. Why disappoint her?

She drifted upstairs, hugging her secrets to herself.

* * *

Mark was halfway to Rocky Hill when he realized that he had turned off his cell phone at the luncheonette and forgotten to turn it back on.

Eleven voice mails, two pages, six text messages.

One very major screwup.

"I took over the meeting for you, pal, but I'm not happy about it. Give me a call. I'm your sponsor and I want some answers. I'll keep my cell on. Call me. I don't care how late it is."

He punched in Scott's number.

"Sorry to wake you," he said. "I was out with Kate and forgot it was Friday." He hoped he made up in truth for what he lacked in responsibility.

"Are you sober?" Scott sounded tired and deeply concerned.

"Totally."

"This is the first time you blew a meeting, pal. We were worried."

"I apologize," he said. "We drove down to Spring Lake and—" He stopped. The details were his business and Kate's and he would make sure they stayed that way.

"So what's the story with you two?"

"We had a good time."

"You can tell me to mind my own business—"

"Mind your own business."

Scott ignored him. "—but Marcy and I were pretty sure we saw something going on between the two of you. Some real sparks."

"I like her," he said. "Very much."

"So did we."

He laughed. "You didn't say more than hello and good-bye to her."

"Ex-cops have good instincts."

Mark heard the sound of whispered conversation.

"Marcy wants to know if you two would like to come over for dinner Sunday."

"I'll ask Kate and get back to you."

More whispered conversation. "We figured she was there with you."

"I'm in my car. She's in her house."

And even more whispers.

"Why don't you put Marcy on," he suggested, "and I'll tell her myself."

"I wouldn't do that to you, pal," Scott said with a laugh. "You want to save another life? Bring Kate to dinner on Sunday and I'll owe you big."

Dinner with Scott and Marcy would lead to a movie with Ann and her husband, which would lead to another dinner and another movie and before you knew it he and Kate were a couple with friends in common and a shared social life, which would be history in less than six weeks.

Why now? He had told her to forget the six-week deadline and enjoy the ride, but that was easier said than done. It hung over his head like the sword of Damocles.

I know there has to be a reason for bringing her into my life now but I can't figure out what it is. I believe in

Your wisdom and trust in Your mercy, but if You could see fit to explain Your plan for Kate and me, I wouldn't mind a bit.

Either that or give them more time.

Eighteen

Kate slept straight through until noon the next day. She had never done anything like that in her life and it was as decadently wonderful as it was disorienting. She felt simultaneously slothful, pampered, and guilty as hell.

What was it Dr. Lombardi had said to her? *Listen to your body.* And she had. Her body had told her in no uncertain terms that she needed to recharge her batteries after that amazing day with Mark at Spring Lake.

Listen to your body. If she had listened to everything her body had to say, she would have ended up trying to seduce an Episcopal priest in the front seat of a Honda Civic.

She wasn't sure what had stopped them from actually making love instead of just making out. The fact that she probably needed her cardiologist's okay? His religious vocation? The memory of his ex-wife? A tiny front seat in the middle of an active parking lot? Cellulite? She hadn't a clue.

They had talked about everything else. Religion. Poli-

tics. Family. Life. Death. Disappointment. Joy. Illness.
Their taste in music and food and movies. Sooner or later
they would have to talk about sex.

She carefully tucked her hair into a hotel freebie shower
cap and showered, then booted up her laptop to check
e-mail while she dressed.

TO: kate@frenchkiss.biz
FROM: gwynnbann@njshorefun.net
SUBJECT: next Saturday—questions

Help! Andrew and I are trying to figure out a menu and
we need to know:

1. what can't you eat?
2. what does Father Mark like to eat? (i.e., does he
   eat fish??)
3. could you bring the wine? (please please—our
   budget won't stretch)
4. e-mail to Gran bounced—would you ask her if
   she'd make a chocolate cheesecake for dessert?
5. I think you forgot to send Andrew that note. Just
   in case, his e-mail is bigfish@threemilelimit.biz

ASAP above!
Love you,
Gwynnie

* * * * * *

TO: gwynnbann@njshorefun.net
FROM: kate@frenchkiss.biz
SUBJECT: RE: next Saturday—questions

1 and 2—Fish is great for both of us
3—ok but we'll need some soft drinks too

4—why don't you phone her?
5—I promise I'll get to it

Love you back.

* * * * * *

TO: kate@frenchkiss.biz
FROM: paul.grantham@weissgranthamreilly.com
SUBJECT: Gwynnie's dinner party

Notice please I didn't call you today and interrupt your outing with your new friend. I'm in London and Paris next week but wouldn't miss Gwynnie's party. I'd swing by and pick you up but have feeling you'll carpool with Super Cleric. Let me know.
If you feel like talking, you have my #.
L, PNG

* * * * * *

TO: paul.grantham@weissgranthamreilly.com
FROM: kate@frenchkiss.biz
SUBJECT: RE: Gwynnie's party

Glad you'll be there and yes, Maeve and I will carpool. We'll talk when you get back.
Safe trip, P.
L from K

* * * * * *

TO: kate@frenchkiss.biz
FROM: mark.kerry@mklj.net
SUBJECT: dinner invitation

It's seven a.m. I hope you're asleep. (insert suitably inappropriate comment here.) Scott and Marcy (you met

them in the parking lot at The Old Grist Mill) invited us
to dinner Sunday night. Command performance for
me but you're free to say no.
Hope you say yes.

* * * * * *

TO: mark.kerry@mklj.net
FROM: kate@frenchkiss.biz
SUBJECT: RE: dinner invitation

Yes.
(Am I going to regret this?)

She slipped into jeans and a yellow cotton sweater
and gathered her hair into a ponytail. She glanced at her
face in the mirror and noted, to her surprise, the faintest
glimmer of color from the sun. Makeup could wait until
later.

Maeve's laptop was set up on the kitchen table, surrounded by empty coffee cups, notepads, and an assortment of pens, pencils, and markers. A copy of the *Kama
Sutra* was propped open to a particularly alarming, if in-
triguing, page.

"I'm doing a workshop at a fifty-five-plus community
in Boca next month," Maeve said. "Do you think number
seventy-eight is too athletic?"

Kate bent down and peered more closely at the crisp,
clear color photograph. "I think you'd better ask an or-
thopedist. I'm not sure anyone outside the Romanian gym-
nastic team could do that."

Maeve's fingers were a blur on the keyboard. "Thanks,
honey. I'll contact a few orthopedists and maybe a cardiologist or two, just to be on the safe side." She tore her
eyes away from the screen and looked at Kate. "Honey,
you have never looked more gorgeous."

Kate felt her cheeks redden. "Thanks. A good night's sleep can do wonders."

"So can sex," her mother said with her usual blunt honesty. "He might be a priest but he's still a man. I hope you used protection."

"Mom!" Now she sounded like Gwynn. "Last week you asked me if I was in perimenopause."

"There are reasons besides birth control to use a condom, Kate."

What twisted fate decreed she would be having a birds-and-bees conversation with her mother twice in one lifetime?

"We haven't had sex. I can't even think about sex until I have my stress test." *It's been so long I'm not even sure I remember how to have sex.*

"Judging by that smile on your face, I think you should call Dr. Lombardi and find out."

Her mother had a point but she refused to acknowledge it. "Any oatmeal left?"

"In the saucepan. Want me to nuke it for you?"

"I'll do it." She spooned the oatmeal into a bowl and popped it into the microwave for forty seconds. "By the way, I asked Mark over for supper."

That got her mother's attention. "I was going to throw together a salad and some soup."

"That's fine. I'll pop some bread into the machine when I get back and figure out what to do about dessert."

"You could stop by the bakery," Maeve suggested, "and get more of those brownies."

"No," Kate said. "I want to make something myself."

She ignored Maeve's comment about hell freezing over and sat down with her oatmeal and the bread machine cookbook.

"You said yes to Gwynn, didn't you?" Maeve asked as she popped a blank CD into her drive and pressed a few buttons. "She really wants to thank Mark for what he did."

"I think she wants us to see her and Andrew together and give our familial seal of approval."

"And you're not inclined to give it."

"I don't have any bad feelings toward Andrew. He seemed like a nice enough young man. I just don't think he's right for my daughter."

"Try to keep an open mind," Maeve urged. "Don't say things you'll regret. There's a chance Andrew is going to become part of our family, and you don't want to get off to a bad start."

Kate looked down at her bowl of oatmeal, sans cream, sans sugar, and sighed. "You know I hate it when you're right, don't you?"

"Of course I do," Maeve said.

* * *

It started small.

Mark came over for supper on Saturday night. Sonia and Liz happened to drop by. Two of Maeve's oldest friends came over for coffee and a friendly game of cards. Before either Mark or Kate realized what was happening, the carriage house was filled with people laughing, talking, playing cards, drinking coffee, getting to know each other.

And checking out Father McDreamy.

Kate quickly lost track of the number of thumbs-up signs flashed across the room by matchmaking married friends who were dying to hook her up with Mark, who was definitely the center of attention. No surprise there. He had the kind of presence that drew the eye, a combination of physical beauty and strength of character that was irresistible.

The next day they drove over to Pennsylvania for dinner at Scott and Marcy's house. The small dinner for four had expanded without their knowledge to include Ann and her husband Charlie, and Matty and Lynn. Kate quickly realized they were all members of the same AA group that Mark led near New Hope, and she found herself impressed by the sense of family that had developed between them and their spouses.

She was also impressed by the deep regard and affection they had for Mark and listened avidly as they tried to persuade him to stay in the New Jersey/Pennsylvania area and forsake his New Hampshire roots.

"You're tempted, aren't you?" she asked as they wound their way along country roads on their way back to her house.

"More than ever." He kept his eyes on the dark and winding ribbon of road. "I've got to admit I never saw you coming."

"You weren't on my radar screen either, clergyman."

"I wish—"

She shook her head. "It is what it is. You have to go back. We both know that. Why waste time debating a done deal?"

Of course her words might have been a whole lot more effective if she hadn't started to cry immediately afterward, but those were the breaks.

"Ignore the waterworks," she ordered him, sniffling into a paper napkin she found in his glove box. "In case you hadn't noticed, I'm not crying half as much as I was last week."

"That's like quantifying the ocean."

"You're going to miss these operatic crying jags when they're gone."

"I'm going to miss you."

He reached for her hand and held it tight the rest of the way home.

The night of Gwynn's party

There was no point to taking separate cars, so Kate, Mark, Maeve, two bottles of Shiraz, two bottles of Pepsi, two bottles of ginger ale, a case of bottled water, and one gorgeous chocolate cheesecake shoehorned themselves into his Honda for the long ride down to Paradise Point.

"I hope your parish in New Hampshire supplies a car," Maeve said as she settled in the backseat next to the bags of food. "This one looks like spring break in Fort Lauderdale."

Kate shot her mother a warning look, but Mark just laughed.

"This old girl's indestructible," he said as he waited for Kate to buckle up. "I thought she would give up the ghost when the odometer rolled past two hundred thousand miles but we're at two-fifty and still climbing." He turned the key and the engine sprang to life. "If she doesn't give up on me, why should I give up on her?"

"That's probably the most deeply romantic sentiment I've ever heard a man express," Maeve said. "I just wish it weren't for a car."

Mark and Kate laughed, but Maeve was on a roll.

"Oh no," Kate said. "She whipped out her battery-operated keyboard. The Muse has landed."

Maeve proceeded to interview Mark on everything including religion, sex, and the deep and passionate relationship between American men and their cars. Kate mounted a fake protest, but she was hanging on every word and intended to demand a transcript from her mother when they got home.

The sign welcoming them to Paradise Point seemed to pop up before they knew it.

"Paradise Point reminds me of Cape May," Mark said as they rolled down Main Street. "Great town."

"They're rebuilding," Maeve said. "They have a way to go, but it's definitely catching on with the tourist trade."

Kate swiveled around to look at her mother. "You seem to know a lot about this town. Has Gwynn been sending you brochures?"

The spacious Victorian bed-and-breakfasts gave way to retail stores that, in turn, gave way to bait shops, boat rentals, O'Malley's Dockside, and her daughter's home.

"Oh God," Kate said as they parked adjacent to the tiny bungalow teetering at the water's edge. "It's worse than I thought."

"It's charming," Maeve said. "Very atmospheric."

"I hope they're insured. A stiff wind will knock them into the water."

"You two go ahead," Mark said. "I'll unload the car."

"Remember what I told you," Maeve warned as they approached the front door. "That young man may be part of our family for the next fifty years. If you can't be happy for them, fake it."

"I thought you said women should never fake it."

"This isn't sex. This is parenthood."

Kate straightened her shoulders, smoothed down her hair, and plastered on her game face as the front door swung open.

"Come on in," Paul said, raising a Corona in greeting. "We've been waiting for you."

Nineteen

It was clear to anyone with eyes that Paul was in a particularly contentious mood.

Kate pulled him aside as Maeve introduced Mark around. "Knock it off," she said. "Lose the attitude or climb behind the wheel of that monster-mobile of yours and go back to Manhattan where you belong."

He didn't deny the obvious. "What happened to those tears of joy you've been crying lately?"

"You know I love you, pal, but this is Gwynn's day and I'm not going to let you screw it up with any ridiculous macho posturing."

"It's not too late to get into law school, French. With a mouth like that, you'd end up one of the Supremes."

Kate opened her mouth to say something blistering as Maeve marched up to them in full maternal mode. "I've been breaking up your fights since grade school. How about we give peace a chance and join the rest of the party?"

"Your daughter's in a bad mood," Paul said. "All I did was open the front door."

"With a Corona in your hand," Kate shot back. "Tell him he should go home before he ruins everything."

Maeve, experienced in the art of peaceful coexistence, placed her hand under Kate's elbow. "Gwynnie!" she called out. "Where's that guided tour you promised us?"

The guided tour took less than three minutes, but it did break up the fight.

"You could make breakfast without getting out of bed," Kate whispered to Maeve.

"It's cozy," Maeve said, ever the optimist when it came to love.

Any cozier, Kate thought, and they might as well live in a furnished closet. If possible, the house was even tinier on the inside than it appeared from the outside. You couldn't turn around in the kitchen without bumping into yourself. And God forbid you needed to use the bathroom, because that required a somersault across the double bed and some fancy footwork once you got there.

And Gwynn, her materialistic, spoiled daughter, seemed oblivious to it all. She was glowing with happiness and so, Kate had to admit, was Andrew.

Not to mention his brother, Don, and their mother, Joanne, who arrived seconds before Ed. If she didn't know better, she would have guessed they'd all been enjoying a nitrous oxide cocktail.

"Good thing Marie stayed home," Ed whispered to Kate as they helped themselves to some iced tea. "We'd have to sit on the roof."

"You're Gwynn's parents, aren't you?" Joanne joined them near the living room window. She grabbed Kate's hands and gave her a kiss on both cheeks. "I can't believe all you've been through! You'd never know it to look at you. Isn't medical science incredible?"

Kate cast around for the right thing to say, but Joanne was too fast for her.

Joanne angled her body away from Ed and lowered her voice. "Did that gorgeous priest really save your life? Andy told me the story, but I have to say I didn't believe it. It sounded like something straight out of Hollywood."

"Mark really saved my life," Kate said. "I wouldn't be standing here right now if he hadn't come along when he did."

Joanne sighed loudly. "I may stop taking my Procardia."

Kate burst into laughter, and Joanne wasn't far behind.

"I told Andy you two would like each other." Gwynn joined them, her face flushed with happiness and heat from the kitchen. "I was right!"

"Gwynnie!" Maeve called out. "What do I do with these steamers?"

"Steamers!" Joanne's face lit up. "Let me help."

Gwynn and her maybe-possibly future mother-in-law dashed the ten steps to the kitchen, where Maeve was staring down a giant bucket of sandy clams. They looked so comfortable, the three of them together in the postage-stamp kitchen. Happy and friendly and *(Go ahead, Kate, admit it)* so much like family that Kate had to turn away toward the window, where Ed was still standing with his iced tea.

"This could be us twenty-five years ago," he said.

"This was never us." Kate took a sip of tea. "We leaped from high school to parenthood without passing Go."

"I think we did pretty well for ourselves, don't you, Katie? We had some good years."

Her eyes filled with tears and she blinked quickly. She had it down to a science. "We had some great years, all things considered."

"All things considered?"

"Considering we were never in love with each other."

"There was love there," he said softly. "Always."

"You know what I mean."

Of course he did. There was a world of difference between loving and being in love. He had found that kind of can't-live-without-you love when he met Marie and had been smart enough to hang on.

"Yeah," he said, draping an arm around her shoulders. "I know what you mean."

She had never envied her ex-husband more than she did at that moment or wished him greater happiness.

The sound of their daughter's laughter drew their attention.

"Gwynn and Andy don't look old enough to vote," Ed said with a shake of his head.

"They're six years older than we were when she was born."

"And we all survived. Gotta be a miracle in there somewhere."

She put her glass down on the windowsill. "Congratulations on the new baby. Gwynn told me the news."

"We weren't going to tell anyone until Marie had the sonogram but—" He shrugged but his pride and excitement were clearly evident. "Good news has a life of its own."

She tried to imagine herself in Marie's shoes, forty-one and pregnant, and to her surprise it wasn't that bad a fit. Those had been happy years.

"Boy or girl?" she asked.

"We're old-fashioned," Ed said. "We don't mind waiting to find out."

"I wouldn't want to know either. Some things are worth waiting for."

Ed gave her a quizzical look. "Are you thinking about having a child?"

"No," she said, laughing. "Of course not. I mean, I just came out of the cardiac unit. I'm still working my way up to driving alone."

"You're a great mother," he said, and once again her eyes filled with tears. "You still have time to start a second family."

"Single, middle-aged mother of an infant?" She pretended to shudder. "I'm not brave enough for that."

"An Episcopal priest," Ed said, a teasing but affectionate glint in his eyes. "You could do worse."

She laughed. "I'm not sure he could. I'm hardly the religious type."

"Don't sell yourself short. This isn't the nineteen-fifties. The world is a more tolerant place. You could always—"

Time for a change of subject.

"Where did the other guys go?" She glanced around. "It's not like anyone could hide in this place."

"Your priest is out on the dock with Andy and Don. I think they're giving him fishing lessons."

"He's not my priest."

So much for the change of subject.

"You can't tell that by looking," Ed said. "For once Gwynnie didn't exaggerate. So what's the story there?"

"There is no story." She told him about the end of May and New Hampshire.

"But you're seeing each other."

She couldn't fight it any longer. "Yes, we're seeing each other."

"I like him."

"You're religious. You can't help yourself."

"He saved your life. I'll admit that gives him an edge, but there's more to him than that." He shot her a look. "And he's in love with you."

She let out a bark of laughter that made Maeve, Gwynn, and Joanne look up from their bucket of steamers with open curiosity.

"He's not in love with me."

"Men aren't as clueless as you girls like to believe. He's in love with you."

"Then I must have the most alluring EKG in town, because Paul decided he was—" She stopped herself. "Oh, forget it. Too silly to even discuss."

Ed frowned, a carbon copy of the frown he used to display in high school when he saw Paul and Kate laughing together. "You heard about Jill?"

"Paul told me the other day."

"He's taking it pretty hard."

"I can't believe the elopement came as such a big surprise."

"Believe it," Ed said. "He was gutshot."

"Did you know he was still in love with her?"

Ed's eyes widened. "You didn't?"

She shook her head. "I thought he just missed his kids."

"Why am I not surprised?" He took a swallow of lemonade. "You and Paul, huh? Maybe it's not so crazy after all. You've known each other your entire lives. You're good friends. No secrets. No surprises. You'd know exactly what you were getting into. There are worse foundations for a relationship."

There had been a time in her life when that would have been more than enough, but not now.

"You know what?" She leaned against the window and listened to the sounds of laughter coming from the dock. "I'm starting to think that the secrets and surprises are what it's all about."

* * *

Gwynn and Andy set up tray tables in the living room. They opened a few beach chairs, tossed some throw pillows on the floor, and announced that dinner was served.

As guests of honor, Mark and Kate shared the tiny sofa. Despite her best intentions to keep her emotions out of the situation, she found herself touched by the sweet innocence of the gesture.

"Where's the wine?" Gwynn asked, darting about like a hummingbird. "We need the wine."

Andy grabbed two bottles from the back porch. "Hold up your paper cups, folks. We've got wine!"

He poured his way around the circle. Only Kate and Mark covered their cups and claimed soda instead.

Kate's reason was understandable. Mark's should have remained private, but Paul decided to play inquiring reporter.

"You're a priest," Paul said, playing to the crowd. "Don't tell me you're a priest who doesn't like wine."

Kate opened her mouth to defuse the situation with a comforting white lie, but Mark was too fast for her.

"I'm a recovering alcoholic," he said easily, "but ginger ale would be great."

Could life really be that simple? No posturing. No social fibs. No cover-up. He told them the truth, they nodded, and even Paul knew that was the end of it. The grudging respect in his eyes took her by surprise. Was it possible to live that way on a daily basis in the beginning of the twenty-first century?

Gwynn was standing in the doorway, looking down at a small white piece of paper clutched in her hand. Andy walked over to her and Kate couldn't help but notice (even though she didn't want to) how solicitous he was with her baby girl, how tender. Would she have noticed any of this three weeks ago, before her heart attack, or would it have slipped past her line of vision and out of reach?

Gwynn cleared her throat and stepped into the room,

which wasn't easy considering every inch of floor space was occupied. She looked so vulnerable, so precious, that Kate did what lately she seemed to do best: she started to cry.

"Mom!" Gwynn waved the piece of paper at her mother. "I haven't even started yet!"

"Ignore me," Kate said, dabbing at her eyes with a paper cocktail napkin from O'Malley's Dockside Bar & Grille. "I cried at the gas station yesterday when the guy cleaned Maeve's windshield."

It got the laugh she had hoped for and gave Gwynn a chance to regroup.

"Andy and I invited all of you here today for a very special reason. Three weeks ago my mom had a heart attack and we would have lost her if Father Mark hadn't been there to save her life.

"We talk a lot about heroes. We have Spider-Man and Superman and baseball players and movie stars, but how often do you meet somebody who actually embodies the real meaning of the word?

"Father Mark breathed life into my mom's lungs. I can't even think about what might have—" She ducked her head and Kate was afraid Gwynn was going to cry, but her daughter was made of stronger stuff than that. She lifted her tear-streaked face and raised her glass to Mark.

"Thank you for being there that morning, Father Mark. Thank you for knowing what to do and not being afraid to do it. Thank you for saving Mom's life and being here today to share our happiness." She started to choke up again but quickly recovered. "Most of all, thank God for bringing us all together tonight to celebrate being a family."

"To Mark!" Maeve said. "Long life and happiness!"

"To Kate," Paul added. "Health, wealth, and a bright future!"

The sound of nine paper cups coming together in a toast might not seem like much, but it was beautiful music to Kate. They cheered her, they cheered Mark, they hugged and kissed and celebrated life. Even Paul seemed to feel honestly grateful to Mark. They were family, all of them, in every sense of the word. She wished Ed's wife and younger children were there too. They were part of this family, part of her daughter's life, and she missed them.

She hugged Gwynn (resisting the urge to brush Gwynn's hair off her face and comment on the eyeliner), kissed her mother, kissed Andy's mother *and* his brother, hugged Paul, hugged and kissed Ed, hugged Andy so hard the poor guy thought it was the Heimlich maneuver, and then without thinking, without worrying if she would live to regret it, she threw her arms around Mark and kissed him in front of God, her family, and anyone else who happened to be walking by.

She had spent her life keeping an eye on her emotions the way a miser kept her eye on her bankbook. Love was a renewable resource, a well that refilled itself the more water you drank from it. But then again, she had never felt anything close to the wild surge of exhilaration she felt whenever Mark was near. If she had, she would have gone to the ends of the earth to hang on to it.

This was what had happened to Ed when he met Marie. This was what Maeve wrote about, examined, explored, lived for. This was why Paul still carried a torch for his ex, why he had looked toward her to ease his aching heart. This was the reason Gwynn looked at Andrew as if he'd hung the moon. You couldn't explain it to someone who'd never experienced it. It was a different vocabulary, a different perspective, like explaining jazz to someone who loved show tunes.

I get it now, she thought. For the first time in her life, she finally got what it was all about.

But what on earth was she supposed to do with it now that she had it?

* * *

It was almost three in the morning when they got back to Kate's house up in Coburn.

"You can't drive back to Rocky Hill tonight," Maeve said to Mark as he pulled into the driveway. "Stay here. God knows, there's plenty of room."

Next to him Kate yawned and stretched. "We're home?" she mumbled.

"We are and it's almost the crack of dawn," Maeve said. "I told Mark he should stay here tonight."

"That's a great idea." Kate gave him a sleepy smile. "It's Saturday night in New Jersey. You're better off waiting until morning."

She couldn't help noticing that he didn't put up much of a fight.

Maeve poured herself a glass of orange juice, gathered up her laptop and notebooks from the kitchen table, and disappeared upstairs to her room.

"How un-Maeve-like," Kate said as they waited for the water to boil for tea. "She's usually good until four or five in the morning."

He touched her cheek with the tip of his index finger.

"I think your mother is trying to push us together."

Kate winced. "I was hoping you hadn't noticed."

"I noticed," he said, moving closer.

"My mother is a born matchmaker. I've spent my entire life trying to dodge her silver bullet. You don't have to stay if you don't want to."

"I'm staying," he said, "but not because of Maeve. I'm staying because I don't want to miss a minute of you."

The rest of the night was a blur to Kate. They kissed in the kitchen, the hallway, the entrance to the living room, near her favorite reading chair, on her big squashy yellow sofa.

And they talked. Silly talk. Sweet talk. Things you would never say in the light of day. Dreams you wished could come true.

"You need your rest," he said into her hair. "Go up to bed. It's almost five."

"I'm staying here."

"You're making me feel guilty."

"I'm Catholic," she said. "That's my birthright."

"You're asleep on your feet."

She giggled softly. "How can that be when I'm lying here in your arms?"

He reached across the armchairs and grabbed one of her pale gold mohair throws and covered her with it. The last sound she heard before she fell asleep was the steady beat of his heart.

Twenty

"You don't have to do this," Mark said as they made their way south on Route 206 toward Princeton. "Charlotte would understand."

"I want to do it," Kate said, flipping down the visor and checking her lipstick in the cracked mirror. "That was probably the nicest luncheon invitation I've ever received."

"She wants to check you out," Mark said, laughing. "Make sure you're good enough for me."

"Is this typical Episcopalian behavior?"

"I don't know, but it is typical Charlotte Petruzzo behavior."

"So I'm going to have to fight Charlotte for your attentions, am I?"

"You never know," he said. "Wait until you meet her and then you tell me."

Two hours later Kate had to admit she'd been bested.

"I love her," she said as Mark started the car. "She should be declared a national treasure." She had sat spellbound as Charlotte spun stories about her adventures in mainland China, her years in Hong Kong, the happy years she had spent in Paris with her beloved husband.

"She thinks you're terrific," Mark said. "She wants you to come back and visit again some time."

"Try and keep me away. I wouldn't blame you if you proposed to her."

"I spoke to her doctor," he said. "Charlotte says she's ready to go whenever God calls her, but Dr. Warren says it isn't her time yet."

Kate raised her hands palm outward. "Not my specialty," she said. "My grandmother was given three weeks to live and she lasted eight years, but her sister, who was given a clean bill of health, died six weeks after her husband."

"We pretend to understand but we really don't," he said. "Nobody does." Mind over matter or matter over mind. Kate's guess was as good as his. "It's going to be hard to say good-bye to her."

"Do you have to say good-bye?" An angry blush flooded her cheeks. "I didn't mean to say that. I know you have to go back."

"I thought leaving New Jersey when the time came would be easy," he said. "I was wrong."

"We have Episcopalians here too," she said. "Churches, pulpits, congregations, full service, no waiting."

"Listen," he said as he stopped the car at a red light, "I got a call this morning that my friend Maggy's father died." Henry Boyd had been a good friend to him and to Suzanne. He had just seen him two weeks ago when he went up to talk to the bishop.

"I'm sorry," she said, a note of caution in her voice.

"I'm flying up to New Hampshire in the morning."

"For the funeral?"

"Maggy asked me to give the eulogy and I said I would."

"Do you want company? I won't go to the funeral, but I could fly up with you and poke around some antiques shops in the area."

He probably refused her offer a little too quickly. He saw the shadow cross her eyes and instantly regretted not taking a second or two longer.

"Listen, Kate," he said, feeling awkward and clumsy, "it's not that I don't want you, but the church is sending someone to pick me up and I'm not sure what they have planned for me."

"I understand."

"We could do it another time."

"Sure," she said, glancing toward the window. "Listen, it was a crazy idea. I don't know what I was thinking."

"I do," he said, "because I'm thinking the same thing."

She looked over at him, her hazel eyes wet with tears. "Less than four weeks," she said. "That's all we have left."

"I'll fly back tomorrow night. I'll take the late flight out and be back here before midnight."

"My house is closer to Newark Liberty than your house. You could sleep on the couch again."

"I'll only be gone a few hours. It'll be like a regular workday."

"I have my appointment with Armitage tomorrow afternoon and I'll put in my normal couple hours at the shop in the morning. I won't even know you're gone."

"I will," he said. Every hour, every minute, every second.

Route 1—the next day

"I'm forty-one and I have to ask my mommy to drive me around," Kate grumbled. "What's wrong with this picture?"

"Have you heard me complain?" Maeve asked as they zipped along Route 1 toward Professor Armitage's office.

"No, I haven't," Kate said, "and quite frankly I don't know how you're doing it. If I were in your position, I'd be bitching up a storm. You've been a total saint."

"My tape recorder is in the glove box," Maeve said. "I want this captured for posterity."

"I don't know what I would have done without you," Kate said. "I—"

"Oh, stop that boo-hooing," Maeve teased. "Servitude is a mother's natural state of being."

"Now I wish *I* had a tape recorder."

Maeve flipped on her turn signal and moved into the slow lane. "I wouldn't have wished that heart attack on you for the world, honey, but these past few weeks have been very special for me."

Kate reached over and patted her mother's hand. "For me too."

"I feel like I've been there with you through some very important transitional moments."

"English, please. I don't speak self-help."

"Gwynnie's engagement."

She groaned. "I'm trying not to dwell on that."

"You've softened. Don't tell me you haven't. I saw you at the dinner party. You can't fool me."

"Just don't spread it around. I have a reputation to up-hold."

"I think they're truly in love," Maeve said, "but it's not going to be an easy road."

"Right now poverty seems romantic," Kate said, "but sooner or later the novelty is going to wear off and she'll be thinking about all the things she gave up for love."

"I don't think Gwynn's like that."

"I don't mean La Perla bras, Mom. I'm talking about her education."

"There's nothing you can do about that," Maeve said. "She's chosen a different path."

"Were you this copacetic when I told you I was pregnant and trading my prom dress for a wedding gown?"

"I took Valium and cried on Grandma Natalie's shoulder until a month after Gwynnie's christening."

"I didn't know that. I thought you just rolled with it the way you seemed to roll with everything else."

"You were seventeen, honey. I was invisible to you. It's nature's way of making separation easier on all of us."

She could have argued the point with her mother. She had more than forty years of ammunition waiting to be fired at her number one target, but what was the point? Twenty years from now it would be Gwynnie's turn to take aim and Kate would be the target. Maybe the truth was you did the best you could, did it with a full heart, and left the rest in the hands of fate or God.

Greenwood, New Hampshire

William Rogers "Billy" Owens was twenty-nine years old, eight years married, three times a father. His wife, Marianne, had a Ph.D. in Theology and had been considering seminary herself before the first of their little girls made her appearance and she fell in love with motherhood. Billy was smart, kind, dedicated, and currently searching for a congregation to call his own.

"He's officiating at the funeral," Maggy said. "Father Winstead is still on the mend after his cancer surgery. I would have told you but—"

"You have enough on your mind," Mark said. "He seems like a good man."

"He is," Maggy agreed. "He and Dad became friendly when Father Billy took over for Father Winstead last summer after his first surgery."

The eulogy, written on the plane, was warmly received by the hundreds of people crowded into the church to say good-bye to Henry. But there was no denying the fact that the crowd belonged to Father Billy Owens. Billy was one of them. His kids played with their kids. His wife taught Sunday school and baked cakes for the PTA. His enthusiasm was infectious.

Mark was looking at Suzanne and himself if God had dealt them a different hand.

And it hurt.

He went back to Maggy's mother's house after the burial and offered what words of solace and comfort he could find to the family and friends gathered there, but he wasn't fully present and he knew it.

What was worse, he was fairly certain they knew it too.

He was trying to find a polite way to extricate himself when he turned and saw Suzanne's mother, Catherine, walking slowly up the driveway on the arm of a woman he assumed was a health care aide.

His first thought as he stepped out the front door to meet her was that she had aged. Losing her daughter and her husband in quick succession had taken its toll on her beautiful face. The lines were etched deeper. Her eyes no longer dazzled with life and joy. Instinctively he knew he was looking at a woman who had given up on life and was ready to say good-bye.

Their eyes met and for a moment the sorrow on her face dropped away, replaced by the kind of love and warmth that fed the soul.

"Mark." Her voice was older too, less resonant, but the sound was pure music.

He was next to her in an instant, embracing her gently, carefully, aware of the fragile bones, the once-indomitable spirit there now only in memory.

She didn't cry, but he came very close.

They found a quiet place to talk on the side porch and he waited while the aide, a lovely woman named Joyce, helped Catherine settle in.

"I saw you in church," Catherine said as Joyce drifted inside to fetch some lemonade. "I was hoping you would be here."

"I thought you were in Florida," he said. "If I'd known you were in town I would have—"

She waved her hand in a gesture reminiscent of Charlotte Petruzzo. "I leave for the airport in the morning." She glanced around and closed her eyes briefly. "Such a mistake."

"Moving to Florida?"

Her eyes opened. "You."

"What are you talking about?"

"You shouldn't have come back."

Her intensity surprised him. The Catherine he knew was a mellow, easygoing woman much as her daughter had been. "Henry was my friend," he said carefully. "It was my privilege to deliver the eulogy."

Again the wave of the hand in dismissal. "Of course you should deliver the eulogy. That isn't what I'm talking about."

Was Catherine heading down the dark road of dementia? He regrouped. "I'm sorry," he said, "but I don't understand."

Her exasperated expression would have been comical under different circumstances. "Your time here is over, Mark. It has been over for a very long time, same as mine. You've made a new life for yourself in New Jersey. I know you feel a debt of gratitude toward your friends here, but life is painfully short. Don't waste a second of it moving backward."

"They have a need; I'm grateful for the chance to fill

that need." He found himself struggling with an unexpected flare of temper. "It's one year, Catherine. I can give them that much."

"One year becomes five becomes ten and you're still in the same place you were at the beginning except you're alone."

"This is my hometown. This is where I grew up. Would it be so bad if it's where I end up?"

Catherine reached over and took his hand in hers. "Our girl is gone, Mark, and she isn't coming back. If you think you're going to find her here amid the memories, you are terribly wrong."

Joyce emerged from the house with lemonade, and he made a show of looking at his watch.

"I'm taking the seven-twenty out of Manchester to Boston," he said. "I'd better get moving."

"Remember what I said," Catherine murmured as he kissed her cheek. "I wasn't a meddling mother-in-law when Suzy was with us, but allow me the right to speak my mind now."

He made his good-byes, eager to get back into his rented car for the trip home.

Wherever the hell home was these days.

Coburn, New Jersey—later that night

"Say that again." Mark polished off the last of the western omelet Kate had made for him. "I don't think I heard right."

"Oh, yes you did. Maeve and Professor Armitage are going out on a date tomorrow night."

"This is the same Armitage you were going to see the day you had your heart attack."

"The very same."

"Nasty little guy with beady eyes and a scruffy beard."

"Nasty little guy who turned into Julio Iglesias the minute he shook my mother's hand."

"Your mother does have something," Mark said, spreading orange marmalade on a perfectly toasted English muffin. "I can understand why he'd be smitten."

"Smitten!" Kate clapped the heel of her hand to her forehead. "That's the word I've been searching for. That mean-tempered old fool is smitten with my mother."

"What about the box of letters? Did he stop flirting long enough to take a look?"

She told him about Armitage's underwhelmed response to her find. "Basically the jury's out. He's going to run them over to the U of P next week and have a confab with some other foul-tempered historians and see what they come up with. I'm preparing myself for disappointment."

"Did you pay a lot for them?"

She shook her head. "That's why I go on buying trips to the U.K. twice a year. One dealer's junk is another dealer's treasure." She poured herself a cup of herbal tea. "You're going to laugh, but I actually thought those letters were going to be my ticket to early retirement."

"You'd retire at forty-one?"

"Probably not, but wouldn't it be nice to have that option?"

They talked a bit about their plans for the next few weeks, about small towns, about family and friends and the connections that strengthen with time and proximity and those that don't, but as they talked she had the distinct feeling that something had changed.

"Are you okay?" she asked as they curled up together on the sofa. "You haven't said anything about your trip."

"The entire town came out for Henry's funeral. He would have been happy to see how many people loved him."

"And your eulogy?"

A second's pause. "It was well received."

She cast around for the right thing to say. "I'm sure it must have been difficult to say good-bye."

"Why waste time talking," he said, "when we could be kissing."

She couldn't argue with that even if she wanted to. He was a man and when men didn't want to talk, they didn't talk. His kisses were spectacular, sweet and hot and addictive. But kisses, even great ones, weren't enough to erase the feeling that, like it or not, reality was waiting for them right around the corner.

* * *

TO: marcy_n_scott@quickaccess.com
FROM: kate@frenchkiss.biz
SUBJECT: Great time

Great meal, great conversation, great poker game! My losing streak is coming to an end. Next week: Texas Hold-'Em!
Love from Kate

* * * * * *

TO: kate@frenchkiss.biz
FROM: annie-s@aol3.com
SUBJECT: bbq

Charlie and I are having a bbq next Saturday—our annual Fire Up the Grill celebration. Mark is one of the regulars and we'd love it if you came with him. It's great to see him so happy. Now if we could just get him to stay in NJ!
Ann S

* * * * * *

TO: kate@frenchkiss.biz
FROM: bigfish@threemilelimit.biz
SUBJECT: thanks

Thanks for dinner Saturday night. We all had a great time, esp. my mom. She doesn't have e-mail but if you could send her a copy of your key lime pie recipe she'd be really happy.
Gwynnie sends love and says she'll call you later.
Andy Dempsey

* * * * * *

TO: mark.kerry@mklj.net
FROM: mboyd@nh2day.net
SUBJECT: housing

There's a small house on Gardiner Lane coming up for sale in June but the real estate agent said you could see it now before it hits the market. That way you'll only have to live a month or two at the rectory. You can do that, right?
Maggy

* * * * * *

TO: mboyd@nh2day.net
FROM: mark.kerry@mklj.net
SUBJECT: RE: housing

Thanks for the FYI but I'll check it out when I get up there the end of the month. Busy tying up loose ends down here but will call soon.
MK

* * * * * *

TO: kate@frenchkiss.biz
FROM: paul.grantham@weissgranthamreilly.com
SUBJECT: on the road

The newlyweds are back and I'm off to Barbados for a few days with Lisa. NYC ain't big enough for the four of us. Yet.

Gwynnie said you just got the all clear from the MD to drive, etc. Good on you. Gwynnie also said you and the preacher are "hot and heavy." Be happy, kid, while it lasts but I just don't see you as the preacher's wife . . .
L, PNG

* * * * * *

TO: gwynnbann@njshorefun.net
FROM: kate@frenchkiss.biz
SUBJECT: privacy

If I wanted your Uncle Paul to know my updated medical status OR ANYTHING ELSE I'd fax him a copy. Use your head, Gwynnie, and ASK ME first. BTW watch the mail: I'm sending the key lime recipe for Joanne.
xoxo Mom

* * * * * *

TO: sonia@frenchkiss.biz
FROM: kate@frenchkiss.biz
SUBJECT: vacation!!!!

I won't be in again until June 1. Believe it or not, I'm taking a 2-week vacation. If you need me, the cell will be on. Otherwise have fun, work hard, and remember all gossip. xoxo Kate

Twenty-one

"Wait, Mom!" Kate flew out the front door and across the lawn toward the driveway. "You forgot your keyboard."

Maeve hit the brakes near the mailbox and rolled down her window. "Thanks, honey! I'd be lost without that."

Kate slipped the device through the open window and took the opportunity to hug her mother one more time.

"I'm going to miss you."

"So you've said six times in the last hour!" Maeve gave her a return hug. "I'm only three towns away. I think we'll be seeing each other."

Kate nodded and stepped away from the car. "Drive carefully. That intersection near the shop is tricky. Look both ways before you make the left onto Church; there's a blind driveway and—"

"I've been driving since I turned sixteen, Kate. I think I can manage."

"Of course. You're right. I'm being silly."

"If you want me to stay a few more days, honey, I'd be happy to."

"No, that's okay," Kate said, although she was tempted to take her mother up on the offer. "Dr. Lombardi said it's time, so it's time." Her stress test went perfectly. Her EKG was great. She was cleared to resume all normal activities.

Including sex.

"Don't be afraid," Maeve said. "Everything will turn out the way it's supposed to."

Kate had to laugh. "Mom, that's been said about everything including the Potato Famine and the Oscars telecast. What does that *mean*?"

"Leap and the net will appear," Maeve said, quoting another one of her favorite aphorisms. "If you do that, you'll be fine."

Kate stood in the driveway long after Maeve's car disappeared around the corner. If she followed her heart, she would leap into her own car, drive down to Rocky Hill, and throw herself at Father Mark Kerry's feet.

For the first time in her adult life, she had two weeks with nothing to do, nowhere that she had to be, nobody she had to please but herself. She could go where she wanted, when she wanted, and stay as long as she wanted.

Mark was systematically closing down his life in New Jersey. His various responsibilities were dropping off one by one in preparation for his return to New Hampshire. They no longer talked about his future plans. They both knew that each day brought them closer to saying goodbye.

His commitment to his old congregation ran deep. She couldn't compete with the forces pulling him back to Greenwood. He had debts to repay, ghosts to put to rest, and until he did all of that they couldn't possibly have a future.

Not that she was thinking of a future. The future was dangerous territory, uncharted and littered with the broken hearts of other women wiser than Kate in the ways of love. But somehow that didn't stop them from trying again. She had never been good at living for the moment, but it was time she threw what remained of her caution to the wind and gave it a shot. It was easy to avoid heartbreak if you never fell in love, but that was no way to live.

Leap and the net will appear.

Maybe it would, maybe it wouldn't. It didn't matter. The time had come to make the leap.

* * *

Change was everywhere. You could see it in the greening lawns, the flowering trees, the gardens suddenly blooming with color and life. The landscape seemed to change on a daily basis as spring finally hit its stride, and so, it seemed, did the landscape of Mark's life.

Spring was supposed to be about renewal, but this year spring was about good-byes and those good-byes were starting to take their toll on him. His New Jersey roots had grown deeper than he'd been willing to admit; transplanting them to New Hampshire wasn't going to be the easy, painless transition he had envisioned when the vestry first approached him about coming back to Greenwood. Catherine's words had hit their mark. He wasn't the same man who had left Greenwood in search of recovery. He wasn't the same man who was content being rector of a small-town parish, raising his kids where he had been raised, growing old with his wife with grandkids and great-grands sprouting around them like dandelions.

Those dreams were dead, but new dreams had shaken off the ashes and managed to flourish when he wasn't looking.

There was a place for him here, a good place, but the timing was all wrong. Two months ago he had looked upon his return to Greenwood as both repayment of an old debt and a sweet challenge. One year or five, it didn't matter. He would follow where it led.

But that was before God decided to send Kate into his life and turn everything upside down.

She was waiting for him on the front porch. Her hair was scraped back in a ponytail. She wore jeans and a bright red sweater and old sneakers that had clearly been around a few years. She jumped up at the sound of the Honda and waved at him, and he nearly drove into the rose bushes at the look of joy on her face. He'd stopped asking himself whether he deserved this unexpected happiness. Only God knew the answer to that, and He wasn't saying.

She ran across the yard and jumped into the car. "Maeve's gone, my tests were perfect, and I've decided the next two weeks belong to us."

"You're not working mornings at the shop?"

"Shop?" She widened her eyes. "What shop?"

Except for Charlotte, his days were free and clear.

"Spring Lake," he said, as a huge smile spread across his face. "I could use a cheeseburger."

She gave him a look. "Ever had your cholesterol checked?"

He started to laugh. "Been to church lately?"

"I'll forget the cholesterol if you forget the church." She started to laugh. "Deal?"

"Deal."

The truth was, nothing was off-limits between them. No topic was too sensitive, too awkward, or too personal. They had talked about their families, their marriages. The future was the only thing they didn't talk about. By tacit agreement, they had stopped acknowledging the fact that their time together had an expiration date, and had started living in the now.

The rain started as they reached the highway and was coming down steady and hard by the time they exited at Spring Lake.

"Springtime in New Jersey," Kate said as they found parking a few blocks away from the luncheonette. "Welcome to the Dark Side."

"There's probably an umbrella in here somewhere." He dug around in the backseat but could only come up with a copy of the *Book of Common Prayer*, Sunday's *Newark Star-Ledger*, three roofing tiles, a box of nails, and an impressive assortment of wrappers from every fast-food place in the state.

"You like McDonald's?" she asked, eyeing the wrappers.

"You've got a problem with McDonald's?"

"I saw one just outside town. Why don't we use the drive-through?"

"Mickey D's isn't much on ambience."

"That's why they call it takeout," she said with mock patience. "We'll take it out to the beach and eat in the car."

Fifteen minutes later they were parked in the lot facing the ocean, cocooned by rain and fog and the steam rising off his Big Mac with fries.

"I'm impressed," he said, gesturing toward her Chicken Caesar. "I wouldn't have had the willpower."

"Sure you would," she said, spearing a piece of romaine with the tines of her white plastic fork. "You had the willpower to give up drinking, didn't you? That impresses me."

"One day at a time," he said. "That's about as much as I can control."

"When you come down to it, that's about as much as any of us can control."

"God wants us to live in the now."

She put down her fork. "That's assuming God asks anything of us."

"So you're an agnostic?"

"I don't know."

They both laughed at the irony of the statement.

"I believe in something, some force, but I don't know exactly what to call it."

"I wasn't going to bring up religion again, but it's part of me." It colored his thinking, his actions, his daily life.

"That's okay," she said. "This gives me the right to deliver one free cholesterol lecture at a time and place of my choice."

"Reality's starting to make inroads, isn't it?" He popped a fry into his mouth.

"I noticed," she said, pushing aside a crouton in favor of a piece of chicken. "I hate when that happens."

Suddenly the rain stopped. The clouds lifted. The sun—well, the sun gave it its best shot. And just like that, reality bit the dust.

"Are you game?" he asked as he gathered up their wrappers and tossed them into the backseat with their brethren.

She flung open the passenger-side door and jumped out. "Try and stop me."

It was like walking through oatmeal. They squished, slid, sank, and laughed as they struggled down to the shoreline.

"Whose bright idea was this?" Kate demanded in her best *Sopranos* Jersey Girl imitation. "What were you thinking?"

"Hey, you saw the rain," he said. "Rain plus sand equals mud."

"A wiseguy in a clerical collar. We should pitch the idea to HBO."

"An Episcopalian mob movie? Sounds like a winner to me."

They held hands as they walked along, batting increasingly silly ideas back and forth, until they were laughing so hard and so loud that they had to stop and hang on to each other for support.

Her body was warm and soft against his. Her hair smelled like flowers and sunshine. Their laughter made a quick shift into something sharper, something that felt a lot like desire.

Reality was massing right beyond the perimeter and it was up to him to keep it at bay as long as he could.

* * *

Three visits to Spring Lake. One drive to the Poconos. A long kiss-filled afternoon at the movies.

Nine days and counting.

She didn't invite him to stay the night and he didn't ask. Their good-night kisses were prolonged and painfully exciting, but she kept the door closed between them and refused to ask herself why.

They rode the train into Manhattan and spent the day wandering through museums and enjoying Central Park.

They drove into Philadelphia to visit Independence Hall and the Liberty Bell.

They went to a good-bye party at Scott and Marcy's house, shared tea and cookies with Charlotte Petruzzo, met Gwynn and Andy for linguine with clam sauce at a little Italian restaurant in Asbury Park.

Three days and counting.

The morning before Mark's house sale closed, they went to Professor Armitage's house to sign a consent form for the documents to be shipped to another expert in Boston. Maeve, looking radiant and happy in a crimson silk wrapper, opened the door. She kissed them both and ushered them into the dim foyer.

It was one thing to know that your mother was dating a

notoriously foul-tempered history professor. It was another to see her rosy in the afterglow of love.

"Chester has a class this morning. He asked if I minded staying around until you came by." She gave both of them a big hug. "As if I'd mind seeing you two!"

Kate made a show of checking out her mother's state of dishabille. "Should I start calling him Daddy?"

Maeve threw back her head and laughed. "We're not at that point yet," she said, "but I wouldn't rule it out."

"The eternal optimist," Kate said. "I don't know how you do it."

"I believe love is possible," her mother said, "even if sometimes the signs point to the contrary."

"Don't pay any attention to her," Kate said to Mark, pretending to cover his ears with her hands. "My mother owns property in Fantasyland."

"Life is short," Maeve said. "If you're lucky enough to have a choice, why not choose happiness?"

Kate and Mark exchanged looks as Maeve went in search of the letter of permission that needed Kate's signature.

Choose happiness.

It sounded so simple when Maeve said it. Given a choice, who wouldn't choose to be happy?

So why was it so hard to do?

Maeve got a little weepy when they said good-bye. She hugged Mark hard and kissed him on the cheek, rubbing the red lipstick smudge away with the pad of her thumb. "Words can't possibly express my gratitude to you," she said, "or my affection."

Kate, who hadn't had a crying episode for almost four days, wept all the way down the front steps, across the yard, and down the driveway to her Miata.

"I really thought I was over this," she said as she

wiped her eyes with a paper napkin. "Leave it to Maeve to turn me back into a crying machine."

They stopped for lunch at a health-food restaurant in Princeton, and for the first time they didn't talk much at all. She wasn't sure if it was her mother's words that had triggered the descent into silence or the fact that very soon they would be saying good-bye.

But there was no denying the fact that they had finally run out of words.

* * *

The closing on Mark's house was set for two p.m. at his lawyer's office in Plainsboro. The Wygrens and Bev the real estate agent showed up at noon for the walk-through as Mark finished packing the last of his things into the U-Haul attached to the back of his Honda. Most of his furniture had been thrift-shop finds that he had donated to a women's shelter in town. The remaining few pieces he offered to the Wygrens, who had gratefully accepted them. Papers were signed. Checks were written. People shook hands and wished each other well.

At five p.m. he handed over the keys to the happy couple and headed north on Route 1. His original plan had included a quick bite to eat and then driving straight through to New Hampshire with two days to spare before he was set to take over.

But that was before Kate.

Choose happiness, Maeve had said, but he wasn't sure he remembered how.

* * *

They tried, they really did, but it was hard to relax and enjoy the dinner Kate had prepared for them with that pink elephant sitting in the middle of the room.

Their time together was running out and instead of savoring every minute, every second, they were acting as if they couldn't wait for it to be over.

When had they become so ill at ease with each other? Kate wondered as they carried their plates into the kitchen and loaded the dishwasher. Their easy camaraderie, the almost otherworldly sense of connection—how could it vanish overnight?

The doctor had warned her that this would happen. One morning she would wake up to find that while she was sleeping life had resumed its normal dimensions. All of those beautiful Technicolor emotions would have muted into pastel and it would be as if the heart attack and the weeks that followed had happened to somebody else.

She just hadn't expected it to happen now, when their time was running out.

The funny thing was that her emotions were still vivid Technicolor reds and blues and greens, sparkling golds and shimmering silvers. Mark was the one who had changed.

He seemed distant, almost a stranger, and she sleep-walked through the motions of making coffee, serving dessert, like a robot in a bad science fiction movie.

By ten o'clock they had run out of things to say to each other. The dishes were neatly stacked in the dishwasher. The pots were scrubbed and put away. The candles on the table outside had been extinguished, and so it seemed had the last flicker of warmth between them.

When he stood up to say good night, she heard his words before he uttered them. His house was sold. He'd said all of his good-byes. Why spend the night in a motel when he could spend it on the road and be in Greenwood by daylight?

Just because he'd saved her life didn't mean she was entitled to the rest of his.

"It's late," he said. "I should—"

Choose happiness . . . choose happiness . . .

"Stay." She reached out and took his hand. "You should stay with me tonight."

Now the choice was his.

Twenty-two

They never made it beyond the hallway. The words had barely escaped Kate's mouth when they crashed together in a clumsy, ardent, wild explosion of heat and longing that stripped them both of everything but the need to touch and be touched.

Her hands slid under his sweater. His fingers unbuttoned her shirt. The shock of flesh against flesh was painful, sweet, breathtakingly erotic.

They undressed each other clumsily, hungrily, never taking their eyes off each other. Sweater, shirt, jeans, skirt, shoes, everything piled together on the floor. Forgotten like the world beyond the front door.

They kissed with eyes wide open, intimate, probing, with nothing held back. They brought everything they were to the moment, all of their hopes and dreams and disappointments.

They dropped to their knees, half on the rag rug, half on the polished oak floor, then fell the rest of the way, limbs entwined. He rolled over onto his back, pulling her on top of him.

For a second she froze, suddenly aware of where she was, the man she was with, the enormity of what was about to happen between them. There was nothing casual about it, nothing simple. Her life would never be the same. They would never be the same.

He was big, wonderfully hard. She loved the way he felt pressing against her belly. She loved his broad chest and muscular shoulders, the way his thick dark hair fell across his forehead. She loved the anticipation building between her legs, the way he stroked her with his fingers, long voluptuous strokes that made her wetter and hotter than she had ever been before. She almost came just from the excitement of knowing that any moment he would be inside her while she rode him until they were out of their heads with pleasure.

She leaned over him, breasts brushing against his chest, laughing softly at the tickle of hair against her skin. He found a nipple with his mouth, circling it with his tongue, sucking hard until she cried out from the jolt of electricity that shot through her body at his touch. He gripped her hips and positioned her over his rock-hard erection. He watched her as she lowered herself slowly slowly onto him, watched her as she cried out again from the sheer joy of it, never once took his eyes from her as she leaned back and began to move against him.

They were there together in every way that mattered. Her skin was exquisitely sensitive to the touch. Her mind was an erogenous zone. She was fully there, more completely herself than she had ever been before, and she knew without asking that it was the same for him.

He rolled her onto her back, covering her with the

delicious weight of his body. He was gentle and strong, wild and powerful, everything she had ever wanted in a man.

She wrapped her legs around his waist and he gasped into her mouth, drawn even more deeply into her body. She felt his heat building, caught the flame and fanned it into a raging fire that burned away everything that had come before.

"Wow," she said later, after they had napped in each other's arms. "That wasn't the way I remembered it."

You're in love, Kate. That's the difference.

He pulled her closer and kissed the top of her head. "This is the way it's supposed to be."

Was this how it was with your wife? Was this what you had and lost?

What she had had with Ed didn't come close to this, and now she knew why.

They were wrapped in a soft blanket, curled up together on the lemon-yellow sofa.

"How did we get here?" She glanced around the darkened room. "The last thing I remember was lying on the floor in the hallway."

"Astral projection?"

"Maybe we dreamed the whole thing."

"Don't move." He slid under the blanket toward the end of the couch and threw her legs over his shoulders. She tensed and he murmured soft words against her belly until she sank deeper into the soft cushions. His breath against her heated skin was warm and moist. He drew a line with his tongue from her belly to her navel to the cleft at the top of her thighs and her last bit of resistance vanished at his touch. When he found her center, logic, reason, and sanity vanished along with it.

For the first time in her life, Kate was well and truly lost.

Much later

"Are you hungry?" Kate leaned up on one elbow and smiled at him. "I make a great fake-egg omelet."

She wore nothing but the creamy pink sheet draped around her creamy pink shoulders and if God decided to end things now, Mark would have no regrets. He had already had a glimpse of heaven.

"Fake eggs?" he answered, brushing a lock of shiny auburn hair back from her face. "Should I be afraid?"

"I was at first," she admitted with a roll of her big hazel eyes, "but they're really not too terrible."

"I'll give 'em a try."

"Don't think you're just going to lie here like a sultan awaiting his handmaiden," she said, laughing. "I need a sous chef and you're elected."

"How long have we been up here?"

"A long time," she said as she slipped into a short cotton robe and belted it around her waist. "A *very* long time and I'm *very* hungry."

He sat up and looked across the expanse of bed to the clock on her nightstand. "It's two in the morning."

"Very good," she said, pretending to clap her hands. "Do you know the alphabet too?"

He leaped from the bed before she had the chance to run, tossed her over his shoulder in a fireman's hold, and then carried her downstairs to the kitchen.

He loved her laughter. There was nothing guarded about her laughter. It was slightly bawdy, slightly goofy, completely irresistible. He set her on her feet and she playfully made to swat him with a dish towel.

She put him to work chopping onions and green peppers while she wiped some tiny white mushrooms with a damp towel and sliced them paper-thin.

"I have fake cheese to go with the fake eggs," she said,

"or, if you like, we could add cubes of fake ham or fake turkey."

"You make it sound so . ... edible."

"What can I tell you?" She plucked a container of cholesterol-free spread from the fridge. "Once you have a heart attack, fake becomes the new natural."

She was clearly at ease in the kitchen. She moved from task to task smoothly, keeping up a line of chatter as she did. He was still working on the peppers while she had moved on to setting the table and pouring orange juice into heavy crystal glasses.

The room was a feast for the eyes. A trio of china chickens watched from the top of the refrigerator. A three-foot-high anatomically correct Holstein stood guard at the French doors that opened out into the yard. A spinning wheel in the far corner was draped with bunches of fragrant herbs hung there to dry. Color was everywhere: flowers bloomed where he least expected them in bursts of yellow and orange and cherry red. The counter boasted a pale ivory wicker basket piled high with golden Spanish and eye-popping purple onions. A braid of garlic hung from a peg over the counter near the well-worn wooden block that held her knives.

This was a real working kitchen and he enjoyed watching as she glided effortlessly between tasks.

"Did you toast the muffins?" she asked as she slid the omelet onto a platter.

"Almost," he said. "Where do you keep the jelly?"

"Top shelf." She pointed toward the fridge. "Raspberry preserves, orange marmalade, grape jam."

"Grape jam? No contest."

The omelet was huge, bursting with green peppers, red onion, mushrooms, crushed red peppers, and herbs. She served it on one enormous platter and was about to divide it onto two separate plates when they looked at each other and started to laugh.

"Grab a fork," she said. "I'll start on the right side. You start on the left. We'll meet in the middle."

They toasted each other with orange juice. He slathered the crispy muffins with jam and fed her bites with his fingers. They polished off the omelet, toasted an extra muffin, and washed everything down with a big pot of herbal tea.

By the time they loaded the dishwasher, the sun was coming up and they stumbled upstairs and fell into bed.

"Do you have a favorite side?" she asked around a yawn.

"The side next to you," he said.

And then they slept.

* * *

TO: maevefrench@threewishes.net
CC: gwynnbann@njshorefun.net
FROM: kate@frenchkiss.biz
SUBJECT: FYI

I'm fine. The cell's turned off. DON'T WORRY! Mark leaves on Saturday. I'll call you Sunday, ok? XOXOX-OXO

* * *

Sometimes the best thing you can do is lock out the world.

Kate's home became their sanctuary, their hiding place from the reality that was waiting right outside the door. Being together was the only reality that mattered. They slept, made love, ate, laughed, and talked and never once looked at a clock, but time was slipping away from them just the same.

In some ways it was probably too easy. Too perfect. There was no period of adjustment. The sex was both sweet and incendiary, intensifying a connection that seemed to run straight to the center of their souls. Their habits meshed perfectly. She liked the window side of the bed, while he preferred being closer to the door. They were open and at ease with each other. She didn't feel as if he had invaded her home. He never felt anything but welcome.

He had spent years blaming God for Suzanne's death and the ruin his life had become, but there with Kate in his arms, he was finally able to see where the journey had been headed all along. He was finally at peace.

If only it didn't have to end in less than seven hours.

They were curled up on her squashy yellow sofa eating ice cream and watching a *Sopranos* rerun, both trying to ignore the fact that by this time tomorrow their idyll would be over. *The Sopranos* turned into *Sex and the City*, which became *Entourage*. Neither one noticed. They were lost in a world of their own creation.

"I want you to do something for me, Kate," he said as they slowly climbed the stairs to her bedroom.

She would do anything for him. Didn't he know that by now?

He didn't want to say good-bye. When it was time to leave in the morning, he would just leave. No tearful good-bye in the driveway. No Lifetime for Women drama on the front porch. Anything that needed to be said they would say in her bed, with their bodies and with their hearts.

Moonlight streamed through the open window and pooled on the floor near the bed. A gentle breeze ruffled the curtains. Spring in all of her painful beauty managed to work her magic even in the dark.

Too bad spring didn't have any magic up her sleeve that could make paradise last a little bit longer.

* * *

Kate awoke to the sound of a car in her driveway. She stretched and buried her face deeper into her pillow. The mail carrier, most likely. Or maybe UPS. It didn't matter. They were part of the real world and the real world didn't exist here in paradise.

She opened one eye and peered across the bed. His side was empty. He had said this was the way he would do it and, true to form, he hadn't lied.

She leaped up, wrapped the pale yellow sheet around her, and dashed to the window in time to see the beat-up Honda moving slowly down Indigo Lane.

Six weeks from beginning to end, like the story arc on a prime-time television show. They meet. They fall into something that may or may not be love. They part. You turn off your television set and move on to the next thing while the fictional stars of the romance live on in some happily-ever-after dreamworld.

Reality wasn't what it was cracked up to be.

She sat near the window for a long time. It wasn't that she expected him to turn around and come roaring back up Indigo, so much in love with her that he would turn away from his dreams and responsibilities to be with her forever. She didn't know what she expected, but this flat echoing emptiness inside her heart couldn't possibly be all that remained of the happiest weeks of her entire life.

If only she could cry. For weeks she had been able to weep buckets of tears over parking spots, baby ducks, the theme song from *Cheers*, but now she was desert dry.

They were two consenting adults who had known where they were headed from the first moment they met. So why did it feel like a surprise? She felt as if fate had pulled a fast one on her, shown her a glimpse of what life could be like, how love could feel, and then snatched it away from her the second she began to believe it could last.

Had she really believed he was going to abandon his plans, the people he cared about, to stay in New Jersey with a divorced agnostic he barely knew? That wasn't the way things worked, and the old Kate, the pre-Mark Kate, understood that better than most.

Follow your heart, they all said. Life is short. What are you waiting for? Choose happiness. The advice was the same whether it came from Maeve or Charlotte Petruzzo. It sounded wonderful and maybe there really were romantic souls out there who could do exactly that but apparently, for very different reasons, she and the good Father weren't among their number.

She had already experienced more happiness in a shorter period of time than she'd ever expected to feel in her life. She should be happy with that and move on.

Same as he had.

*　*　*

He made good time through New Jersey, crossed the Tappan Zee around eight o'clock, then barreled north on the New England Thruway. Around ten-thirty he pulled off the road in search of an Egg McMuffin and cell reception.

She picked up on the first ring.

"Did I wake you?" He knew what she looked like when she slept, how she sounded and smelled.

"I heard you leave," she said. "I kept hoping you would turn back."

"I wanted to." He cradled the phone closer to his ear and tried to block out the traffic noise all around him. "I almost turned around."

"I wish you had."

"I wish—" There was no point to any of it. The next year belonged to the good parishioners of St. Stephen's, and after that it was anybody's guess.

"Finish the sentence."

"I wish things could have been different."

"I wish we'd met ten years ago," she said and he heard her sharp intake of breath as she realized exactly what she was saying. "I'm sorry. I didn't mean to—"

"I know." She had done the math. If Suzanne had lived, they wouldn't be having this conversation. If her marriage hadn't fallen apart . . . if he hadn't started driving . . . moved to New Jersey . . . if God hadn't put them in that Princeton parking lot on that sunny morning—

"I miss you," he said.

"It's only been a few hours." She tried to laugh but the sound was false and strained. Then, "I miss you too."

"Three hundred miles isn't so much."

"Of course it isn't," she said. "Just a long commute."

"We'll figure this out, Kate."

"I know we will."

What they didn't know was how.

Twenty-three

French Kiss—two weeks later

"Are you sure you're okay?" Sonia whispered to Kate as they finished unpacking a shipment of eighteenth-century salt cellars from an estate sale in Virginia.

"I really wish people would stop asking me that question," Kate said, popping her thumb along a strip of bubble wrap. "Blood pressure, EKG, CBC, everything's just fine."

"That's wonderful," Sonia said, "but that's not what I'm talking about." She paused a second, but Kate refused to fill the silence with information. "Have you heard from him?"

"I had an e-mail just last night." A hurried note long on work minutiae and short on sentiment. A fine point the old Kate wouldn't have noticed.

"And you've talked on the phone?"

"What is this, the Second Inquisition? Of course we've talked. Would you like me to bring in the tapes?"

"So when are you going to see him?"

"Sonia, really. Now you're going too far."

"It's important," Sonia said. "Don't believe absence makes the heart grow fonder. The only thing absence does is screw up a good thing."

Kate excused herself and stepped out onto the back porch so her assistant wouldn't see her cry. Better Sonia thought she was annoyed than for Kate to admit to the world that she missed Mark so much that each day without him felt like a lifetime.

He had phoned her twenty-three times that first day, pulling over at every rest stop between New Jersey and New Hampshire to hear the sound of her voice. He had left no doubt about the way he felt.

And Kate hadn't made the slightest attempt to shield her heart from danger. When he turned on his laptop that first night to download his e-mail, she had made sure there were twelve silly animated greetings waiting for him and four long mushy high-school-girl-in-the-throes-of-first-love letters.

Those first few days apart had been excruciatingly lonely and so painfully sweetly romantic that she finally understood the crazy things women and men did in the name of love.

Like believe that a lapsed Catholic in New Jersey and an Episcopal priest from New Hampshire have a chance in hell?

Geography, religion, and life experience were all stacked against them, and that was just for starters. He was deeply committed to his responsibilities in New Hampshire. Her roots extended deep and wide in the fertile soil of the Garden State. Long-distance relationships worked for some couples, but she knew in her heart that she and Mark weren't one of them. She missed the dailiness of their time together. The phone calls, the quick trips down the shore, watching him talking to Maeve at the kitchen table.

Extreme circumstances begot extreme reactions. She had a heart attack and he saved her life. It didn't get much more emotionally extreme than that. Was it any wonder that they had been drawn together?

Of course that didn't explain the heat, the need, the deep well of affection and respect and understanding that in the real world, her old world, took years to build. If you ever found it at all.

Sonia was right. A year was a very long time. And a year in a brand-new relationship was longer still. Maybe young love thrived on separation, but it had taken her forty-one years to discover what falling in love was all about, and it would have been wonderful if the object of her affections weren't three hundred miles away rebuilding a life that had nothing to do with her.

Greenwood, New Hampshire

"You've been here three weeks," Maggy said, "and you're still staying at the Motel 6. That's really not acceptable for the rector of St. Stephen's. People are starting to talk, pal."

Mark made a left on Sprucewood and headed toward the open-house flags waving at the end of the block. "I've looked at a lot of places, Maggy, but I haven't found the right one yet."

"You're worse than a girl," Maggy said with a roll of her eyes. "This isn't New Jersey. We're not all about choice. We have ranches and we have shacks. Pick one and get it over with."

The one on Sprucewood wasn't right. Neither were the ones on Drake, Fremont, and Garretson.

"This is a small town," Maggy reminded him over coffee at the Pancake Platter. "There's just so much available. You'll have to settle like the rest of us."

"I can look in Bedford."

"No, you can't. You're the rector of a small-town parish. You have to live in the same small town as your parishioners."

"That wasn't in the contract."

"It would have been if we'd had any idea you were thinking of looking in Bedford." She leaned across the table. "What's the problem, Mark? I know how you feel about living in the rectory, but it's beginning to look like you feel that way about the whole town."

"That's not true."

"Then convince me I'm wrong."

"Most of the places were too big. I don't need three bedrooms and a family room."

"The one on Marcotte was a two-bedroom with a workshop in the garage. What was wrong with that one?"

"Nothing," he admitted.

"So why didn't you make an offer?"

"What do you want from me, Maggy? I haven't found the right place yet."

"Okay," she said, leaning back against the bench seat. "Don't tell me. But if you're afraid I'm going to tell Sam your secrets, I swear I won't. Just because Sammy and I are engaged doesn't mean I'm going to betray a confidence. I'll put your secrets in the vault, same as I always have."

He didn't say anything.

"That's a *Seinfeld* reference," she said.

He really needed to watch more TV.

"It's about that woman, isn't it?"

It was and it wasn't, but romance was the safer conversational road to follow with Maggy.

"I thought I was covering up pretty well."

"Not to me."

"It's been a long time since I've felt this way, Mags, but I don't know if she feels the same about me."

"Did you ask her?"

He shook his head.

"What did she say when you told her how you felt?"

"I haven't told her."

"You haven't told her that you're in love with her?"

"No."

"Then you're a bigger jerk than I thought."

"Would you talk to Father Billy like that?" Billy Owens was still awaiting an assignment to a church of his own. In the meantime the young cleric had been helping Mark get settled and, as a result, growing even more popular (and indispensable) by the day.

"If he were a jerk, you bet I would."

"The right house will come along," he said. "I'm not in a rush."

"I know," Maggy said. "I'm just afraid the right house is in New Jersey."

* * *

TO: mark.kerry@mklj.net
FROM: kate@frenchkiss.biz
SUBJECT: big news

I tried your cell phone but was flipped to voice mail so here I am.

I really wanted to tell you in person (okay, voice to voice) but I can't hold it in a second longer.

Gwynn is pregnant! She told me today over lunch and it was one of those times when I wished I was still a practicing Catholic because I needed all the help I could get to keep a big smile on my face. Of course I'm happy that she's happy. (She and Andrew were beaming like the couple on top of a wedding cake.) But she has no idea the responsibility she's taking on and there's no way I can tell her that she'll understand. I guess we all make our own choices, don't we?

Ed and I spoke about it for a long time this evening. He's feeling as overwhelmed as I am. Not at the thought of being a grandparent (although 41 does seem young to me) but at the memories this is digging up. I always thought my pregnancy was a "mistake" but I can see now (hindsight being what it invariably is) that there was no mistake involved in it at all. I wanted a family. I wanted a steady, dependable home life. And I knew somehow (even at that tender age) that Ed could provide all of that. Love, real love, never entered into it. I saw a chance to create my own stable home and I made it happen. No regrets, though. We have a beautiful daughter, a grandchild on the way, and a sustaining friendship to show for it. But I can't help hoping it's more than that for Gwynn. I'm hoping she's found love.

The baby is due in late January so they've decided to move up the wedding from next spring to September 15th. Gwynnie wants to know if you could possibly come down to officiate at the ceremony. She ~~feels like you're part of the family~~ thinks so highly of you.

Did you find a place to live yet? I checked out Realtor.com and was surprised how high the prices are. No wonder you're having so much trouble.

Professor Armitage (Chester to his intimates . . .) put me in touch with John at Christie's and John thinks I'll see somewhere in the low six figures for the collection. I've decided to follow through on the idea I told you about and use the money (assuming there is any, fingers crossed) to buy a house for Gwynn and Andy

(and the baby). What do you think? I don't want to em-
barrass either one of them (esp. A) but the inheritance
from the senator's son changed my life. I'd like to do
the same for Gwynn but while I'm still alive! I'd appreciate any advice.

Hope you're well. ~~I miss you so much I think my heart
is going to break in two~~. Talk to you soon.
PS: I visited Charlotte Petruzzo yesterday. We shared
tea and conversation. She sends her love.

Mark leaned back against the motel headboard and
read the e-mail a second time. It didn't read like Kate. It
was chatty, sure, but the warmth, the depth of affection
he'd grown accustomed to, was missing.

Hope you're well. That was the way you talked to a
business acquaintance or the cousin you hadn't seen in
twenty years. You didn't say it to the man who'd shared
your bed and, he'd believed, your heart.

He'd been warned. He couldn't say he hadn't been.
This isn't the real me. The "life is beautiful" syndrome
would run its course in time, but that didn't mean they
couldn't have a future together.

He had repeated that mantra over and over again as he
crossed the states between New Jersey and New Hampshire and now, for the first time, he wasn't sure he believed it any longer.

Worse than that, he wasn't sure she believed it.

They weren't twentysomething kids with clean slates
who crashed into each other like a pair of guided mis-
siles. They brought the full measure of their life experience with them. You didn't check the last twenty years of
your life at the door when you met someone. That wasn't
the way things worked.

She had a mother and daughter in New Jersey, a wedding to help plan, and a grandchild on the way. She had a successful store in a town where she was loved and respected, a town that was her home in every sense of the word.

You didn't ask a woman like that to throw it all away to follow a widowed Episcopal priest to a place where he didn't belong in the first place. She had a great life. She didn't need his complications, his responsibilities, his mistakes.

A better man would let her go. It would be easy to do. Geography had already done part of the job for him. And if what he suspected was true, the return of the real Kate was doing the rest.

That was what a better man than he would do.

He, however, asked her up to Greenwood for the holiday weekend because he was a priest and priests believed in miracles.

TO: kate@frenchkiss.biz
FROM: mark.kerry@mklj.net
SUBJECT: RE: big news

I'd call but it's too late. I was out looking at more houses, then had to make an emergency hospital call. Sarah Spruell has been fighting cancer for six years. They thought she had it beat but it's back and winning the battle. I'm typing this from a machine at the nurses' station (using Web mail, in case you're wondering) and watching Sarah's husband and kids as they keep vigil. The doctor told them it might be a few days but I think he's wrong. I think it's going to be tonight and I'm hoping that I'll be able to find the right words.

I read your news about Gwynn and said a prayer for her and Andrew and the baby. I have a good feeling

about them. You did a fine job with Gwynn, and Andrew's a good man. Let me think about your house
idea. There's a way to do it without tipping the balance
of family power. You'd figure it out without me but I'm
glad to help.

We could talk about it on the Fourth of July weekend.
The town is celebrating its 300th anniversary and we're
marking it with a barbecue and fireworks festival. It's
not a bad drive (seven hours) and I guarantee great
food and company.

~~I see you everywhere, Kate. I hear your voice. I can still
taste you.~~
The Chinese food's better in New Jersey. Consider
yourself warned.
M K
PS: I spoke to Charlotte this morning. Your visit worked
wonders.

* * * * * *

M K?

Kate leaned closer to the screen and read the e-mail
twice.

M K??

No love. No sense that they had shared anything more
than friendship. He didn't even sound like a good friend,
just a friendly acquaintance with an extra room to let for
the holiday weekend.

This was what she got for going where sane women
feared to tread. A polite invitation from a man whose own

basic sense of decency required that they end things properly and not just let the three hundred miles between them do it for him. One trip to New Hampshire and she would see for herself that it could never work.

Besides, no good could possibly come from an involvement between a lapsed Catholic and an Episcopal priest. You didn't have to believe in a higher power to see disaster written all over it.

Maybe the thing to do was accept it for what it was—six weeks of paradise—and then let it go before her battered heart suffered a blow it couldn't bounce back from.

She wished with all her heart that she could still cry.

Kate's house—the last day of June

"Mom's not going, is she?" Gwynn dipped a fresh, fat strawberry into a bowl of nonfat whipped cream and popped it into her mouth. "How could anyone say no to Father Mark's invitation?"

Maeve, who was making short work of the real whipped cream, nodded. "Mark has invited her into his world. This is the next part of their journey. Of course she's not going. That would be putting herself out there, and we know Kate doesn't do that."

Kate, who had been toying with her iced tea spoon, let out a primal shriek that stopped the conversation cold. "Quit talking about me like I'm not here."

"Fine," Maeve said, turning to look at her. "Kate, we're terribly disappointed in you."

"Totally," Gwynn agreed. "We would've driven up there with you if you'd said yes."

"Thanks for the offer, ladies, but we're having a big sidewalk sale that weekend at the shop. I can't spare the time."

She hadn't realized her mother and daughter used language like that.

"Tell me how you really feel," she mumbled into her iced tea.

"You're making a terrible mistake," Gwynn said. "True love is a once-in-a-lifetime thing."

Clearly Gwynn's hormones were doing things to her judgment.

"He's putting himself out there," Maeve said. "He's inviting you to see him in his own milieu, to meet his congregation. What kind of signal are you sending him by saying no?"

"You're reading too much into this invitation."

"What else can it possibly mean?" her mother demanded. "He wants to continue the relationship."

"Or end it."

Her mother and daughter exchanged glances.

"Besides, I already told him I couldn't make it."

"You did what!?" Maeve and Gwynn shrieked in unison.

Oh God. And here she had thought she was over the crying jags. "We never talked about a future, okay? We never once mentioned anything about what we were going to do after he went back to New Hampshire." Except for the joke about the three-hundred-mile commute, the topic was still unexplored.

"So now he *is* talking about it." Her mother was relentless. "What are you afraid of, honey? That it might not work out the way you hope?"

"We were living in the present. Not the past. Not the future. Isn't that what you've been trying to get me to do?"

"I've been trying to get you to let go and be happy, and this isn't the way."

"I'm not having this conversation." She pushed back from the table and stood up. "I'm going to load the dishwasher."

Gwynn looked up at her with her huge weepy eyes. "You were so happy with Father Mark," she said, her beautiful and foolish pregnant daughter. "I was so hoping you two could make it work."

"Maybe he wasn't so happy with me." She stopped cold. "What do I know? He has a life up there, ladies. I knew that from the beginning and I'm okay with it." Who would have known she was such a good liar?

"And he wants you to be part of his life," Gwynn said, waving the printout of his e-mail. "Why else would he invite you up there?"

"Reread that note, darling daughter," Kate said. "He wants me to be part of a barbecue." She started toward the door. "It doesn't matter anyway. Like I said, I told him I'm not going."

"Who is this woman?" Maeve said to Gwynn. "I can't believe she's one of us."

"I don't know," a sniffling Gwynn said mournfully. "It just makes me so sad . . ."

A little more than twelve weeks after her cardiac incident and everything was officially back to normal. Once again it was Maeve and Gwynn on one side of the romantic divide and Kate on the other.

Alone.

Greenwood, New Hampshire—July 2

Mark was at the computer, trying to make sense of the church budget. There was talk of implementing a day care center in the Sunday school space, but projects like that took a commitment of money as well as time. He was trying to determine how much they would need, how much they already had, how much more they would have to raise in order to turn the idea into reality.

So far he had been staring at the screen and getting

nowhere. He'd been back at St. Stephen's for more than a month now, and he still hadn't managed to settle into anything that approximated a normal routine.

His heart, it seemed, was still in New Jersey with Kate.

He missed her. His life seemed incomplete without her, as if he had left an essential piece of his soul in her keeping. He had been sleepwalking since his arrival in Greenwood, going through the motions the best he could but not truly connecting with the process.

The plain truth was, he didn't belong there anymore. He knew it and, unless he missed his guess, everyone in town had figured it out by now too. Bishop Clennon would probably get an earful when he returned from his trip to California. Even the good people at Motel 6 were beginning to talk.

He still loved the town and its people. The memories he had of life as the rector of St. Stephen's were sweet ones, but they belonged to the past. His life had changed and so had his interests, his skills; those skills had found a better fit in New Jersey.

It felt good to be able to say that and feel its truth inside his bones.

His first day back he had driven up the mountain to the cemetery where Suzanne lay buried next to her father and grandparents and he finally said good-bye. It had taken him five years to reach this point, and it felt right. Suzanne would live on in his heart forever but the time had come to move on.

He was pretty sure God still had a plan for him, but he was having trouble figuring out what that plan was.

He was three hundred miles away from the woman he loved, mired in the first month of a one-year contract with his old home parish, living in a Motel 6 off the highway on fast food and regrets.

When had New Jersey turned into the center of his universe?

Why hadn't he told her he loved her? Why hadn't he thrown a lifeline into the future, something they could both hang on to until they were able to be together? He hadn't a clue what she was thinking right now. Her e-mails were opaque. He couldn't see through them to the warm-blooded woman he had held in his arms.

She had turned down his invitation to spend the Fourth of July holiday with him. Her voice-mail message gave him no clues at all.

Thanks for the invitation, Mark. I wish I could drive up for the celebration but we're having a store event that weekend and I need to stay in town. Sorry we missed each other. Talk to you soon.

He had it memorized. The words. The tone of voice. The distance between them that couldn't be measured in miles.

"Father Mark."

He looked up and saw Billy Owens, the young cleric, standing in the open doorway.

"Can I come in?"

"Sure thing." He took off his glasses and tossed them down on the desk. Just looking at the guy made him feel ten years older than the number on his driver's license. He pointed toward the chair adjacent to his desk. "Make yourself comfortable."

Billy took note of the church ledgers stacked on the floor next to his chair. "The day care project?"

"I'm trying to see if there's some way we can close the gap between what we have and what we need."

Billy looked like a kid wearing a priest costume on Halloween. He had a thick shock of red hair, bright blue eyes behind a pair of plain black eyeglasses, and an infectious smile. He also had a sharp intellect and an almost intuitive understanding of human nature that made people open up before they had a chance to duck behind their defenses.

"You probably already thought of this," Billy said, "but there must be surplus from the tower restoration project a few years ago."

"Tower restoration?"

He had to hand it to the kid. In his shoes, Mark doubted he would've been able to keep from gloating.

"They put it together while you were gone," Billy said easily. "Bring up the projected budget for two thousand three. It should be there." Billy explained that the vestry had also agreed that the church bell was in dire need of repair and had decided to have it lowered and then shipped to a man in Georgia who specialized in the arcane art of repairing cracked church bells.

"Run that by me again," Mark said. "It cost *how* much?"

The figure didn't sound any more sane the second time around.

"The man died," Billy said, "and the job was cancelled. The bell is in storage and the money is there waiting to be put to good use."

He found himself impressed again by Billy Owens's selflessness. "Would you be interested in heading the committee I'm putting together to push the day care idea forward?"

"Actually that's sort of what I want to talk to you about. I've been offered a pulpit in Missouri. A small church with a growing congregation in a suburb of Kansas City. I spoke to Marianne about it, and while she'd rather stay here too, we both feel it's an opportunity that we can't ignore."

An idea began to take shape in the back of Mark's mind. "I think I can speak for everyone in town when I say we don't want to lose you."

"And I don't want to be lost, but our savings are pretty

well depleted at this point. We have three kids and this offer has come along at the right time."

"When do they need an answer?"

"I said I'd let them know after the Fourth of July
weekend but I don't see much point to waiting."

Mark was silent for a while. "You wanted the pulpit
here at St. Stephen's, didn't you?"

Father Billy nodded. "I fought the good fight, but the
best man won."

Mark looked at the young man and smiled. "I'm not so
sure of that."

Pinecrest Village

"Looks like you're ready for the Fourth around here,"
Kate said as she kissed Charlotte on both cheeks. "Uncle
Sam is manning the reception desk out front."

"That's Kenny Gruenwald," Charlotte said with a laugh.
"He was John Raitt's understudy in *The Pajama Game*
years ago. If I'm still here at Christmas, you can catch his
Christmas show."

The words *Of course you'll still be here* wanted to pop
out, but Kate knew better. Charlotte was long since past the
need for empty reassurance. She had somehow learned
the secret of enjoying every day and not worrying about
the clouds gathering on the horizon.

"Let me see you." Charlotte motioned for Kate to turn
around.

"This is a great dress, isn't it?" Kate pirouetted. "I've
had it for years but—"

"You look terrible."

"I knew it was too young for me. I'm going to be a
grandmother. I probably should pass this on to Gwynn
and—"

"What's wrong?" Charlotte demanded. "Have you seen

your doctor? Have that overpaid son of a seacook run some tests. Make him earn his money. Are you nauseated? Are you having any pain?"

"I'm fine," she said, faking a laugh. "Although I'm not too crazy about hearing how terrible I look."

Charlotte considered her long and hard. "I thought you would be on your way to New Hampshire by now."

"I thought I told you I wasn't going."

Charlotte shook her head. Her sparkly chandelier earrings brushed her fragile shoulders. "You didn't tell me. Father Mark told me when he phoned yesterday."

"Oh."

"Oh, indeed." Charlotte's look could only be described as imperious. "I'm disappointed. I thought you were your mother's daughter."

Kate's eyes widened. "You know my mother?"

"We all know your mother. She spoke at our Living the Good Life Longer Festival two years ago." The imperious expression on her face grew downright saucy. "If only she'd shown up when I was in my eighties and Tony Biondino was still alive . . ." She sighed lustily. "I would have shown him a thing or two."

Kate poured them each some juice from the carafe on the side table. "Maeve is definitely memorable."

"You sound disapproving."

"Not at all. I'm all in favor of living life to the fullest."

"Well, then, dear Kate, why aren't you doing it?"

She sat up a little straighter. "I think I am."

"I don't think you are."

"And, with all due respect, Charlotte, I don't think you know me well enough to pass that judgment."

"I know a coward when I see one."

Had Charlotte been thirty years younger, Kate would have walked out. Unfortunately she had been raised to respect her elders and so, seething, she stayed where she was.

"I resent that statement," she said with as much restraint as she could muster.

"You would have no need of resentment if you were on the road to New Hampshire."

"Charlotte, I'm not sure what you think you know about Mark and me, but what happened between us is nobody's business but ours. I appreciate your concern, but you don't know what you're talking about."

"The world changes, young lady, but people don't. You may think you're the first woman to experience love but you're just one in a long, long line that started with Eve." She leaned back against her pillow and closed her eyes and for a moment Kate was afraid something terrible had happened, but then Charlotte's eyelids snapped open and she was a young woman again, a woman who was willing to do whatever it took to be with the man she loved.

"My George worked for a British firm and he was being sent to Hong Kong. He asked me to marry him but I hesitated. I couldn't imagine leaving behind all of the new freedoms and opportunities, so when he left, he left alone."

Kate listened as Charlotte spun out the story. Charlotte and George corresponded for months. He was an ardent, persistent suitor but then one day a letter arrived that seemed different to her. Charlotte sensed that maybe she had waited too long, that her reluctance had been perceived as disinterest when what it really was, was fear.

"Love was a dangerous thing," Charlotte said. "At least that was what I believed when I was twenty-two. I had seen my sister take to her bed and turn into a recluse because the man she loved didn't want her any longer. The thought that that could happen to me was terrifying."

But even more terrifying was the chance she might lose the love of her life. So Charlotte did the only thing she could do: she went to Hong Kong to tell George what was in her heart.

"You traveled alone from New Jersey to Hong Kong?" Kate was awestruck in the true sense of the word. "Weren't you terrified?"

Charlotte shook her head slowly. "Once I made up my mind, nothing could stop me. We all have a choice to make when it comes to our lives, and I chose to be happy."

"I know your story has a happy ending," Kate said, gesturing toward the array of family photos propped on the nightstand, "but what if it hadn't? What if the worst happened and you traveled all the way to China to be with him and he didn't want you anymore? Your heart would have been broken!" Not that she saw a parallel between Charlotte's situation and hers . . .

Charlotte reached for Kate's hand and held it tight. "A broken heart isn't the worst thing that can happen, Katherine. Never giving your heart to another is. Haven't you figured that out by now?"

Twenty-four

July 4—French Kiss

"Whoever came up with the idea for the Sidewalk Sale should be severely chastised," Kate said as she stifled a yawn.

"I second that." Sonia poured herself a double espresso. "Eight a.m. on a holiday is a punishable offense."

"We're an antiques shop, not Target," Kate grumbled over her decaf. "I absolutely refuse to put anything over twenty dollars out there on the street for people to paw over."

"Guess that rules out the Georgian china you bought on your last trip."

"I'd say it rules out just about everything in the inventory," Kate said.

"Look what I found!" Liz popped out of the storeroom with two 1940s-era Uncle Sam figurines and a set of red, white, and blue stars-and-stripes plates from the early 1960s. "They're not antique, but they sure play into the Fourth of July theme."

They were off and running. By the time the first tourists hit Main Street, they had an eye-catching display set up on the table.

"You keep looking at your watch," Sonia remarked as they left Liz outside to keep her eye on things. "Got an appointment or something?"

"Nope." It was nine-fifteen. If she drove the speed limit, she could be at the Greenwood Fourth of July Barbecue by five. Not that she was planning to do anything that crazy. Just a what-if. "I'm surprised we have activity so early."

"You did it again."

"Did what?"

"Looked at your watch." Sonia put down the early Wedgwood beaker she was wrapping for an online customer. "Do you have to be someplace?"

And just like that she knew what she had to do.

"I'm sorry to leave you in the lurch, Sonia," she said as she gathered up her belongings and stuffed them into her enormous leather bag, "but you're right. There is something I have to do."

"Are you feeling okay?" Sonia looked puzzled and a little concerned. "Maybe you should sit down."

"I'm fine." She had never felt better in her life. "I'm going to take a few days off, Sonia. You and Liz can hold down the fort, right?"

"Sure we can." She grabbed Kate's arm. "You're going back into the hospital! I've heard that sometimes those procedures have to be redone and—"

"I'm not having another angiogram," Kate tossed over her shoulder as she dashed for the back door. "I'm going to New Hampshire."

She cut across the parking area they shared with Blake's Flowers and Geneva's Spice Shop.

"Nice display, Kate," Geneva called out as she emptied

some trash into their mutual Dumpster. "Hope I get some of your overflow."

She didn't have time to stop and shoot the breeze with Geneva or the crowd at Danny's Coffee Shop or the gang from the bakery. She didn't even wait for the light to turn green at the corner of Stuyvesant and Main. She darted into traffic (all three cars of it) and practically polevaulted to the other side.

She felt like an explorer heading into uncharted territory. She had no map or guide, only her heart to keep her on course, and her heart was telling her to hurry before it was too late.

She broke into a run. She hoped Dr. Lombardi knew what he was talking about when he said she was one hundred percent. Maybe she should phone Maeve and ask her to ride along with her, or maybe she could grab a flight out of Newark Liberty. What was wrong with technology anyway? Why hadn't anyone figured out a way to transport love-struck people to their lover's doorstep before they had time to lose their courage?

She ran past the Goodwins' crazy Irish setter, the Mac-Dougalls' skateboarding grandson.

What if she couldn't find him once she got there? She didn't know the town or the people. She couldn't wander up and down the main street asking for the pastor's address. What if he wasn't even there? He had friends in New Hampshire. He had family. He could have begged off on the festival and gone off somewhere else . . . with somebody else.

No. She refused to think like that. He would be there. He would listen to what she had to say. He would—

Actually she had no idea what he would do. She knew what she hoped he would do, what she prayed he would do, but when the moment came only God and Mark had a clue.

She started to laugh. That was what happened when you fell in love with a priest. You started thinking like one. The truth was, there were no easy answers. Sometimes there were only questions. But that was no reason not to take a stand.

She turned onto Indigo, slipping on a patch of wet grass near the Terhune house. She glanced at her watch. Almost ten o'clock. Five minutes to grab something to eat. Five minutes to pack. Another five for the unexpected. She could be on the road by ten-fifteen, on the highway by ten-thirty.

She ran past the Drake house, the Eliott house, the empty Voorhees house, and then skidded to a stop at the foot of her driveway.

A beat-up pale blue Honda with New Hampshire plates was angled next to her Miata.

A tall, lanky figure rounded the corner of the house and for the second time in her life she thought her heart would stop beating. His head was down. His dark hair glinted with gold and red highlights in the summer morning sun. He wore jeans and the Grateful Dead T-shirt and suddenly she couldn't remember a time when he hadn't been part of her life, her heart.

He took another step and then glanced up. Their eyes locked and suddenly she was in motion, flying up the driveway straight into his arms. Her defenses were down. Her heart was wide-open to love for the first time in her life.

"I drove all night," he said, kissing her hair, her forehead, her nose, her mouth. "I had to see you."

"I ran all the way home," she said, running her hands through his hair, down his shoulders, across his chest. "I was going to drive up to New Hampshire to be with you."

"I can't live without you, Kate." He looked exhausted but happy, deeply happy, and her heart soared with hope. "I'm coming back to New Jersey."

"I like New England. I could—"

"You're not listening." His eyes met hers. "I'm coming home." It would take another month to straighten out the details, but he had worked out a plan to hand over the reins of St. Stephen's to Father Owens in a way that made everybody happy. "I should be back down here around Labor Day," he said. "To stay."

The question "Why?" burst out before she could stop it.

"Because I love you." There was nothing forced about the declaration, nothing fake or practiced. He spoke directly from his heart. He cupped her face with his hands. "Why were you driving up to New Hampshire?"

"Because I wanted to tell you—" Her throat closed against the enormity of the words. This was it. The point of no return. Once she said those words her life would be changed forever. She would be changed. "I wanted to tell you that I love you."

There were kisses that turned a woman inside out. There were kisses that melted her bones. And then there were kisses that promised her a future more wonderful than anything she had ever hoped for.

"I want you to know what you're getting into."

"I read the Mitford books," she said and he laughed. "I know it won't be easy."

"My days as a small-town parson are probably over. Right now I don't know what the future holds for me." He wanted to continue working with the elderly and people battling substance abuse, but he had closed those doors when he went back to Greenwood. Only time would tell which ones would reopen for him.

"I'm not exactly the ideal companion," she said cautiously. "I've been poring over books about Episcopalianism, but nothing's changed. I'm not sure what I believe in or why. I haven't been to church in years. I don't want to be a liability."

"I know who you are, Kate, and I don't want you to change for me or for anyone. We'll figure it out as we go along."

That was the most beautiful declaration of love she could ever ask for.

"Change is good," she said. "If I hadn't changed I wouldn't be standing here with you right now." Sometimes change hurt but it was all part of living.

"You Jersey girls don't scare easy, do you?"

"The thought of losing you scares me." The thought of how close she had come to living her whole life without knowing how it felt to be in love terrified her.

He dropped to one knee in the gravel driveway and took her hands in his. "You don't have to give me your answer right away," he said, "but I don't want you to have any doubts about where this is going."

He wanted her heart, her body, her soul, her future, and he was willing to give her everything he had in return. He wanted to build the rest of his life with her and he wasn't afraid to put his own heart and soul on the line and tell her so.

Life didn't come with guarantees. You never knew what the fates—or God—might have in store for you somewhere down the line. She could hide from love forever or she could take that leap and hope the net really would appear.

There were a thousand questions yet to be answered, but only one that really mattered.

Choose happiness . . . choose happiness . . .

It turned out she was her mother's daughter after all, and so she did the only thing a French woman could do: she chose happiness.

She finally chose love.

Epilogue

Coburn, New Jersey—one year later

The first time was always the hardest.

Daniel Mark Dempsey was eleven weeks and four days old and his very tired, very young parents were going to spend their first night without him.

"We should've stayed at your place," Mark said as Andy lugged in the last of the baby bags. "Is there anything left at home?"

Andy grinned at his father-in-law. "Gwynnie wanted me to dismantle the crib and bring it along, but I had to draw the line somewhere."

"Good thinking," Mark said. "Any more stuff and you'll have to hire a sherpa."

"Gwynnie!" Andy shouted up the staircase. "If we don't leave now we'll miss check-in!"

"It's a long drive," Mark called out, "and lots of traffic. Better get moving."

"She doesn't want to leave the baby," Andy said. "She wanted to bring him with us."

Mark grinned at the young man he had come to respect and love. "I think Kate and Maeve might have something to say about that." The two women had been counting down the hours until Danny was all theirs to fuss over and spoil.

Finally the baby was safely tucked into his travel crib and Andy was nudging his wife toward the door.

"Are you sure you have the diaper bag?" Gwynn asked for the tenth time.

"Both of them," Mark said.

Gwynn cast her eyes around the foyer. "I don't see them."

Maeve gave her granddaughter a big hug. "One's upstairs and the other is downstairs."

"What about the milk I expressed?"

"Properly stored," Kate said.

"His binky!" Gwynn clutched her husband's sleeve. "We forgot his binky!"

Mark held up the little rubber object. "Binky," he said and was rewarded with a wave of laughter.

"I wish I had that on tape," Kate said. "They'd love to hear that down at St. Michael's, wouldn't they?"

Life had taken him down a few interesting professional roads in the last year. Not only was he doing his chaplain work with the elderly once again and keeping up with the program with his old crowd in New Hope, he had begun counseling men and women with substance abuse problems at St. Michael's Hospital near Basking Ridge. It was a full life and a happy one.

"Maybe you'd better not bathe him tonight," Gwynn said. "It's a little chilly and—"

"Gwynnie," Kate interrupted, "I think I know what to do."

"And if she doesn't, I do," Maeve said. "Between us we have a lot of experience."

"Don't look at me," Mark said, laughing. "I'm still in training."

Poor Gwynn. His heart went out to her. She looked so young, so excited, so nervous, so much in love with the life she was living. "I know I'm being silly," she said, "but it's just this is the first time and—"

"It's a long trip," Andy said, holding the front door open. "We'd better hit the road."

Gwynn was clearly torn between motherhood and the prospect of an unbroken night's sleep complete with room service. "Do you have the number?"

"Of course we do," Kate said.

"On speed dial," Mark added.

"I'm keeping my cell on all night," Gwynn said. "If you need me for anything, I don't care what time it is, call me!"

Maeve walked them out to the car while Kate and Mark watched from the front porch.

"I'm off," Maeve said after she helped them unpack all of the baby paraphernalia. "I have a lecture tonight at the Bernardsville Library."

"Alone at last," Kate said as her mother's car disappeared down Indigo. "I thought they'd never leave."

Mark pulled his wife close and buried his nose in her fragrant hair. "I was thinking maybe we could—"

Daniel Mark Dempsey was tiny, but he had a powerful set of lungs. His cry made them jump apart like guilty teenagers.

"Better get used to it," Kate said with a smile. "Only four and a half more months until we're the ones looking for a babysitter."

"Happy?" he asked her.

She met his eyes. "Happier than I ever thought possible."

Mark placed his hand on his wife's rounded belly and felt the faint stirring of life deep inside her. Nothing he had learned in seminary had come close to explaining the basic wonder that was life. That was the one thing he had to learn for himself in his own time. Who would have guessed he would find his own glimpse of heaven in a carriage house on a country lane in central New Jersey?

"Uh-oh," Kate said as Daniel Mark Dempsey tested his lungs once more. "I think he's hungry."

Mark took his wife's hand and together they went inside to see what their grandson wanted.

Turn the page for a preview of
Barbara Bretton's next novel,

It's In His Kiss

Coming soon!

Goldy's Bakery—Lakeside, New Jersey

Hayley Maitland Goldstein was battling a sheet of rolled fondant when Trish, one of the counter girls, burst into the kitchen.

"There's a guy outside and he's unbelievably hot." Trish was seventeen, the age when any biped with a Y chromosome rated a breathless announcement.

"That's great, Trish." She centered herself and draped the sugary sweetness over the bottom layer of carrot cake. Rolled fondant was like edible vinyl flooring. It required a sure touch and seamless application or else you might as well have your cakes decorated at Home Depot.

"Mrs. G.?" Trish handed her a pair of sharp kitchen shears. "About that guy—"

Hayley clipped the excess around the perimeter of the cake, then stepped back to survey her handiwork. Good thing it was the anchor layer and she would have five more chances to get it right. "Go back up front, Trish. You know Rachel doesn't like being alone at the counter."

"I know, but about that guy." Trish was practically hopping in place with excitement. "He wants to see you."

"And I want to see Russell Crowe." Hayley smoothed a tiny ripple with the flat edge of a knife. This was her punishment for delaying the job until the last minute. What she really needed to do was start all over again, but there just wasn't time. "We don't always get what we want."

Trish lowered her voice. "He looks like one of those rock stars from, you know, way back in the eighties."

Ouch. She had been Trish's age in the eighties.

"A rock star?" she asked, lifting a brow.

"A rock star," Trish confirmed. "And he's wearing leather."

There was only one reason an aging leather-clad hottie would show up at Goldy's Bakery at four o'clock on a Wednesday afternoon, and it had nothing to do with brownies, cheesecake, or bagels.

"Tell him to get lost," she said. "I'm not bailing Michael out of another one of his messes."

"But he didn't ask for Mr. Goldstein. He asked for you."

Of course he did. She was the one with a bank balance. Leather Boy was probably one of the half-dozen bookies her ex-husband was currently ducking up and down the Jersey Shore. She wished she had a dollar for every angry enabler who had shown up at Goldy's in search of the reluctant Mr. Goldstein. She'd be able to buy him out once and for all and still have money to spare.

"Trish, I have a six-layer cake to finish for the Cumberland County Association of Female Realtors gala tonight. Tell him I'm not here."

"But, Mrs. G., I already told him you were."

"Then you'd better go out there and tell him you were wrong. If it's that important he can leave a message."

Trish rearranged her pretty features into an even prettier frown. "He really wants to see you, Mrs. G. Maybe—"

Hayley had no choice. She whipped out The Look, the same look every mother on the planet had down cold, and aimed it in Trish's direction.

"I'll tell him," Trish said, then pushed through the swinging door to deliver the bad news.

The Look had stopped working on her daughter Lizzie, so it was nice to know she still had enough maternal fire power at her command to keep her young staff in line.

She couldn't make out Trish's words through the closed doors, just the high, apologetic string of sounds that was followed by a male rumble. Leather Boy, no doubt. He had a good voice, baritone, a little smoky. She couldn't make out his words either, but Trish's answering giggle conjured up some painful memories of herself at that age.

First a girl giggled, then she sighed, and the next thing you knew she was in Vegas taking her wedding vows in front of a red-haired Elvis with an overbite. You knew you had made a bad choice when Elvis slipped you his divorce lawyer's business card while you were still shaking the rice from your underage hair.

She paused, a fresh sheet of fondant rippling in the breeze, and listened closer. Trish said something girly. Leather Boy rumbled something manly. This time Rachel, the other counter girl, giggled too, a sound that sent Hayley's maternal early-warning system into DEFCON 3 mode.

Rachel was a serious straight-A student bound for Princeton next year on full scholarship. Rachel Gomez had probably never giggled before in her life.

If Rachel giggled, then even Lizzie might not be immune. She thanked the patron saint of single mothers for making sure her daughter was safely tucked away upstairs, working on her physics homework while her iPod pumped hip-hop directly into her bloodstream.

Lizzie was a good girl, a throwback to her maternal grandmother, who preferred the life of the mind over the pleasures of the flesh. But she knew even good girls had their limits.

Once upon a time Hayley had believed that the love of a good woman (her) could turn a bad boy (her ex) into a knight in shining armor (pure fantasy). Ten years of marriage to Michael Goldstein had finally drummed the truth into her head. People didn't change with time. They just became more of who they were to begin with.

In the real world bad boys didn't turn into knights in shining armor. Bad boys grew up to be even worse men, and the world would be a much happier place if little girls were taught that basic fact along with their ABCs.

Why didn't women teach their young how to cope with the things that were really important instead of how to walk in your first pair of heels? Why didn't they make a point of sitting their girl children down and telling them the truth about men instead of letting some guy in a leather jacket seduce them over a tray of black-and-white cookies?

Those idiotic girls out there were like ripe fruit on a very low-hanging branch. The slightest breeze would be enough to shake them from the tree and into the waiting arms of Leather Boy or someone just like him.

Well, it wasn't going to happen on her watch. The Cumberland County Association of Female Realtors would have to get in line.

She laid the sheet of fondant down on a clean tea towel, then elbowed through the swinging doors.

Leather Boy was draped across the counter, all lean muscle and attitude. He might as well have had a skull and crossbones painted on the back of his jacket. He was too old, too jaded, too sure of himself, and if he so much as crooked one of those bony nicotine-stained fingers in their direction, those two idiotic little girls would follow him right out the door and into the biggest mistake of their lives.

Twenty years ago she had done the same thing, and it would be nice if somebody finally benefited from her mistake.

"Trish!" She sounded like a Marine drill sergeant on steroids. "Rachel! I need you two in the kitchen."

Rachel stared at her wide-eyed. Trish looked like she was in a trance.

"Now!" Hayley barked, and the two teenagers sprinted past her.

Even Leather Boy straightened up.

She could get used to this.

"I'm Hayley Goldstein," she said as she rounded the counter, "and if this is about Michael I can't help you."

"Who's Michael?" He looked a whole lot less dangerous when he was puzzled. Maybe she'd shooed the girls away too soon.

"You're not looking for my ex?"

"I'm not looking for anybody." He gestured toward the street, where an enormous black SUV had pride of place in front of the shop. "I'm Anton and I came along for the ride."

And here she had done some of her best work for nothing. They stared at each other for a full second or two. He really did look like an eighties rock star. Once upon a time he would have been her dream man, but fortunately that time had come and gone.

"Anton, unless you're looking to buy a lemon meringue pie or—"

Anton raised his hand to stop her. He wore a heavy silver ring on his middle finger and a wide leather strap around his wrist. A rocker's version of Armani. "Wait," he said. "Let me get the boss."

The boss? She didn't like the sound of that. Her ex didn't exactly run with the Mensa crowd. Visions of an Anthony Soprano wannabe with a chip on his shoulder sprang to life, and she debated the wisdom of locking the front door and putting up the CLOSED sign while there was still time.

Anton approached the SUV parked at the curb. She watched, fascinated, as the passenger door opened and a Suit stepped out. The Suit towered over Anton. His shoulders were as wide as a running back's, something that was either the result of good genetics or an even better tailor. Anton looked like an undernourished boy next to him.

Her younger self might have had a weakness for bad boys in leather jackets but her current self leaned more toward grown men in suits. A woman could trust a man who wore a suit. Men in suits knew how to keep a job. Men in suits paid their bills on time and owned houses and cars they could actually afford.

Of course some men in suits were Mob bosses or CEOs with a yen for embezzlement, so maybe her theory needed a little fine-tuning.

She busied herself wiping imaginary fingerprints from the glass countertop as he said something to Anton, straightened his tie, then strode across the sidewalk to the front door.

"You were looking for me," Hayley said when the door closed behind him. She had never been good at playing games.

"You're Hayley Maitland."

"Hayley Maitland Goldstein," she corrected him.

"I thought you were divorced."

"Excuse me?"

"One of your counter girls said you were divorced."

She needed to have a long talk with Trish. "I am divorced," she said. "I never got around to switching back to my maiden name." *Not that it's any of your business.*

"She also said you weren't here."

"Is there a point to any of this? Because if there isn't, I have a lot of work to do."

He should have been offended but strangely he didn't seem to be. He wasn't the usual caliber of bill collector sent to find her ex.

"Are you this rude to all of your paying customers?"

"I thought you were here to—" No need to play the terrible-ex-husband card until she had to.

"I'll pay double the going rate if you'll finish that sentence." He managed to say it with such good humor that even she had to laugh.

"First, tell me what you're buying and I'll decide if it's worth my while to spill family secrets."

"Fair enough. I need a cake in the shape of a set of drums."

"I can do that." *In my sleep with my spatula tied behind my back.*

He grinned. "And the bass drum has to feed two hundred."

"We did a wedding reception for five hundred last spring. The cake was in the shape of a pair of swans. I can show you photos if you like."

"I've already seen them."

"But Trish didn't—"

"I do my homework, Mrs. Goldstein. In the last year you handled the Citibank reception at McCarter in Princeton, two very successful election night parties in Harrisburg and Trenton, and some private functions for some very well-known families."

"You really did do your homework. Tell me your name so I can do my homework too."

"Finn Rafferty." He handed her a business card with his name and numbers on it.

She looked up at him. "You're a lawyer?"

"I represent Tommy Stiles. You might have heard of him."

Heard of him? That was like saying you were vaguely familiar with Elvis or the Beatles. "He's—uh, he's a singer." A singer who had happened to make his bones alongside Springsteen and Joel, Stewart and Clapton.

Rafferty's eyes twinkled with amusement. "Yeah," he said. "He's a singer. He'll be performing at Convention Hall in Atlantic City next month and he wants you to handle the cakes for the after-party."

She hated herself for asking the question but the "Why me?" slipped out just the same.

"Because you're the best between here and New York, and Tommy only deals with the best."

She had always believed in herself but the fact that Tommy Stiles even knew she was on the same planet seemed to have rendered her temporarily speechless.

Rafferty picked up the slack.

"We'll supply you with hotel rooms for yourself and your staff. I'll make arrangements for you to have full access to the kitchen's facilities. Whatever you need to get the job done, it's yours."

She didn't have the heart to tell him she usually baked the cakes right here at Goldy's then schlepped them to the venue in the back of her van, praying the whole way that they'd arrive in one piece.

"So what do you say? We know your going rate and we're willing to sweeten the deal."

Tommy Stiles of Tom and the Afterlife? Was this really happening?

"I'll—maybe I can—how about I work up a proposal and fax it over to you tonight."

"I have a better idea. Why don't we hammer out the details right now? I didn't come all this way to go home empty-handed."

She tried to think of a reason why that wasn't a good idea but her mind was a total blank. All she could think of was what this job would do for her bank account. This could be the difference between just getting by and getting ahead. With a reference from someone like Tommy Stiles, she would be catapulted into a whole different level of success.

When a superstar like Tommy Stiles did something, he did it with full press coverage. There would be photographers from *People* and *InStyle* and film crews from *Entertainment Tonight* and E! They always did a full spread on the catering at important parties. She had thumbed through countless celebrity magazines, soaking up the details on who served what and how. Sometimes the caterer's phone number and website were published, which was the equivalent of finding the Holy Grail in your hall closet.

All she had to do was create a spectacular, mindblowing confection for two hundred people who had seen it all at least ten times over, and pray that her Cinderella moment was finally here.

*   *   *

Hayley Maitland Goldstein might be a baker, but she had the soul of a first-class litigator. Hammering out the contract took longer than Finn had expected, and that was after he had agreed to all of her demands.

It was dark when he finally left the bakery. He felt like he had gone ten rounds with a Supreme Court justice.

Anton caught sight of him as he approached the Hummer, and the engine sprang to life.

He tapped on the window and the glass whirred down

softly. "Give me a minute," he said to his friend. "I have to make a call."

Anton nodded and the glass window whirred back up.

Tommy picked up on the first ring. "Did you see her?"

"I saw her. I presented the proposal and she signed on the dotted line. She'll be at the Taj Mahal on the twenty-ninth for Flash's party."

There was a moment's hesitation, then Tommy cleared his throat. "And—?"

Finn thought about her quick laughter, the flashes of temper, the unexpectedly familiar green eyes with the flecks of gold. The capable hands with the odd little quirk to the right ring finger. Only one other person on earth shared that ring finger jog.

He would recommend they go the DNA route because he was a lawyer and he was trained to cross every *t* and dot every *i*, but the results would only prove what he already knew in his gut to be fact.

"Better sit down, Tommy," he said. "I think this time we found you a daughter."

USA Today Bestselling Author

BARBARA BRETTON

Someone Like You

"A master at touching readers' hearts,"*
Barbara Bretton explores the emotional journey
of two sisters and the healing truth of an
unforgettable family legacy when an
unexpected reunion inspires a better
understanding of secrets and sacrifices.

PRAISE FOR THE NOVELS OF BARBARA BRETTON:

"GRAB THIS ONE WHEN IT HITS THE SHELVES!
A PERFECT 10!"
—*ROMANCE REVIEWS TODAY*

"ONE OF TODAY'S BEST WOMEN'S
FICTION AUTHORS."
—*ROMANCE READER*

978-0-425-20388-0

Available wherever books are sold or at
penguin.com

Penguin Group (USA) Online

What will you be reading tomorrow?

Tom Clancy, Patricia Cornwell, W.E.B. Griffin,
Nora Roberts, William Gibson, Robin Cook,
Brian Jacques, Catherine Coulter, Stephen King,
Dean Koontz, Ken Follett, Clive Cussler,
Eric Jerome Dickey, John Sandford,
Terry McMillan, Sue Monk Kidd, Amy Tan,
John Berendt…

You'll find them all at
penguin.com

*Read excerpts and newsletters,
find tour schedules and reading group guides,
and enter contests.*

Subscribe to Penguin Group (USA) newsletters
and get an exclusive inside look
at exciting new titles and the authors you love
long before everyone else does.

PENGUIN GROUP (USA)
us.penguingroup.com